Miss Delphine's Dangerous Game

HISTORICAL REGENCY ROMANCE

EDITH BYRD

Copyright © 2021 by Edith Byrd All rights reserved.

No part of this book may be reproduced in any form or by any electronic or mechanical means, including information storage and retrieval systems, without written permission from the author, except for the use of brief quotations in a book review.

About Edith Byrd

Edith Byrd comes from a long line of Ohio natives. She left her little Ohio only for educational purposes to study geography at Montreal where she also met her husband. Upon their marriage they both returned to Ohio where they've been living for the better part of the
last two decades.

For Edith, writing didn't come naturally, and she never had the strong urge to publish her thoughts. Her creativity sprung when her second-born son was diagnosed with Asperger's, so she had to come up with alternatives for him to focus on any subject. This constant practice in creating stories for her son and her interest in literature pushed her to eventually write books.

In her free time, she volunteers for people with disabilities, studies Ohio's history, and enjoys long walks with her husband and two dogs.

Prologue

London, England, 1812.

"You'd better come quickly, Delphine, he's dying," Bessie called out, hurrying to meet Delphine, who had just returned to the inn from running errands on the docks.

She put down her basket, pulled off her bonnet, and followed the maid up the backstairs of the inn to her father's bedroom. When she had left, he had been sleeping, but now Delphine could hear him coughing and spluttering, choking in the throes of agony.

"Father, try to lie back. Open the window, Bessie, then fetch some water from the pump," Delphine cried out, rushing to her father's side, and putting her arm around him.

He lay back on the cushions, his eyes wide, his breathing short and erratic. Spittle was running from his mouth, and Delphine pulled out her handkerchief to dab at his moist lips. He had been ill for some time, but in the past few days, his condition had grown worse, and Delphine feared this was the end.

"I... I can't go on," he gasped, but Delphine shook her head and squeezed his hand in hers.

"Nonsense, Father. You're as strong as an ox. You can go on. I know you can," she replied, even as she felt uncertain of her own words.

The doctor had told her there was nothing more he could do, though Delphine was not certain the doctor had done much, save pocketing the large fee he had charged. There had been tonics prescribed, and much speculation, but nothing had worked. Delphine's father had complained of stomach cramps two months previously, and his condition had deteriorated rapidly from there.

"No, Delphine, I can't," he groaned, as Bessie returned with a cup of water, standing in the doorway with an anxious expression on her face.

"Thank you, Bessie. Tell Alice to prepare a broth – Father always likes that," Delphine said, trying to ignore the fact of her father's despair.

He had been a constant presence in her life, and the thought of losing him was too much to bear. Together, they ran The Seven Bells – a handsome inn in the City of London – just as her grandfather and her great-grandfather had done before them. To imagine the inn without her father behind the counter in the taproom was simply impossible. He was its landlord, the confidant of so many. The inn was a place where many an aristocrat and rich gentleman had sought refuge from the wagging tongues of the outside world. It had a certain reputation in the City of London, a place of discretion, where those who wished for privacy could have it. Delphine did not know what she would do if her father died, and she was left to run the inn alone.

"No broth. I don't need anything, just my daughter," Delphine's father groaned.

"But you must eat something, Father. Please, try to drink a little water. It'll do you good," Delphine said, but her father shook his head and gave her a weak smile.

"Water pumped out of that filthy river. No, I'd rather have a sip of wine, my favorite vintage, you know the one," he said, squeezing her hand.

Delphine nodded, glancing at Bessie, who hurried off to fetch the bottle of wine from the cellar. Delphine's father was something of a connoisseur, and the cellar was filled with dusty bottles of the finest vintages. Delphine sighed and sat down on the edge of the bed, still clutching her father's hand in hers. She was trying hard not to cry. She knew the inevitability of what was to come, even as the thought of it filled her with dread. She and her father had always been close. Her mother had died when she was very young, and it was her father who had dried her childhood tears, encouraged her in her childhood ways, and helped her grow into the woman she now was. She loved him with all her heart, and could not bear to see him suffer so.

"Father...you..." she began, but her father interrupted her.

"It's my time, Delphine. A sip of wine and my daughter – what more could I ask for as I close my eyes for the last time," he said.

Delphine could no longer hold back the tears, which rolled down her cheeks, as she clung to her father, who tried to comfort her.

"I can't do it, Father. I can't do what you do. I can't," she exclaimed, knowing the burden of responsibility which would be hers when her father died.

She would be the landlady of the inn, with all the duties it entailed. The thought of it terrified her, even as she knew it was unavoidable.

"But you can, Delphine. You're ready. You've done it whilst I've been confined to this accursed bed," he reminded her, giving her a weak smile.

Bessie now returned with the wine bottle and a glass. She poured some out and handed it to Delphine, who helped her father to drink from the glass. His hands were trembling so much he could not hold it steady, but having taken a sip, he gave a sigh of deep satisfaction.

"Don't leave me, Father," she whispered, but her father's eyes were now closed.

His breathing was becoming labored, and it was as though he had made his peace and was now ready to depart this world.

"I love you, Delphine," he whispered, and with that, he breathed his last.

Delphine wept, and the glass fell to the floor where it smashed. Bessie hurried forward to comfort her, throwing her arms around Delphine, and the two women mourned the passing of her father.

"Oh, ma'am, I'm so sorry. He was such a good man," Bessie exclaimed, pulling out her handkerchief to blow her nose.

"I don't know what I'll do without him, Bessie. I can't...oh, he can't be gone," Delphine replied.

But as she stared down at her father's lifeless body, his eyes closed, his breathing ceased, she knew a chapter of her life had ended. He was no longer the landlord of The Seven Bells, no longer the confidant of so many, no longer the cheerful face at the barrel. All of that now fell to her, and she knew her father wanted it to be hers.

"I'll do my best, Father. I promise," she vowed.

Chapter One

"William Thomas Ivory, Landlord and Publican of The Seven Bells. Born 8th December 1750, died 4th June 1812. Aged 62," the headstone read.

Delphine had had it erected shortly after her father's burial a month ago, in the churchyard of Saint Mary-le-Bow, and she had visited it every day since. The churchyard was only a short walk from the inn, and she would come and sit by the grave and talk to her father. She would often bring a posy of flowers, and she always made sure the gravestone was clean and brushed. She did not want it to fall into decay like those around it, where moss and lichen covered the memory of those interred below.

I won't ever forget him, she promised herself, rising from the ground in front of the grave where she had been sitting for the past half an hour.

It was a warm summer's day, and a gentle breeze was blowing from the river as Delphine walked back towards The Seven Bells. The weeks following her father's death had passed like a dream, and Delphine still expected to find him sitting behind the counter in the taproom or rolling barrels up from the cellar. Her father was the inn, and the inn was her father. News of his death had been greeted with much sadness by those who knew him, and a subscription had been raised to allow for a fitting memorial in his memory.

Delphine was grateful for the kindness of so many, but in truth, she felt lost without her father – lost, and unable to see where her future lay. The inn, of course, continued as it had always done. It had been her grandfather who had first turned a back street hovel into a handsome coaching inn, one frequented by the great and the good, as well as the poor and lowly. It was a fine building; whitewashed, with the window edges painted in blue. A large sign above the door depicted the seven bells of its namesake, and an arch to one side led to stables at the rear.

The inn was well known amongst London society as a place of refuge and privacy. Rooms could be taken with no questions asked, and there was always an aristocrat or two who would come in from the countryside to take refuge from a scandal, whilst others came simply for the comfort of a place to stay in London, with good food and a fine wine cellar. Delphine had seen all of life during her childhood growing up there, and her father had often commented that the inn was a world in itself, a place where every side of life found its place.

And now it's all mine, Delphine thought to herself, sighing as she let herself in through the kitchen door from the stable yard.

Delphine had always known that responsibility for the inn would one day be hers. Her father had told her as much from an early age. She had no siblings, and there was no one else to whom the responsibility could pass. The inn was hers. It would soon be her name above the door – "*Delphine Ivory, licensed purveyor of spirits.*" She had so far resisted removing the sign with her father's name on it. To do so seemed a finality, one she was unwilling to accept, even as she knew she had to do so eventually.

"Was everything all right up at the churchyard, ma'am?" Bessie asked, as Delphine entered the kitchen.

Bessie Buttersworth had been the inn's maid and housekeeper for twenty years. She lived in the attic, along with the cook, Alice Ducker, and did everything from changing the beds to serving the guests their meals. She was a kind and faithful creature, and Delphine relied on her, not only for her work, but for her friendship, too.

"I scraped some of the moss off from the base. It grows so quickly. It's no wonder the other graves are falling down. There's no one to care for them. It's so sad," Delphine said, shaking her head as she sat down at the kitchen table and sighed.

"I'll make you a cup of tea, ma'am. It's not good for you to go up there every day to the churchyard. They say a person who clings to death isn't far from it themselves," Bessie said, shaking her head and tutting.

Delphine knew what *they* said, but she did not care. She wanted to feel close to her father, and visiting his grave each day allowed her to be so. She knew she was clinging to what she had lost, but it was the only way she felt able to cope with the overwhelming sense of sorrow she was feeling. Life was lonely for Delphine, and despite her responsibilities and the busyness of her life, she felt terribly alone, even as she knew she had Bessie and Alice to support her.

"I don't know what else to do, Bessie. I can't just stop feeling like this," Delphine replied.

Bessie looked at her and shook her head.

"It takes time, ma'am. It won't happen overnight. But I've got something to take your mind off your troubles," the maid said.

Delphine looked at her curiously.

"Yes...what is it?" she asked, and Bessie smiled.

"It's the earl and the marquess, ma'am. They arrived whilst you were out," she replied.

Delphine rolled her eyes. This was the last thing she needed. Robert Grantham, the Earl of Paxton, and Jacob Rollins, the Marquess of Renfrew, came as a pair. They were the closest of friends, but also the worst of combinations. They would arrive unannounced on a whim and take rooms at the inn for as long as their fancy desired. Their presence usually caused disruption on a grand scale – everything had to be just *so*. The earl liked his eggs cooked in a certain way and had particular feelings regarding goose feather pillows, the marquess demanded hot water at all hours and drank only a certain type of coffee, they ordered carriages to take them here and there, and returned when they pleased, expecting refreshments, sometimes in the middle of the night. Delphine sighed.

"I see..." she said, shaking her head.

But it was not only the particular demands of the highly strung aristocrats which caused her to bemoan their arrival but also their feelings towards her, for both the earl and the marquess held a torch for Delphine. They had both asked her to marry them on no less than a dozen occasions, and on each of those occasions, it had been her father who had refused on her behalf.

He would always give them the same answer.

I can't have my daughter getting married. She's got work to do here."

Polite but firm, always said with such an affable smile, one could hardly take offense to the dismissal.

But without her father there to speak for her, Delphine wondered how she would deal with the inevitable advances of her guests.

"I've put them in their usual rooms. No doubt we'll soon hear from them," Bessie said, and just as she spoke, the bell from the front bedroom jangled in the kitchen.

"That'll be the marquess calling for his hot water, I presume?" Delphine said, as Bessie rolled her eyes.

Delphine knew she had no choice but to welcome her guests. She wondered what had brought them from their country estates and how long they intended to remain in London – whatever the reasons and however long they remained, Delphine knew it would be a trial. The earl and the marquess were not bad men. They were simply tiresome, and in her present condition, Delphine was by no means prepared for their arrival.

"He'll be wanting something particular for his dinner, too, no doubt," Alice said, appearing from the pantry where she had been sorting out the inn's store of jams and preserves.

She was a homely-looking woman with a round red face and gray curly hair covered with a cloth cap. She wore a black dress and white apron, which was stained and marked through its many years of service.

"He always does," Delphine replied with a sigh, rising to her feet and brushing down her dress.

It was time to face her public. Her father had once told her that running an inn was like performing in a theater. There was a backstage, where chaos and strife could rain, but once one stepped through the doors into the taproom or the parlor or the dining room, the performance had begun. There was no chance for rehearsal, and the script was one's own.

"Ah, Delphine, there you are," the earl said, as Delphine emerged from the kitchen into the parlor.

It was a large room, with windows facing onto the street. Tables and chairs stood all around, and a large hearth took up the far wall. A fire was kept blazing there – even in the summer – and the walls were covered with all manner of pictures and paintings, so that the room had a homely and welcoming feel. The earl was sitting in an armchair by the window, but the sight of Delphine caused him to rise, and there was no doubt in Delphine's mind that the earl was pleased to have caught her first, before his companion had had a chance to speak with her.

"My Lord...how...good it is to see you here," Delphine said, always aware of her performance, even as the truth of her words was open to question.

"My dear Delphine, how sorry I was to hear of your father's death. I had Mass said for him," the earl replied.

He was unusual amongst the English aristocracy for professing the Catholic faith. A tall man, with bright blue eyes and a high forehead. He was much older than Delphine, his hair going gray, and his face somewhat lived in, even as he remained in full possession of his faculties. He was a patron of the arts, and frequented the London theaters, even as his own abilities at musical performance left something to be desired.

"You're very kind, my Lord. Do you intend to stay in London long?" she asked, hoping the answer would be a resolute no.

"I don't know as yet. But it's always a pleasure to be here with you. I know it's not the same without your father. You'll be all right, I'm sure," he said, and he took her hand in his and raised it to his lips.

At that moment, a crashing sound, followed by a cry caused them both to jump, and Delphine turned to find the marquess – a portly man whose clothing was always ill fitting owing to his own vanity – rolling from the staircase leading up to the bedrooms. He had fallen, and Delphine rushed to his side.

"Goodness me, my Lord. Are you all right?" she exclaimed, as the marquess looked up at her in a dazed state.

"I came to see where the hot water was. Is Bessie bringing it?" he asked, seemingly unaware of what had just occurred.

"You've just fallen down the stairs," Delphine said, as she and the earl helped the marquess to his feet.

He laughed and looked around him.

"Oh...so I have. Where's the hot water?" he asked, just as Bessie came running from the kitchen to see what the fuss was about.

"I just heard a terrible...oh, you've dealt with it, ma'am," the maid said, curtseying to them all and blushing.

"Just the hot water, please, Bessie," Delphine replied, rolling her eyes – the next few days were going to be a trial indeed, of that, she was certain.

"My dear Delphine, how pleased I am to see you," the marquess said, as Delphine helped him into a chair by the window, and Delphine began to wonder if his falling down the stairs had merely been an act to garner her attention.

"I'm sure I'm very pleased to see you, too, my Lord," she replied, as the earl cleared his throat.

"Your condolences, Jacob," the earl said, and the marquess blushed.

"Ah…yes, forgive me. We were both very sorry to hear about the death of your father," he said, adopting a somber tone.

"You're both very kind. I hope you have a pleasant stay in London. If there's anything we can do to make your comfortable…" Delphine said, allowing her words to hang in the air.

She knew the earl and the marquess would have no qualms in making their wishes known.

"The hot water," the marquess ventured, just as Bessie emerged again from the kitchen carrying a steaming jug.

"I'll take it up for you at once, my Lord," the maid said. Delphine was thankful to the maid for her swiftness in providing that which the marquess desired.

There would be many more requests of this nature in the days and weeks to come.

"We're staying for a while. You'll be pleased to know," the earl said, smiling at Delphine, who nodded and returned his smile through gritted teeth.

"And do you have plans whilst you're in town?" she asked, hoping there was something specific which had brought them there and would keep them occupied for the duration.

"Oh…the usual round of soirees, balls, dinners. It's all very exciting, the sort of thing one does when one moves in the circles we do," the marquess said, as he rose to his feet.

"But I'm sure we'll be very comfortable here, as we always are. I wonder…could the cook oblige us with some of her delicious mutton chops? The anchovy sauce...it's simply delicious," the earl said.

Delphine nodded. She could hear Alice's voice when she told her of the earl's request. But for now, she merely smiled and edged towards the kitchen door.

"I'm sure something can be arranged, my Lord," she said, and with a curt bow, she retreated from the parlor.

"They're just the same as always," Bessie muttered, as she returned a moment later with the empty water jug.

"I think we're in for a busy few weeks," Delphine replied, shaking her head.

"They always make more work, but I suppose they keep us in business, and for that, we must be grateful," Bessie replied pragmatically.

Her words reminded Delphine of something her father had once told her.

"The guest comes first, Delphine. It's the guest that puts food on the table, and fuel on the fire. Treat them well, and they'll come back," he had said, and that was precisely what Delphine intended to do.

Chapter Two

"Anchovy sauce, more anchovy sauce – I've never known a man to eat gravy in such a quantity," Alice said, tutting as Bessie entered the kitchen with an empty sauce boat calling out for a replenishment.

Delphine had found Alice's reaction to the earl's request for mutton chops with anchovy sauce to be as she had expected, but the request had been fulfilled, and the earl had ordered seconds.

"It's delicious, worth the ride from Oxfordshire alone. I could eat it every night," he had said.

Delphine had not recounted these exact words to Alice, who planned her menus meticulously and would not take kindly to the earl ordering the dish each evening. But she had obliged that first night, and the mutton chops and anchovy sauce had been duly produced.

"The marquess wants more potatoes," Bessie said, and Delphine spooned out another half dozen boiled potatoes from a simmering pot on the range.

It had been a busy evening, for they were almost full, and all of their guests were dining at the inn, along with those who made The Seven Bells their regular watering hole.

"I'll take them to him, you bring the sauce," Delphine said, and the two of them hurried out of the kitchen, into the parlor, and through to the dining room, where a clamor of voices filled the air.

"Excellent mutton...delicious sauce...will you pass the salt cellar?" said the guests, who were sitting at various tables around the room, some alone, some in groups, but all tucking vigorously into their food.

Delphine felt glad to be continuing her father's legacy, even as she felt like a gracious swan, desperately kicking its legs beneath water, whilst remaining calm and serene on the surface. There was so much still for her to learn, and so much that could easily go wrong. Her father had dealt with the financial affairs of the inn himself, and the administrative side of the business largely remained a mystery. Delphine was not good with figures, and she feared making some dreadful mistake in the conduct of her affairs. But with the dinner service in full swing, she had little time to think of such matters, as the earl addressed her.

"I want something specific for breakfast," he said.

A lesser person might have uttered an exasperated cry at these words. The pudding had not yet been served, and already the marquess was talking about his breakfast. But Delphine was not like that. She remembered her father's words, and nodded, offering the earl her full attention.

"If I can get it for you, I certainly will," she said, and the earl smiled.

"Kippers. Smoked kippers. I saw a place that smokes them on the way here, and it set my mind to it. Kippers or herring. I don't mind which, served with bread and butter and a poached egg," he replied.

As luck would have it, Delphine knew the place the earl spoke of – a smokehouse in the shadow of Saint Paul's Cathedral. Alice did not like cooking kippers for breakfast. She complained the smell lingered – which it did – but Delphine wished only to be obliging, and she nodded to the earl, who clapped his hands together in delight.

"I know the place, I'll get some for you," she said, and it seemed the earl was appeased – until another request entered his mind, that is.

"You're too good to them, ma'am. No wonder they keep coming back," Bessie said, as they returned to the kitchen a few moments later.

Delphine knew the maid was right. She always made sure her guests had what they wanted. It was a trait her father had employed, too, one he had learned from his own father before him. That was why the inn was so popular, ensuring that men like the earl and the marquess returned there frequently.

"Well…my father entrusted the inn to me, and I want to make sure I do right by him," Delphine replied.

The rest of the evening passed in a whirl. Alice had made a steamed treacle pudding with custard, and all of their guests commented on how delicious it was. The earl and the marquess sat up late drinking brandy, and it was not until the bells of Saint Paul's had chimed the midnight hour that they finally went to bed. Delphine knew she would have to rise early if she was to buy the kippers for the earl's breakfast, but there was still a great deal to do, and now she, Bessie, and Alice began to prepare the inn for the next morning.

"I hope I've got enough eggs," Alice said, counting through a basket.

"Two dozen – that's more than enough. Mr. Simmonds isn't having breakfast. He's leaving first thing, and the two Miss Aldershotts don't eat them," Bessie said.

Delphine was scrubbing the kitchen table, and Bessie had just made a pot of tea for them – as was their custom. At the end of a long day and before bed, the three women liked to sit down to a cup of tea and catch their breath. It was a hard life, and they were always on their feet. There was always another job to do or a task to see to.

The life of an innkeeper never stops.

It was something Delphine's father used to say.

"And I've kippers to poach in the morning, too," Alice grumbled, shaking her head and tutting.

"He'll only want them once. You know what he's like. He gets these ideas into his head and that's that. It was black pudding last time," Delphine said, stifling a yawn as she sat down at the freshly scrubbed table.

Alice came to sit opposite her, and Bessie brought the pot of tea and placed it in front of them, along with three china cups and saucers.

"We never get any peace when they're here. There's always some demand or other. They want this and that, fetch this, carry that. I feel sorry for their servants. It must be a relief for them when they go away. Where do they both live?" the maid asked, as she poured out the tea.

Delphine smiled. The earl and the marquess had made it their business to inform her at great length of their domestic situations and had gone to pains to tell her that – under no circumstances – were they interested in pursuing marriage in their respective districts.

"The earl has an estate in Oxfordshire. Paxton Hall, I believe it's called, and the marquess resides in Windsor. They went to Eton together, and then Cambridge. They've been friends their whole lives long. They come as a pair. I think they'd be lost without one another," she said, smiling at the thought of the earl and the marquess, who, despite their many faults, had something of an endearing quality to them.

"But they can't remain like that forever, ma'am. It's you they keep coming here to see. And one – or both – are going to be disappointed," Bessie replied, shaking her head.

Delphine sipped her tea. The matter of the earl's and the

marquess' affections had long puzzled her. She did not know what two ageing aristocrats should see in the daughter of an innkeeper. Their worlds were hardly akin, and Delphine could think of nothing worse than being married to a noble. The inn was her life – now even more so – and she had no intention of giving that life up, not for an earl, or a marquess, or anyone.

"Both, I think. But let them have their fun, I suppose. I can hardly refuse them to stay here, and they do spend a lot of money," she said.

Both the earl and the marquess were liberal with their pocketbooks. They drank the finest wines in the cellar, they stabled their horses at the inn, and demanded unusual foods at odd hours – all of which came at a price.

"Just don't let them take advantage of you," Alice said, wagging her finger at Delphine, who smiled.

"I won't. Don't worry. They're harmless enough – if somewhat tedious at times. They'll both ask me to marry them, and I'll refuse them both, too," she said, causing Bessie and Alice to glance at one another with worried looks on their faces.

"Do you think…will you marry, ma'am? We hate to see you without your dear father. The two of you were so close, but now he's gone, you need someone to take care of you," Bessie said.

Delphine sighed. She knew they were only trying to help, but the subject of marriage was not one she wished to discuss. As far as Delphine was concerned, she wanted only to continue her father's legacy. She had known suitors in the past – not least the earl and the marquess. Working in her father's inn entailed a certain amount of attention from the opposite sex. But Delphine had never been interested in such attentions and was content with the thought of living out her life, just as she was.

"I don't need anyone. I don't need someone to take my father's place. I don't need a man to take care of me," she replied, fixing the maid and the cook with a stern gaze.

"You might not need it, ma'am, but it would make you happy, I'm sure," Bessie replied.

Delphine rolled her eyes. Alice had lost her sweetheart at sea many years before, and it had always been her greatest sorrow not to have married. Alice had never expressed interest in a man, nor had she ever lamented the fact. Between them, they knew little of the ways of men, and Delphine was content for that to remain so.

"Right now, what would make me happy would be to go to bed. Come now, we should retire. It'll be morning before we know it, and I've got to get up early and find the earl his kippers," Delphine replied.

They finished their tea, snuffed out the kitchen candles, and locked up for the night. The inn was quiet, and Delphine made her way to bed, holding aloft a candle to light the way. Her bedroom was in the attic, and she could hear the earl snoring in the room below. She climbed into bed with a weary sigh, pulled the blankets over her, and yawned. It had been a long day, and more of the same was to come the next. Not for the first time, she wondered if this was truly the life for her. Her father had entrusted her with the inn, but the choice to stay or go was hers.

But I made a promise, she told herself, and with refresh resolve, she fell into a deep sleep.

Chapter Three

Fermony Grange, Berkshire

"You're not leaving are you, my Lord?" the butler asked, as Maximilian snatched up his traveling cloak and hurried across the hallway.

"There's nothing to keep me here, Dalton. Nothing at all. Tell my father I've left, and have my things sent on. They can find me at…oh. What's the name of that place where father stays in town?" Maximilian asked, as the butler looked at him with a concerned expression on his face.

"The Seven Bells, in London, my Lord. But…to leave so suddenly. Are you sure?" he asked, and Maximilian nodded.

"I can't remain here a moment longer. I *won't* remain here a moment longer. Not after what she's done. I'm leaving, and that's final," he exclaimed, wrapping his cloak around him and buckling the clasp at his neck.

"But my Lord…where will you go after The Seven Bells?" the butler asked.

Maximilian had not thought the matter through. All he knew

was he had no intention of remaining at Fermony Grange a moment longer.

"I don't know. I don't care. I'll stay at The Seven Bells until you send my things. Perhaps I'll go to the continent, or north to Scotland. Anywhere but here," he replied, and pulling on his riding boots, he marched out of the door, followed by his father's butler, who continued in his persuasive overtones.

"But my Lord, your father...he'll want to know why you've left so suddenly. He'll be terribly upset," Dalton said, hurrying after Maximilian, who was marching towards the stables.

"He'll soon know why I've left. It'll be the talk of every drawing room in the *ton* by tomorrow. What *she's* done," Maximilian replied.

He could barely speak her name, even to himself. He would not speak her name, not out loud. Maximilian was humiliated, and Lady Frances Stott was laughing behind his back. The butler's face fell.

"Your betrothal, my Lord? Has it..." he began, and Maximilian nodded.

"It has, Dalton. Spectacularly so," he replied.

They had reached the gates of the stables, which lay on the far side of the house. Fermony Grange was a rambling, ivy-covered house, which had been the seat of the Barons of Fermony for ten generations. It had been Maximilian's home his entire life, but the events of the previous few days had left a bitter taste in his mouth, so much so, he could no longer bear the thought of residing in the district and finding himself the object of the ridicule and gossip that he knew would follow.

For a man to find himself humiliated by the woman he had loved and believed loved him was the cruelest of blows, and the insult Maximilian had suffered was enough for him to distrust all women for the rest of his life. He wanted to go far away – to the continent, to the New World, to anywhere he could forget his troubles and make a new start. Frances had broken their engagement, and she had done so with the revelation she loved another man and would be married to him by the end of the summer.

"My Lord…your father should be told. It's right that you tell him," the butler said, but Maximilian's mind was made up.

"No, Dalton. He'll find out soon enough. I'm leaving. My decision's final. Goodbye," Maximilian replied, before calling out for one of the stable boys to bring him a mount.

The horse was saddled and brought forth. Rain was in the air and the skies were gray and cloudy. But Maximilian did not care. He wanted only to get away, to escape from his humiliation and hide away somewhere he would neither be known nor recognized. London was the obvious choice, and The Seven Bells was a name he had often heard his father speak of.

"My Lord, I beg you to reconsider," the butler exclaimed, but Maximilian flung himself into the saddle and urged the horse into a gallop from the stable yard.

"Have my things sent on after me, Dalton. To The Seven Bells," he called out, as the sound of the horse's hooves echoed across the forecourt in front of the house.

Fermony Grange lay in Berkshire, a day's ride from the capital, and Maximilian rode hard, spying the dome of Saint Paul's Cathedral by the time the early evening had arrived. He was weary – not only from the ride, but from everything that had happened to him in the days gone by. His humiliation had been cruel and entirely unexpected. He had believed Frances to be in love with him, and despite what she had done, his own feelings for her remained.

I was a fool not to see it coming, he told himself, and not for the first time.

There had been the ball at the home of Sir Alfred Blenkinsopp, when Maximilian had seen Frances and the man – Lord Douglas Benn – walking together in the garden. He had refused to believe it then, but the signs had been there. The way she looked at him, the way he looked at her, the strange excuse they had made as to why they walked arm in arm – the stone in her shoe… Maximilian had believed it, or rather, he had not dared to believe the alternative. But the previous day, Frances had come to him and told him of her desire to marry Douglas and to break her engagement with Maximilian.

She's welcome to him, he thought to himself, as he rode through the streets of London, searching for The Seven Bells.

He knew it lay in the shadow of Saint Paul's, on the south side, and as he came to the steps of the cathedral church, he chanced on two well-dressed gentlemen hurrying past.

"Excuse me, sirs, I say, do either of you know the way to The Seven Bells inn?" he asked.

The two men looked at one another and smiled.

"Oh, yes," one said, nodding his head.

"We certainly do," the other replied.

They had a certain eccentricity about them. One was tall, the other short, one was thin, the other rotund, one had hair, the other was bald. They were each dressed in tailored frock coats, with cravats at the neck, and well-polished shoes – though both pairs were splattered with the mud of the city.

"I'm looking for a room tonight and heard of the inn's reputation," Maximilian said.

The two men looked at one another and nodded.

"We're staying there ourselves. We'll take you. You're not...a friend of the landlady, are you?" the short one said.

Maximilian thought this to be a strange question indeed. He knew nothing of the landlady and wanted nothing to do with her save take one of her rooms for however long it took for Dalton to send him his things.

"I don't know any landladies," he replied, feeling a certain sense of exasperation at the odd behavior of the two men.

"That's excellent then," the tall one said, and they both bowed together before beckoning Maximilian to follow them.

"Do you stay often at The Seven Bells?" Maximilian asked.

"Oh, yes. But forgive us...we've not even introduced ourselves.

My name is Robert Grantham, and this is Jacob Rollins," the tall man said, offering his hand to Maximilian, who was leading his horse by the reins.

"Maximilian Blane," Maximilian replied, shaking hands with both men, who now looked at one another excitedly.

"*The* Maximilian Blane? Son of the Baron of Fermony?" the one called Jacob exclaimed.

Maximilian sighed. He had not wanted to be known in London, and whilst it was doubtful that news of his failed betrothal had yet reached the drawing rooms of the capital, he knew it would only be a matter of time.

"That's right, yes," Maximilian replied.

"But we know your father – and he knows us. I'm the Earl of Paxton, and this is the Marquess of Renfrew," the one called Robert said.

This news surprised Maximilian. He had not thought the two gentlemen – as well dressed as they were – to have aristocratic credentials. He had heard of the Earl of Paxton and of the Marquess of Renfrew, though he knew nothing of them, even as they now escorted him in the direction of The Seven Bells.

"You'll find the inn a most convivial place to spend a few nights. We come to stay here often. We're close personal friends of the landlady, you see," the earl said, sounding somewhat haughty, as though a friendship with the landlady was a privilege enjoyed only by a few.

Maximilian thought this was a strange turn of phrase. A landlady was not usually on friendly terms with an earl and a marquess, and he wondered what the true nature of their relationship might be…

"Is that so?" he said, and both men nodded.

"She's a delightful creature. Miss Delphine is her name. She recently lost her father. It's such a tragedy. But she's doing a sterling job as innkeeper," the marquess said.

They were in sight of the inn now. It was a handsome building, whitewashed and with the window edgings painted blue. A large sign hung over the door, depicting seven bells on a blue background, and in the lower windows, Maximilian could see men drinking ale and conversing. He led his horse into the stable yard, followed by the earl and the marquess, who seemed intent on escorting him inside.

"Are you here on business?" the earl said.

Maximilian had not thought of a suitable explanation for his flight from Berkshire, and he merely nodded and gave some vague explanation as to seeing his father's lawyer.

"I don't know how long I'll remain in London," he said, as the earl and the marquess followed him towards the door of the inn.

"You'll find The Seven Bells a hospitable place," the marquess said, and the earl nodded.

"Very hospitable," he repeated.

Maximilian was growing tired of their company. They were a strange pair, and he was uncertain as to their motives. He stepped through the door of the inn and found himself in a comfortably furnished parlor, where a babble of voices filled the air, and a woman bustled back and forth, fetching drinks to a group of men sitting in the window.

"And two more ales, Bessie, my dear," one of them called out.

"Is that the landlady?" Maximilian asked, turning to the earl and the marquess, who both shook their heads.

"No, good heavens, no. That's just the maid, Bessie. I don't know where Miss Delphine is," the earl replied, gazing around him with a disappointed look on his face.

Once again, Maximilian thought it odd to hear the aristocrat refer to the landlady is such familiar terms, but the maid now came hurrying over to him with a welcoming smile on her face.

"Is it a room for the night you're wanting, sir?" she asked, and Maximilian nodded.

"For several nights, if possible. I've come to London on business. I'm having my things sent on from Berkshire. A bed and full board, if you please," he replied.

The maid nodded and turned to consult a large ledger which sat on a table next to the door.

"That'll be two shillings a night, sir. What name shall I put?" the maid asked.

"Blane, Maximilian Blane," Maximilian replied.

The maid's response was non-committal, she had clearly not heard of him, and to Maximilian's amusement, she appeared to be ignoring the earl and the marquess, who continued to loiter nearby.

"Shall I show you to your room, sir?" she asked, and Maximilian nodded.

"I'd be very grateful. I've stabled my horse in the yard. I hope that's all right?" he said, and the maid nodded.

"Quite all right, sir. This way, please," she said, pointing Maximilian towards a staircase which led off from the parlor.

"We'll see you shortly. Do join us for a drink," the earl called out, and Maximilian gave a vague affirmation, not wishing to find himself embroiled in the company of the two men, who settled themselves down at a table by the fire.

Maximilian followed the maid upstairs to a landing, and when they were out of sight of the earl and the marquess, she turned to him with a sympathetic gaze.

"You've had to endure the attentions of our two most persistent residents, I see, sir," she said, and Maximilian could not help but smile.

"I met them by chance on the steps of Saint Paul's. I asked them for directions, and they seemed only too happy to oblige," he replied.

The maid rolled her eyes.

"Yes, they would be. The earl and the marquess. The poor mistress has no end of trouble with the pair," she said, tutting and shaking her head.

The more Maximilian heard about the landlady, the more intrigued he felt. She sounded like a formidable woman, and Maximilian wondered why the earl and the marquess should so admire her when she clearly had not the time of day for either of them.

"She tolerates them?" he enquired, as the maid led him along the landing to a door at the far end.

She produced a bunch of keys and proceeded to select one, turning to Maximilian and nodding.

"She's too good to them. She is. I'd sling them out. But the mistress…no, she runs around after them, always seeing to their needs, appeasing their wants. She's like that with all her guests, though. You'll see, nothing's ever too much trouble. The other day, she was up with the cock crow hurrying to the smokehouse for kippers – and then the earl complained there were too many bones in them. What does he expect, of course they've got bones in them. They're both in love with her, of course," the maid grumbled, shaking her head as she opened the door.

It led into a comfortably furnished room with a large bed, a washstand, an armchair and a small table. The window looked out over the stable yard, so that Maximilian would be able to see the comings and goings – and keep an eye on his horse. He thought the maid overly familiar, though he could hardly speak in defense of the earl and the marquess, given his own first impressions of them.

"Is there something about her that should cause them both to be?" Maximilian enquired, now feeling even more curious about the landlady, an image of whom was slowly being formed in his mind.

"They're both mad, that's what. Not that the mistress isn't a pretty young lady who could have any man she desired, but because they think she might choose one of them. Whenever they come here – and it's frequently – they make a grand gesture, or a proposal, or some foolishness. She lost her father just over a month ago, and I'm worried they'll do something to upset her, not that I wish to judge them, of course, but they cause no end of mischief," the maid said, shaking her head.

"I'm sorry to hear that. Is she...will they...does she have someone?" Maximilian asked.

The maid looked somewhat indignant and nodded.

"She has me and Alice – that's the cook. We manage well enough. Now then, sir. You're welcome to dine any time after six o'clock this evening. We serve breakfast early or late, depending on your preference. If you need hot water, then please come and ask. We've had some warm nights lately, but if you need an extra blanket, we've plenty in the store. I hope you'll be very comfortable with us," she said, and curtseying to Maximilian, she left the room.

Maximilian surveyed his surroundings. It was a comfortable room, and he could see why his father had chosen to stay there on occasions when he had visited the capital. He glanced out of the window and could see his horse stabled below, peering out from one of the stalls. He sat down on the bed and lay back with a sigh. It felt strange to have fled Berkshire so quickly and arrived in London under such circumstances.

He thought of Frances, and of his own humiliation at her hands. Maximilian had no desire to see her again, and he wondered if he would ever be able to trust another woman for as long as he lived. She had betrayed his trust and made him the laughingstock of the district. She would know soon enough of his disappearance, but would she care? She had told him she loved him, and accepted his proposal, whilst all along embroiling herself in a clandestine relationship with Douglas Benn. It made him sick to think about it, and he cursed the day he had laid eyes on her.

The foolishness of the heart, he told himself, shaking his head and vowing never to fall in love again so long as he lived.

Chapter Four

Maximilian was surprised when he opened his eyes and found that darkness had fallen. He had fallen asleep, and he did not know what time it was or for how long he had slept. He sat up and looked around him. The room was dark, but moonlight was coming through the windows, and he could hear a babble of voices from the taproom below. Hoping he was not too late for dinner, he got up and felt his way to the door, opening it to find the landing lit by candles burning in sconces on the wall.

I hope there's still something to eat, he said to himself, as he made his way downstairs.

The atmosphere in the parlor was merry. An accordion player was sitting by the hearth playing tunes on a battered old instrument, and several groups of men were sitting playing cards. A pleasant scent of cooking wafted from the kitchen, and the remnants of a meal lay on a table in the corner. Bessie was bustling back and forth, and she smiled at Maximilian, who nodded to her.

"Something to eat, if you please," he said.

"Rabbit stew and parsley dumplings. Will that be all right?" she asked.

Maximilian shrugged. It was a more rustic choice than he was used to, but his stomach was rumbling, and it seemed he had no choice but to be grateful for what was offered.

"Very well," he said, just as a familiar voice called to him from the far side of the room.

"My Lord, come and join us," the earl called out, and Maximilian sighed.

He had hoped to eat his dinner in peace, and now he looked over to see the earl and the marquess beckoning to him. Reluctantly, he joined them at the table, and Bessie brought a large plate of rabbit stew with four parsley dumplings sitting on top. Maximilian had to admit it smelled delicious, and he took up his knife and fork and attacked the plate with vigor.

"Do you find your quarters adequate?" the marquess asked.

The two men were drinking ale, and the marquess had the top button of his breeches undone, suggesting the two had already eaten.

"They'll do, yes," Maximilian replied.

"We always have the same bedrooms. Facing the front of the inn. Very comfortable," the earl said.

Maximilian was not particularly interested in the details of their accommodation. The bed was adequate, the room comfortably furnished. He needed nothing more than that to satisfy his needs.

"The landlady makes certain of it," the marquess interjected.

"Do you always speak so readily of the landlady?" Maximilian asked, for it seemed the earl and the marquess could converse on no other topic, and that whatever they said, the talk always returned to the woman whom Maximilian had yet to lay eyes upon.

"She's worth speaking readily of. You wait and see. But...we wouldn't want you to think..." the earl began, but the marquess interrupted him.

"To think you were interested in her," he said.

Maximilian stared at them incredulously. They were quite the strangest characters he had ever encountered, and he wondered what on earth should possess them to question him in such a way.

"Interested? I've never met her. I know nothing about her. It's hardly suitable grounds for interest, is it? Besides, I'm finished with women," he said, setting down his knife and fork and pushing his plate away.

The earl and the marquess looked at one another with what Maximilian could only term as relief.

"A sadness in your own life, perhaps?" the earl asked, but Maximilian had heard enough.

He was tired and did not relish the thought of recounting his treatment at the hands of Frances to these two oddities.

"It's complicated," he replied, rising to his feet, but as he did so, the door to the kitchen opened and into the parlor came a woman who attracted the attention of all.

"Ah, Miss Delphine – come and meet your new guest," the marquess called out, beckoning the woman to join them.

* * *

It had been a long day for Delphine. She had risen early to run errands and had spent the morning in the kitchens helping Alice. In the afternoon, she had gone to visit her father's grave, where she had laid a posy of flowers and sat for a while telling him about the earl's request for kippers and lamenting the responsibilities which were now hers. The rest of the day had been spent seeing to the accounts and ensuring the inn could pay its way for another month. She had only just finished and was grateful to Bessie for keeping the show going whilst she was otherwise engaged.

"Just one new guest this afternoon, ma'am. A gentleman by the name of Maximilian Blane. He's here for a few days on business. I don't know how long he'll be staying here," Bessie said, as Delphine entered the kitchen.

"I'll speak to him at dinner. Did the rabbit stew go down well with the guests?" she asked, and Alice nodded.

"I made parsley dumplings to go with them. I've saved you a plateful," she said, and Delphine smiled.

"What would I do without the two of you?" she said, smiling at them both.

Having hastily eaten her supper, Delphine stepped out into the parlor to greet her guests. Almost immediately, the sound of the marquess' voice came from the far side of the room.

"Ah, Miss Delphine – come and meet your new guest," he called out.

Delphine smiled to herself. She felt sorry for the new guest if he had found himself under the influence of the earl and the marquess. They would keep him up all night drinking or bore him half to death with their dull stories and anecdotes. Delphine turned to find the marquess beckoning her towards him. He was sitting with the earl in the snug by the fireplace, and Delphine could see a man at their side. Well dressed and with a handsome face, he looked up as she approached.

"Maximilian, your landlady. Miss Delphine, this is Maximilian Blane, son of the Baron of Fermony," the marquess said.

Maximilian rose from his chair and gave her a curt bow.

"A pleasure to meet you, I'm sure. I'm grateful to you for your hospitality," he said, and Delphine smiled.

She was used to greeting strangers, and as such was used to gaining the measure of a person almost immediately. But the man who stood before her was hard to read. He wore a disinterested expression, and it seemed he was only saying what was expected of him. She wondered who he was. She had never heard of the Baron of Fermony, nor his son.

"You're most welcome. I trust you found the room to your liking?" she asked.

He nodded.

"It'll do, yes," he replied.

"Good...and your dinner? I've just tried the parsley dumplings myself. They're quite delicious," she said, and the man nodded again.

"I liked them well enough, though I'm not used to eating rabbit," he said.

Delphine's face fell. She liked her guests to be happy, and she was not convinced her new guest was entirely so.

"Perhaps there's another dish you'd like," she replied smoothly, thinking back to the mutton chops and anchovy sauce favored by the earl.

"There's really no need," the man replied.

"Kippers for breakfast, perhaps?" the earl ventured.

"You complained about the bones," Delphine replied, for she was growing tired of the earl and the marquess, whose constant demands were wearing her down.

"I don't care for kippers. I don't like the taste," the man replied.

An awkward silence fell, and Delphine began to stack the plates on the table.

"You're here on business, I understand. Do you return to the country or go on from here?" she asked.

Every guest at the inn had a different story to tell. Some were gentleman of leisure, with plans to tour the capital's sights, others had business or were traveling on to the continent. Some, like the earl and the marquess, only wished to make mischief. She hoped her new guest was not cut from the same cloth as his fellow aristocrats. But he shook his head and rose to his feet.

"No, I plan to travel abroad. I'll remain here until my things are sent on. That's all," he said, and with a curt nod of his head in their general direction, he crossed the parlor and hurried up the stairs.

"A strange man," the marquess said.

Delphine gave him a withering look.

"Have you said something to him?" she asked, knowing how difficult the earl and the marquess could be.

"What could we possibly say to him, my dear?" the earl replied.

Delphine sighed. She did not know what to make of her new guest, but it would not have surprised her if the earl and the marquess had been purposefully difficult towards him. They hated competition – both from one another and anyone else. They each believed in their own chances of securing Delphine's affections, and any hint of threat was greeted with robust rebuttal.

"You sent Mr. Hardwick packing," Delphine reminded them.

Mr. Hardwick had dared invite Delphine to the theater with him one evening the previous year. The earl and the marquess, having got wind of this pleasantry, had hounded the man to the point of madness, and he had left, vowing never to return. Delphine had gone to the theater anyway and had refused to speak to either the earl or the marquess for a week.

"He was different," the marquess replied, though he made no attempt to explain why.

Delphine shook her head, glancing at the stairs and wondering if she should try to make a more favorable acquaintance with her new guest before bed.

"What do you know about him? I've never heard of him before, not his father, although...oh, I wonder...did he stay here once or twice, perhaps?" Delphine asked, thinking back to the name of Blane, and believing she had once hosted a man of that same name.

"I believe so, yes, and I believe he's running away," the earl said, with a knowing look.

Delphine hated it when the earl and the marquess spoke in cryptic terms. They liked to think they knew things and that they possessed information which others did not. This they lauded over others with an annoying sense of superiority. Delphine gave him another one of her withering looks.

"And what's he running away from?" she asked.

"Love, of course. Why else do men runaway? He's going to the continent, he's fleeing. It's either love or money, and since he seems to have plenty of money, I can only presume he's been spurned," the earl replied.

The marquess nodded in agreement.

"We've not ascertained his full story, of course. But…well, it's simple enough to tell, don't you think?" the marquess said.

Delphine did not think it so. Another of her father's rules had been to avoid speculation.

Our guests deserve our discretion, he would say, and it was another rule Delphine tried to keep.

It did not matter why the man had taken a room at the inn. That was not for Delphine to concern herself with. What he did with it, and why he was there, was of no consequence.

"I'm sure I don't have a clue why he's here. What does it matter?" Delphine replied.

She had finished stacking the plates now and was glad for an excuse to return to the kitchen.

"Did you see him? The new guest, I mean?" Bessie said, as Delphine set the plates down on the kitchen table.

"I spoke to him briefly. He'd had the benefit of making the acquaintance of the earl and the marquess," Delphine replied, shaking her head and smiling.

"Yes, they arrived together. I felt quite sorry for him. They'd talked to him all the way here from the steps of Saint Paul's. Still, it's his business whose company he keeps," Bessie replied.

Delphine began to wash the plates in a bucket of water by the stove. Despite remembering her father's words, she could not help but wonder as to the reason for their new guest's arrival. Was he, as the earl had suggested, fleeing from love?

"I'm sure we'll know all about him soon enough if the earl and the marquess have anything to do with it," Delphine said.

Alice turned to her from the stove and tutted.

"They're a terrible pair, those two. He was in here earlier, asking me to make more anchovy sauce for his dinner tonight. I told him he could wait until next week when it's on the menu again.

"We must try to be accommodating, Alice. The two of them may try our patience, but they pay their bills on time, and leave a handsome tip behind them," Delphine said, raising her eyebrows at the cook, who tutted.

"Anchovy sauce, indeed…and if I hear another word about the bones in those kippers…what does he expect? A fish without bones?" she said in an exasperated tone, shaking her head as she turned back to the stove and clattered the pots and pans.

"I'm sure it's merely a compliment to your cooking, Alice. People come from far and wide to taste your dishes," Delphine said.

"They can stay far, that's all I'll say. Those two…" Alice said, and she shook her head again as Delphine glanced at Bessie and smiled.

"I'll take in the steamed pudding. It's a shame the baron's son didn't stay down any longer. Marmalade pudding. It's one of your best recipes, Alice," Bessie said, picking up the large plate on which sat a steaming marmalade pudding in all its glory.

"I'm sure the earl and the marquess will find something wrong with it," the cook replied with a sniff.

Bessie rolled her eyes and took up the plate, whilst Delphine followed with a stack of bowls and spoons. There was a merry atmosphere in the dining room, even as she felt sorry their new guest had not remained. The more she thought about him, the more intrigued she was, and as she served out the pudding to the earl and the marquess, Delphine could not help but ask them further questions.

"Do you really think he's fleeing from love?" she asked, placing a bowl of steaming marmalade pudding in front of the earl.

"Undoubtedly, my dear. His sort always does. A rogue, that's what he is. Yes, a fop, a rake, a womanizer. He's left a trail of destruction and broken hearts behind him. You don't want to get mixed up with him. Not for one moment," the earl replied, taking up his spoon and digging into his pudding with gusto.

Delphine gave a wry smile. It would suit the earl and the marquess to portray the new arrival in the most disparaging way possible. They believed every man who crossed the threshold of the inn was a threat to their own hopes of romance. But Delphine had no intention of romancing either of the two men, who, despite their wealth, offered little else by way of attraction. Delphine had not grown up in aristocratic circles. She was used to work and working hard. The idle life of the aristocracy held no interest for her, and she was not about to become a lady who paid calls on other ladies who had equally little to do.

"He only arrived today. I don't know anything about him. He probably won't stay for more than a few nights. He's having his things sent down," Delphine said.

The earl and the marquess looked at one another.

"Let's hope he doesn't stay too long, my dear," the marquess said, as Delphine rolled her eyes.

"Another spoonful of that delicious pudding, but tell the cook it needs more sugar to balance the tartness. Oh, and I'd like deviled kidneys for breakfast, if you please," the earl said.

Delphine made no reply, spooning out the pudding before returning to the kitchen.

"He wants deviled kidneys for breakfast," she said, as Alice turned towards her.

"I'll devil him..." she said, scowling at Delphine, who could not help but laugh.

"And the earl says the pudding was delicious, but needed more sugar," Delphine added, as Alice snatched up a large spoon and shook it towards the door into the dining room.

"More sugar! I'll give him more sugar..." she exclaimed.

Chapter Five

The earl and the marquess did not go to bed until well past midnight. They sat up drinking brandy, and it was only when Bessie raked out the fire and closed the shutters in the parlor that they made their way upstairs, calling out a reminder for their deviled kidneys.

"And early, too, we want to attend matins at the cathedral," the earl had called out, for the following day was a Sunday and the earl and the marquess always went to church on a Sunday.

Their religious devotion may have seemed admirable, but Delphine knew it had a mischievous streak to it. The two aristocrats liked to sit in their respective stalls – a gift from Queen Anne to their families – and laud it over the congregation, whilst talking loudly about the finer points of the sermon. Delphine had once observed this spectacle and the angry looks on the faces of the clergy, who were not used to having their theology picked at during its delivery.

"I'm going to put enough mustard in the deviling to blow his head off," Alice said, shaking her head as she sat down on a chair at the table.

Bessie yawned and sat down next to her. Delphine sat across. Alice had made a pot of tea, and the three of them were sitting until tiredness overcame them. The fire was burning low in the hearth, but Delphine had lit candles around the kitchen, which gave off a flickering light as Bessie poured the tea.

"There we are, nice and strong. I need it after the evening we've had," she said, shaking her head.

Delphine smiled.

"And I don't think that's the last of them. Anchovy sauce, more sugar in the pudding, endless brandies...the list goes on," she said.

"And what of the new guest, too? He didn't even stay for his pudding. Just marched off upstairs," Bessie said, shaking her head.

But Delphine did not think the behavior of their new guest to be that strange. Not everyone who stayed at the inn came with the exuberance of the earl and the marquess. Most wanted only a bed for the night and to be left in peace. There was Sir Horace Ingelby who came to town to see his mistress, staying just one night before returning to Yorkshire and the settled life of a country squire, and Lord Fairfax, who business brought him to London with "no questions asked," not to mention the dozens of gentlemen who passed through the inn each month, attending balls and dinners, striking business deals, or going on towards the continent. The Seven Bells was a place of passing, a place where no one stayed forever, and where Delphine prided herself on offering the hospitality which she now viewed as her father's legacy.

"Wouldn't you march off up to bed too, if you'd endured the earl and the marquess in your ear during a nice dinner? It would put me right off my parsley dumplings," Alice said, tutting.

Delphine smiled. She enjoyed these moments with her two friends. Bessie and Alice were the most loyal of friends, and she did not know what she would do without them. They were the closest thing she now had to family, and she was grateful to them for standing by her during the past few months of tragedy.

"I'm sure we'll see him at breakfast and..." she began, but at that moment, there came a loud banging on the door of the inn.

Bessie jumped, and Alice looked up fearfully, glancing at the clock which had long passed midnight.

"Who could that be?" Bessie said, glancing at Delphine, who had risen to her feet.

It was not unusual for latecomers to arrive at the inn, but it had always been Delphine's father who had admitted them and only if they were of sober mind.

"It's probably someone who wants a bed," Delphine said, just as another bang came at the door, accompanied by a muffled voice calling indignantly for admittance.

"Open up, open up, I say!" they called.

"Open up, indeed. And at this hour – robbers, ma'am," Alice exclaimed.

"I can't just leave them out there. If they keep banging, they'll wake the whole inn up. Can you imagine what the earl and the marquess will say if they're disturbed during the night?" Delphine said. She took up the poker from the hearth, just as another loud banging came at the door.

"Open this door!" the voice shouted.

Bessie and Alice followed cautiously, each carrying a candle, as Delphine made her way out into the parlor. The door of the inn was made of oak; ancient and studded with iron bolts. It would take a battering ram to break it open, and Delphine had earlier pulled the bolts across and turned the large iron key in the lock. There was a metal slide at eye level, a remnant from the days when admittance to the inn had been conducted by password and the parlor the haunt of smugglers from the docks. With her hands trembling, Delphine reached out and pulled it back, just as another banging came at the door.

"Who's there?" she called out, peering through the open slide into the darkness beyond.

"A supposed guest," came the reply, and now Delphine felt confused.

She thought she recognized the voice. There was something vaguely familiar in it. She thought through her guests, trying to place the voice to a face. It was neither the earl nor the marquess, of course, and it couldn't be Mrs. Fairfax, for it was a man's voice. Mr. and Mrs. Digby always went to bed at a respectable hour, and though their son Thomas was something of a rascal, his distinctively plum accent was easily recognizable.

"Oh, forgive me, your name, sir?" she called out, feeling terrible at admitting defeat, but not wishing to open the door until she was certain he was friend and not foe.

There were terrible stories about inns being ransacked by marauding outlaws, though admittedly these were in the depths of the countryside or the wilds of the north and not in the shadow of Saint Paul's Cathedral.

"Maximilian Blane, Lord Maximilian Blane," came the exasperated response, and Delphine's eyes grew wide with horror as she realized it was the son of the baron who was calling for admittance.

She breathed a sigh of relief as Bessie pulled back the bolts and opened the door. The guest stood on the threshold with an angry look on his face.

"I'm sorry, my Lord. We didn't realize it was you. We thought everyone had gone to bed," Delphine said, as the baron's son pushed past them.

"Well, they hadn't. I go out for a few hours and return to find the place a veritable fortress. What are you guarding here? The crown jewels?" he demanded.

Delphine felt terrible. She prided herself on keeping her guests happy, and this incident would hardly be good for business. If she and the others had not been sitting up late, then the baron's son may well have slept on the doorstep, and Delphine could only imagine his anger if that had been the case.

"Well...we always lock the door after the last guests have retired for the night. We didn't realize you'd slipped out," she said, and Maximilian's face turned red with anger.

"Slipped out? Am I under custody? Is this a prison? I'll go where I please and do as I wish. I eat a poor dinner, endure the conversation of two imbeciles, and then find myself locked out when I go in search of entertainment and diversion. The sheets are scratchy, I couldn't find the maid to bring me hot water earlier on, and now I'm questioned as to why I dare leave this...this *establishment* of my own accord," he snarled.

Delphine shot a warning glance at Alice, whom she knew would have something to say about his remarks over the dinner.

"It won't happen again, sir. Please. Let me show you up to bed – I've plenty of candles. I'm sure you'll pass a tolerable night and feel better in the morning. We truly didn't realize you were still out, otherwise we'd have left the door open for you. As for your dinner, I'm very sorry it wasn't to your taste. We'll happily make you whatever you wish, and I'm sure a table away from...those men can be arranged. Bessie can fetch some new sheets at once, and some hot water. We've always plenty on the stove," Delphine replied.

She had seen her father deal with unruly guests in this manner on many occasions. Any complaint could be turned on its head, and appeasement was the simplest way to discourage argument. But the baron's son did not appear to be appeased.

"Yes...well, I'd like to splash water on my face and go to bed. These things should've have been seen to before," he replied.

Delphine pointed towards the staircase and tried to force a smile onto her face.

"This way, please" she said, glancing at Bessie, who nodded and hurried off into the kitchen to fetch the hot water.

Alice gave Maximilian a withering look, but she made no comment, and the inn door was shut and bolted, as Delphine led the baron's son upstairs. She was thankful the disturbance had not roused the earl and the marquess and, as they passed along the landing, Delphine could hear snoring coming from their bedrooms. Maximilian's room was at the far end, and she opened the door for him and set the candle down on the bedside table.

"You can light the others. I'll sit up for a while," he said, pulling off his boots.

Delphine did as she was told, and soon the room was bathed in flickering candlelight.

"I trust you had a pleasant evening?" she asked, and Maximilian nodded.

"Pleasant enough, until I found myself locked out of my own lodgings and banging so hard on the door, I might've woken the dead. There was a ball at the house of a Mrs. Grigson – a socialite of sorts. She has three sons. I know the middle one by acquaintance, so I called in. It was hardly worth it," he replied.

Delphine was uncertain what to say. He seemed perpetually discontented and simmering with anger set to boil over at any moment. Delphine quietly finished lighting the candles around the room and retreated to the doorway. She would be pleased when her new guest had left.

"Can I get you anything else? A nightcap, perhaps?" she asked.

The baron's son looked up and nodded.

"Yes, fetch it for me. I'll sit and read, though I couldn't find much by way of a library here. What do your guests do to entertain themselves?" he asked.

"They…talk to one another, mainly," she replied. The baron's son gave her a withering look.

"Bring me a nightcap, some fresh sheets, and some hot water. That's all I want. It's not that difficult, is it?" he asked as Delphine gave a curt nod in reply.

Delphine wanted so desperately to please him and make amends for the problems of the evening. She felt ashamed for being unable to placate him as she knew her father would have done, even as she knew offering him a brandy was the right thing to do

"I'm not interested in talking to anyone, and if the conversation is limited to that of those two blithering idiots, then God help me," he replied.

"I'll fetch you those things now, and I'm sure I can find some books for you tomorrow," Delphine said, even as her heart was beating so fast she felt it might explode.

She closed the door behind her and hurried off down the corridor. Bessie was just coming up the stairs with a jug of hot water and fresh sheets, but Delphine stopped her.

"I'll take them. I'm just going to fetch the baron's son a brandy," she said.

Bessie looked at her in surprise.

"A brandy? At this hour? Does he really want a brandy now?" she asked, but Delphine shook her head.

"No, but I offered him a nightcap. I thought it might…smooth over his complaints," she replied.

"Was he nasty to you, ma'am?" Bessie asked, and Delphine blushed.

"We must get used to difficult guests," she replied.

Delphine was only doing what she believed her father would do in the same situation. She had often heard her father offer a guest a drink on the house, or the use of one of the horses for the morning – little things which served to appease a complaint and prevent ill-words from spreading. The inn traded on its reputation, and if a guest was not happy, then that unhappiness could easily spread.

"I'm sure he'll be appeased, ma'am. Might I go to bed now? I'm asleep on my feet," Bessie said, and Delphine nodded.

"Certainly, Bessie. You've worked hard today, and I fear tomorrow will be more of the same. Goodnight," Delphine said, taking the jug of hot water and the sheets from Bessie and smiling at her, even as she felt like crying.

Alice, too, had gone to bed, and now Delphine poured a large brandy into a glass and balanced it on a tray, holding the sheets under her arm and the jug in her other hand. She made her way back upstairs, setting the tray down on a table on the landing as she knocked gently on the baron's son's door.

"Yes, come in," he called out, and opening the door, Delphine picked up the tray and went inside.

Maximilian was standing by the window. It was a moonlit night, and he had drawn back the curtains so that the silvery light of the moon cast its rays across the rug by the bed.

"I've brought the hot water and the sheets," Delphine said, but as she stepped over the threshold, she stumbled and almost lost her balance.

"Foolish woman, can't you do anything right? Here, let me take that," Maximilian exclaimed, and he hurried over to Delphine and took the jug from her hand.

For a brief moment, their hands touched, and Delphine felt humiliated at having almost fallen over.

"Thank you... I...was carrying too much. I'm not usually like this," she said, as Maximilian set the jug down on the table and tossed the sheets onto the bed.

"Don't you have the maid to bring things for you?" he asked in irritation.

"I told her she could go to bed. It's been a long day for us all," Delphine replied, as she set down the glass of brandy.

"You run the inn on your own, do you? I must say, I was surprised to find three women here," he said, and Delphine smiled.

"We're quite capable of running an inn, I assure you. It's been in my family for several generations, but...well, my father passed away recently, and the responsibility is mine now," she replied.

Maximilian looked at her with a searching gaze.

"I see. Well, you've a lot to learn, all of you," he replied.

There were no words of sympathy, only the evident criticism he had, and Delphine sighed, wondering if she could do anything right.

"I'm sure we're learning. I'm sorry for your inconvenience this evening," she said, trying her best not to show her anger at his arrogance and rudeness.

"Let's hope tomorrow's better," he said.

"I'll leave you in peace. Goodnight," she said, and he nodded to her.

"Yes, I'm sure it is," he replied.

Delphine closed the door behind her with a sigh. She was tired, but her mind was filled with thoughts of her encounter with the baron's son. She knew she had done the right thing in appeasing him, and she knew her father would have told her so, even as he had remained difficult and angry.

I just hope I haven't ruined things, she said to herself, as she made her way sadly to bed.

Chapter Six

"Too much mustard, take it back," the earl exclaimed, spitting out his deviled kidneys and grimacing.

Delphine looked at him disdainfully.

"What did you expect? You wanted deviled kidneys, and Alice made you deviled kidneys," she said, taking up the dish.

"But not with enough mustard to blow my head off. My mouth's on fire. Fetch me a glass of milk," the earl exclaimed.

The commotion had caused the other guests taking breakfast to look up and shake their heads, and Delphine returned to the kitchen with the offending dish, knowing precisely what Alice would say in response.

"I'll devil him, the devil. Too much mustard? Too much mustard? I'll..." she said, rolling up her sleeves and glancing at the rolling pin she was using to roll out a large piece of pastry for a pie.

"I'll just scrape a little of the sauce off and cover it in melted butter," Delphine said, going to the stove.

The earl's bark was worse than his bite, and it would not take much to appease him. She melted some butter in a pan and poured it over the dish of deviled kidneys, mixing it in to dilute the ferocity of the mustard, which Delphine suspected Alice to have added in deliberately larger quantities.

"Everyone else just wants eggs and bacon," Bessie said, and Alice nodded.

"Eggs and bacon are easy enough. Is our new guest down yet?" Alice asked.

"He went out first thing to walk by the river. I don't know if he's coming back for breakfast," Bessie said, as she hurried out of the kitchen with a plate of sliced bread and butter.

Alice rolled her eyes.

"It's a madhouse. Comings and goings, demands for this and that. He was very rude to you last night, I thought," she said, turning to Delphine and shaking her head.

"He was... I fear he won't be an easy guest," Delphine replied, knowing that was the diplomatic answer.

She had been thinking a lot about Maximilian since their encounter the night before. Alice was right – he had been rude, exceedingly so, and his lack of empathy over the death of her father, and his intimation that three women could not run an inn by themselves, was insulting. He had said nothing about going out early, and now she wondered where he could have gone to such an early hour.

"A strange thing, indeed. Out at all hours, early rising, late returns. Does he expect us to wait up for him every night?" Alice asked, shaking her head.

Delphine did not know the answer to that question, or to any of the other speculations surrounding their new guest. Where he went and what he did was his own business, as inconvenient as it may be for them. She took up the dish of deviled kidneys and returned to the dining room.

"I've changed the sauce," she said, as the earl looked down at the plate and narrowed his eyes.

"Less mustard?" he asked, taking up his fork.

"Less mustard," Delphine replied.

The earl tentatively tried a forkful and nodded.

"Yes, much better. You can tell the cook I'll have it like this tomorrow," he said.

"And I'll have the same," the marquess said, for he usually wanted whatever the earl had and vice versa.

Delphine could not imagine one without the other. They were a strange pairing, and whilst they exasperated her, they formed part of the furniture –The Seven Bells would not be the same without the earl and the marquess.

"Aren't you both going to matins this morning?" she asked, hearing the bells of the cathedral begin to chime.

"We time it just right. It takes only five minutes to walk from here to the cathedral, and we take our places just as the bell rings for the voluntary. There's at least another five minutes of organ music before the clergy reach their places. I'd say we've got time for another cup of coffee and one of those excellent sweet buns I saw the maid serving earlier on," the marquess replied.

Delphine smiled. She had no doubt the two of them would arrive at the cathedral at precisely the right time to cause a fuss or implement some mischief or other. But at least they would be someone else's problem until they returned for luncheon.

"I'll fetch you some," Delphine replied, but the earl stopped her.

"How is...the new guest?" he asked, lowering his voice.

The earl enjoyed intrigue. He liked to be in the know and to know other people's business. Delphine narrowed her eyes.

"I'm sure he's quite all right. He went out early this morning, apparently," she replied. The earl gave her a knowing look and tapped his nose.

"A clandestine affair, perhaps. He's been spurned, you know," the earl said, and the marquess nodded.

"Yes, spurned by Lady Frances Stott. She played him quite a merry game, by all accounts," the marquess said.

Quite how the two aristocrats had come by this information

remained unclear. They enjoyed dangling gossip for others to be baited by, and Delphine was not about to trust them to be telling the truth.

"And how do you know this?" she asked.

The earl looked somewhat offended by her question.

"We know things," he said, and Delphine knew this was his way of saying he would not tell her but would impart further information as to the situation if she desired it.

"What things?" she asked, for despite herself, Delphine *was* interested.

She knew what her father would have said – that idle gossip was the preserve of idle women and not to be entertained in a respectable establishment. But there was something about the baron's son which fascinated her, despite his anger. He had not been merely angry about scratchy sheets and a lack of hot water. There was a simmering anger beneath his façade, and he had a sense about him of a man carrying a terrible burden. There was no doubt he was escaping from something, but what that something was, Delphine could not for the life of her imagine – unless it was as the earl suggested.

"That he was spurned. He was in love with her, but all the while, she was involved in an affair with another man – Sir Godfrey Redbald. They're getting married, apparently," the earl said.

Once again, Delphine marveled at the ability of the earl and marquess to glean such information, having apparently not left the inn since Maximilian's arrival the day before. But they were always talking to this person or that, and it was not beyond the realm of possibility that another guest should have furnished them with the information they had sought.

"He fled from Berkshire with nothing but his horse and the clothes he stood up in. He's making for the continent, apparently," the marquess said, and the two men glanced at one another and nodded knowingly.

Delphine pondered these words. She felt sorry for Maximilian – despite the manner in which he had treated her. For a woman to spurn a man in such a way was a humiliation, one which was not easily recovered from. To remain in Berkshire after such a dreadful occurrence would surely only lead to further sorrow, and it was hardly surprising to learn Maximilian had fled.

"Well...good luck to him," Delphine replied, for she could hardly pass judgement on a man who had been so ill-treated, and whilst she had not enjoyed his barbed comments, they were at least understandable in a man who had been treated in such a way.

"The sooner he leaves, the better," the earl replied, and Delphine gave him an exasperated look.

"I do need other guests rather than just the two of you, you know," she snapped.

The earl and the marquess had driven other guests away before – those they had taken a disliking to, believing they were a threat to whatever strange and misguided thoughts they entertained. Delphine had no intention of marrying either of them, and she was not about to lead them to believe she was, even as they believed quite the opposite.

"Yes, but not...men like that," the marquess replied.

"And if he did stay...what would you say then?" she asked.

The earl and the marquess glanced at one another.

"Well...he shouldn't stay, should he?" the earl said, but Delphine could see no reason why he should not.

"But if he did. He's paid his bill. He's no different from anyone else," she replied, pressing the earl, who now became flustered.

"It's your choice...I suppose. You may have whoever you wish to stay here. It's an inn, after all. But we would worry about you. Yes, we'd worry," he said, appearing to regain his composure.

Delphine laughed. She knew precisely why they did not want Maximilian to remain at the inn. It was because they were both in love with her, and the arrival of any man, whatever his character, proposed a threat to them.

"Shall I fetch you those sweet rolls?" she asked, but both the earl and the marquess had risen to their feet.

"No...we'll be late for matins. Come along, Robert," the marquess said, glancing at Delphine with a look of incredulity.

The two of them stormed out of the dining room, the earl leaving his deviled kidneys unfinished. Delphine smiled and shook her head.

What a strange pair they are, she thought to herself, returning to the kitchen.

After breakfast, when Delphine, Bessie, and Alice took their morning break and shared a pot of tea, she decided to venture her thoughts on the earl's words.

"The earl and the marquess seemed in a hurry this morning," Bessie said, as she poured the tea.

"Let them stay out all day. He didn't even finish his deviled kidneys, and it'll be something else he wants tomorrow. Coddled eggs – that's what it was last time. He wanted coddled eggs every day. Coddled eggs, indeed," Alice said, shaking her head.

Delphine smiled. The running battle between Alice and the earl and the marquess would be fought forever. They would demand, and she would retort. It was as it always had been.

"I think I rather annoyed them," Delphine said, and the maid and the cook looked at her in surprise.

"Is that so? How?" Alice asked, and Delphine explained the conversation which had taken place earlier on.

Both Bessie and Alice laughed at the description of the earl's indignation.

"I'm sorry, ma'am, but that's too delicious for words," Alice exclaimed, slapping her leg as she laughed.

"They think every man that comes here is a threat," Delphine replied.

"Well, what if one was. Ma'am?" Bessie asked. and Delphine looked at her curiously.

"What do you mean?" she asked, for she had never taken the indignation of the earl and the marquess seriously.

They were simply being foolish, for no man had ever intrigued her.

"Well, what if you did play them along? The earl and the marquess, I mean, and pretend to fall in love with someone? The new guest, perhaps," Bessie replied.

Delphine thought about this for a moment. It was certainly a novel idea, but as she thought about it, the more it made sense. If the baron's son was to fall in love with her, perhaps he would stop being so beastly towards women. After all, the fairer sex could not be held collectively responsible for his own failings with Lady Frances Stott. And if it were seen that that their new guest *had* fallen in love with Delphine, then the earl and the marquess might realize the folly of their own designs and at last leave her alone.

"You're not going to play them along, are you, ma'am? You mustn't encourage them," Alice said, glancing at Bessie and tutting.

"But imagine if our new guest was to fall in love with me, or at the very least show interest in me. How do you think the earl and the marquess would feel then? And our new guest, too? Perhaps he might realize the error of his insults towards us women." she replied.

It *was* a mischievous idea, and its consequences could be very problematic, but Delphine liked the thought of seeing the earl and the marquess realize they were not entitled to exercise their perceived ownership over her. She had no intention of marrying either of them, and it would be far better if they realized that fact sooner rather than later. If Maximilian was to fall in love with her, then the earl and the marquess might finally realize the folly of their own intentions and leave her alone. Likewise, it would do no harm for Maximilian to have his own opinions altered and his attitude changed. She felt sorry for him in his breakup with his betrothed, but that was no excuse for treating the whole of womankind as a pariah.

"Well...they'd not be happy, ma'am," Alice said, with a worried look on her face, but Bessie reached out and took Delphine's hand in hers.

"I think it's a good idea, ma'am." she said, but Delphine nodded.

"It's your idea, Bessie. But yes, I think so, too," Delphine replied.

It would only be a bit of fun, and she could not imagine for a moment the baron's son would reciprocate. If his heart had been broken, he would surely not wish to risk it being so again. Delphine herself did not wish to fall in love with anyone. She had her own responsibilities and the thought of marriage had hardly occurred to her. But she needed something – anything – to distract her from her thoughts of the past. She missed her father terribly, and she was still uncertain as to what the future would hold. She no longer wanted to be the object of the earl and the marquess' constant attentions, and if a little deception was required to achieve this end, then so be it. There was so much that could go wrong, so much potential for disaster. But she still felt like the graceful swan, kicking its legs frantically beneath the surface, and the thought of something to take her mind off those thoughts was very appealing.

"It's an idea, certainly. But I'm tired of the earl and the marquess demanding so much of my attention. I want them to realize I'm not interested in their advances. They won't listen to me if I tell them – you know what they're like – but perhaps if I show them...well, they might come to understand. And as for the baron's son...well, he was so rude to us all. I didn't like it. He shouldn't take out his anger on us," Delphine replied.

"But what of the baron's son? What if they hound him like they did that poor gentleman before?" Alice replied.

"It might give him something to distract him from his troubles.

Besides, I rather think our new guest might enjoy sparring with the earl and the marquess. He's the sort of man who seems to give as good as he gets. He'll be just as rude to them as he was to us" Delphine replied.

She was under no illusion that Maximilian was a man who did not suffer fools gladly, and that he would be more than a match for the earl and the marquess – whatever ploy they tried against him.

"It might be fun to watch," Bessie said, but Alice still did not look convinced.

"But what about you, ma'am? Do you really think you should? You've been through so much already. We don't want you to get hurt," she said, but Delphine's mind was already made up.

"I won't. I need something to take my mind off things. Something to stop me dwelling on everything that's happened to me. A fresh start, that's what I want. I can't bear the thought of the earl and the marquess forever breathing down my neck. They won't be told, so they need to be shown. Besides, I doubt it'll come to anything. I just think...well, he seems...an interesting character, as rude as he" she said, smiling at the thought of playing the earl and the marquess at their own game, and teaching the baron's son a little respect in the process.

"But what will you do, ma'am? How can you make him fall in love with you?" Alice asked.

Delphine had not worked out the particulars of her plan. That would come later. The idea was new – it had only occurred to her during her conversation with the earl and the marquess at breakfast. But it would surely not be difficult to lay the possibility of romance before the baron's son. If what was said about him was true – that a lover had spurned him, and he had fled Berkshire in disgust – then he would surely be looking for a sympathetic ear and perhaps even a shoulder to cry on.

"I'm sure there're ways. But I don't want to hurt him. He's been hurt already. That's not my intention. I can teach him a lesson – that not every woman is like this betrothed who spurned him. Wit and charm, intelligence, and kindness – those are the virtues which most women possess. He needs to be reminded of that fact, and not judge all women according to his own limited experience," she replied, smiling as she spoke.

It was not out of a desire for vengeance that Delphine wished to act, but the teaching of a lesson. The earl and the marquess needed to realize they could not simply demand her attentions, and the baron's son needed to realize there was more to the fairer sex than the sadness of rejection and the holding of power. Delphine was glad of Bessie's idea, even as she now made it her own.

"Will he be back for breakfast?" Alice asked, for Maximilian had not yet eaten and the other guests had long since departed the dining room.

"He can have it when he gets back. He can have whatever he desires," Delphine replied, for the details of the plan were forming in her mind, and she was eager to begin at once...

Chapter Seven

Maximilian had risen early that morning. He had heard the earl singing in the next room – an unpleasant warbling which had prevented any further recourse to sleep. But having passed a tolerable night – until his rude awakening – Maximilian had left the inn to walk by the river. He liked London. It was a city of anonymity, a place where one could disappear into obscurity. Back home, in the district of Fermony Grange, Maximilian was known by everyone, and to have remained there in the wake of the scandal which had engulfed him would have been intolerable.

It was Sunday morning, and the bells of the city churches were peeling out the summons for matins. Maximilian was not a religious man, but he could appreciate the comfort which such beliefs offered, and he had a keen eye for architecture and art. Finding himself close to the church of Saint Andrew by the Wardrobe, he stepped into its cool and dusty interior. The organ was playing gently, and he heard the beginning of matins as a surplice clad clergyman rose at the front.

"Dearly beloved brethren, the Scripture moveth us in sundry

places to acknowledge and confess our manifold sins and wickedness; and that we should not dissemble nor cloke them before the face of Almighty God our heavenly Father; but confess them with a humble, lowly, penitent, and obedient heart..." he began.

Maximilian slipped into a pew at the back and listened for a few moments. His father would be at the church on the estate listening to the same words, and he thought of Frances, sitting in her family's pew in the village church that morning and wondered if she would acknowledge her manifold sins and wickedness.

Don't think about her. You'll only grow bitter, he told himself, as the service continued.

Maximilian did not want to be that sort of person. It would be too easy to fall into the trap of resentment and to think of Frances as the end of the possibility of romance. Maximilian had been hurt, his heart was broken, but he now realized the folly of dwelling on such feelings, when Frances would not be feeling the same way. She had made her decision and turned her back on him. That was that, and dwelling on the matter would do nothing to change it.

But can I really put it behind me? he asked himself.

Fleeing to London had been a knee-jerk reaction to a bigger problem. What was Maximilian to do now? He had thought his life would follow a predictable and well-defined course. He would marry Lady Frances Scott, and they would live together at Fermony Grange. In the fullness of time, Maximilian would inherit his father's title and become the Baron of Fermony. There would be an heir and other children, too. He and Frances would have grown old together, and that would have been that.

But cruel circumstances had prevented that, and Maximilian was now left with nothing but possibility. He would still inherit his father's title, but everything else was open to question. The thought of going abroad returned to him, and he wondered where he might go – Florence? Venice? Rome? Or further – to Sicily or Malta. He had heard stories of aristocrats who had traveled into the far east and the Indian sub-continent. Perhaps that was to be his destiny, and he pondered the possibility of where fate might take him.

I can go anywhere I choose, he told himself.

The prospect was both exciting and terrifying in equal measure. He had not listened to the rest of the service, nor to the sermon, but emerging from the church, Maximilian felt himself to have a renewed sense of purpose. He would put Lady Frances Stott behind him and have nothing to do with the fairer sex ever again. It seemed a strange ultimatum to make, but one which Maximilian felt a certain sense of justice in determining. Women were all cut from the same cloth – or so he reasoned – and he had no intention of ever allowing another to break his heart as Lady Frances Stott had done.

Maximilian's stomach was rumbling, and he realized he had not eaten anything since the somewhat unpleasant dinner of the night before. The rabbit stew had not been to his taste, and the parsley dumplings had been hard.

I hope the breakfast might be a little better, he said to himself, for it could not be difficult to fry an egg and some bacon to satisfaction.

The inn was only a short distance away and he hoped he would not have to suffer the attentions of the earl and the marquess. The clock on Saint Paul's had just struck ten O'clock as he pushed open the door of the inn and stepped into the parlor.

At least it wasn't locked this morning, he thought to himself.

The parlor was empty, though a fire was burning in the hearth, and he took off his hat and gloves, just as the door to the kitchen opened and his hostess appeared, beaming at him.

"Good morning, my Lord," she said, and Maximilian was somewhat taken aback.

He had not insisted on the title, and he was not entirely sure if he had told the landlady of his background. He thought back to their encounter of the previous evening. He had been sharp with her, sharp enough to expect an icy reception, but her demeanor was quite the opposite, and there was a smile on her face.

"Good morning...Miss Delphine?" he said, struggling to recall her name.

The landlady nodded.

"I trust you've had a pleasant walk. Did you hear the bells?" she asked.

Maximilian nodded.

"I heard them, yes. The cathedral...quite a peel," he replied, and Delphine smiled.

"You must be hungry. Won't you come and sit in the dining room? I'll bring you your breakfast in a moment, and there's a pot of coffee on the stove. Will you have some bread and jam, too?" she asked, beckoning him to follow her to the dining room.

Maximilian had not been expecting such a show of hospitality. After his arrival and the events of the night before, he had imagined the inn to be merely a front to chaos and its proprietor overwhelmed by her responsibilities. But this morning, everything appeared calm, and nothing was too much trouble.

"Bread and jam, yes...thank you...and a pot of coffee. What's for breakfast? Not kippers, I hope," he said, for he feared the influence of the earl on his dining choices.

But Delphine shook her head and laughed.

"Kippers are...an acquired taste. No, I've got eggs and bacon, some black pudding, sausages, and mushrooms. There're fried potatoes, too, if you wish," she replied.

Maximilian did wish – it sounded like a feast, and he was only too happy to indulge in it. Delphine led him to a table by the window, which had been laid with a fresh linen cloth and what appeared to be the best silverware and crockery.

"How delightful," he said, as Delphine pulled back the chair for him and the maid appeared with a pot of coffee.

"It's freshly brewed," she said, smiling at Maximilian and taking up his cup to pour.

Delphine deftly unfurled a starched napkin and placed it on Maximilian's lap, before hurrying off to the kitchen and reappearing a few moments later with an enormous plate of breakfast. Everything on it was doubled – two eggs, two sausages, two slices of black pudding, two pieces of bacon as thick as chops, two large field mushrooms cooked in butter, and an enormous pile of fried potatoes. There was bread and butter, three different sorts of jam, along with pots of honey and marmalade.

"Can I get you anything else? The mustard jar, perhaps?" Delphine asked, but Maximilian shook his head.

"This is more than enough," he replied, and Delphine smiled at him.

She was really very pretty, he thought to himself. Her long red hair hung down over her shoulders and she had large green eyes and rosy cheeks. She was tall and slender and modestly dressed in a white dress and cloth cap. He had not appreciated her the evening before, for his mind had been so filled with thoughts of what he had fled, and hardly on the present.

"You must tell me if there's anything else I can get you. And after breakfast, I'd like to move you to a different room, if you'd like, that is. It's larger, and the bed is far comfier. I embroidered the sheets on it myself," she said, and Maximilian smiled.

"You don't have to go to any trouble on my account. My quarters are perfectly adequate," he replied, though secretly the thought of escaping the sound of the earl's singing was appealing.

"It's no trouble at all. I'm only too happy to oblige. I've made the room up already. Once your things arrive, there'll be much more space for them there," she said, and Maximilian nodded.

He would not refuse her hospitality, even as it seemed overly generous. She left him to eat his breakfast in peace. The dining room was deliciously quiet without the constant noise of the earl and the marquess maintaining their endless diatribe. Maximilian wondered if he had been too hasty in his judgement of the inn – and its landlady.

It's really not that bad a place, he said to himself, as he cleared the last of his plate and sat back with a satisfied sigh.

Now he began to examine his surroundings in more detail. It was a comfortable room, well furnished, and the walls were covered in all manner of portraits and pictures. His eyes rested on a large wine rack in the corner and a door, which presumably led down to a cellar below. Maximilian knew little about wine, but he enjoyed it, and he resolved to ask his hostess to tell him more about the vintages the inn had for sale. Just then, the kitchen door opened, and Delphine herself emerged, bearing a large frying pan, from which she offered Maximilian further breakfast sustenance.

"I cooked another round of everything, just have whatever you want," she said, and Maximilian hardly felt able to refuse, so that when he had finished, he was forced to loosen his belt buckle by several notches.

"That was delicious," he said, as Delphine cleared away his empty plate.

"I'm very pleased to hear it. Will you have another cup of coffee? Some more bread and jam, perhaps?" she asked, but Maximilian shook his head.

"I couldn't possibly eat or drink another thing. I was going to go for another walk, but...well, sitting in the window with a book to read might be preferable," he said, though he realized then that he had nothing by way of reading material to keep him entertained, the offerings of the inn having brought little by way of inspiration.

He had left Berkshire in such a hurry that he had come only with the clothes he stood up in and the saddle for his horse, which was now being looked after in the stables of the inn.

"Would you like one of the periodicals? London's full of penny newspapers. I can send out for some if you wish. The sun comes into the parlor at this time of day. You could sit in the window there. You won't be disturbed. Or should I show you to your new bedroom first?" Delphine asked.

It seemed nothing was too much trouble for her, and Maximilian was curious as to why the landlady should be so eager to please him all of a sudden. She had certainly not been rude the day before, but the details of service he might have expected had been lacking. The scratchy sheets, the lack of hot water, the underwhelming dinner...all of that had been replaced with service which surpassed anything he might have expected. This was like being at Fermony Grange, surrounded by an army of servants to do his bidding.

"The bedroom, perhaps, and then the periodicals," he said, and Delphine nodded.

"Certainly...come this way, my Lord," she said, and beckoning to Maximilian, she led him up the stairs to the landing, where they turned right, rather than left, and up a short flight of stairs to another level, where a large door stood before them.

"In the roof?" Maximilian said, and the landlady nodded.

"It was called 'the captain's quarters' once. The inn used to be a place for smugglers to congregate, but now things are more civilized," she said, taking out a key and unlocking the door.

It opened into a magnificent bedroom cum drawing room, which reached almost the entire length of the inn. A large four-poster bed stood in the center, with drapes hanging down at its side. There was a desk and chairs, and a freestanding stove with a chimney which was built up into the roof. There was a washstand, and a row of little windows, almost like portholes, which looked out over the front of the inn towards the docks.

"What a splendid bedroom," Maximilian said, and Delphine gave a slight bow and looked around her proudly.

"Yes, my father did all the work himself. But we keep this room for...only certain people," Delphine replied.

Maximilian turned to her curiously. He did not know what she meant by "certain people." Was he somehow entitled to special treatment? He had done nothing to deserve it. If anything, he had been overly critical of the inn and excessive in his demands. Rude, even. Perhaps that was it…he had complained about the scratchy sheets, the lack of hot water, and the mediocre dinner. Delphine was merely trying to make amends, and Maximilian was grateful to her for doing so.

"I see…well, it's a very pleasant room, and if you wish me to occupy it, then I shall," he said.

His words seemed to please Delphine, who smiled at him and handed him the key.

"Why don't I show you down to the parlor again and send out for the periodicals? You could have a cup of coffee and then it won't be long until luncheon," she said.

Maximilian did not believe he would eat another thing, but the thought of dozing in an armchair in the parlor window certainly had its appeal, and he followed Delphine downstairs, glad to have put their uncertain first introductions behind.

"Something light to read. I don't want to hear about the doom and gloom in the world," he said, settling himself down in the armchair which Delphine now proffered.

"I'll send Bessie – the maid. *The Gentleman's Magazine*, perhaps?" Delphine said, and Maximilian nodded.

"Yes, and something with the caricatures in. I like to see the Regent taken down a peg or two," he replied.

Delphine went off to issue instructions to the maid, and it was not long before Bessie appeared with the requested copies and a fresh pot of coffee.

"Miss Delphine says I'm to bring you anything you wish, my Lord. A slice of cake, perhaps?" she said, as she set down the periodicals on the table next to Maximilian.

"Just the coffee, thank you," he replied, thinking just how much he was enjoying this lavish treatment, even as he wondered again as to Delphine's motivation…

Chapter Eight

"What might you wish to dine on at luncheon, my Lord? Cutlets of lamb? Boiled beef? A chicken stew?" Delphine asked, just as the clock on the parlor mantelpiece struck the half hour after twelve.

Maximilian had been dozing. The sun was warm, and the armchair was comfortable. He had read the magazine and amused himself with the caricatures, laughing at a particularly rude one which depicted the Regent in a bathing suit with Maria Fitzherbert peering out of a bathing machine whilst Queen Caroline peered through a pair of opera glasses from her carriage.

"Oh... some cutlets would be delicious, thank you," he said, smiling at Delphine, who nodded.

"I trust you've had a pleasant morning. Would you care for a glass of wine before luncheon?" she asked, but before Maximilian could reply, a commotion at the door caused both to look up.

"I'm telling you, it was heretical. He got it all wrong. I'm all in favor of young canons preaching fervently, but he went too far. I don't want to sit there and be told I'm about to suffer fire and brimstone," the earl was saying.

"Me, neither. We had every right to tell him the error of his ways. I don't know why the verger was so put out about it, and for the beagle to have us escorted out of the cathedral. I'm going to write to the dean. I'll write to the bishop. I'll write to His Majesty. He's the head of the Church of England. He'll have something to say about it," the marquess replied.

"I've a good mind never to set foot in Saint Paul's for as long as I live, I..." the earl began, but he suddenly realized he was being observed, and turned to look at Maximilian and Delphine with surprise etched on his face.

The marquess did the same, and both men looked somewhat taken aback to find the parlor thus occupied. Maximilian would gladly have left. He had come to the conclusion that the earl and the marquess were troublemakers and not to be trusted. He had not enjoyed their company the evening before, nor did he wish for it that day, either.

"Oh, Delphine, are you taking orders for luncheon? We'll start with a bottle of claret. Then the beef – you do have beef, don't you?" the earl said, and Delphine nodded.

"Boiled beef, yes, and Yorkshire puddings. You can have those first, and then some slices of beef with gravy," she replied.

"The wine first, and some bread and butter. Yes, we must have bread and butter. And mustard for the beef. Is there anymore of the marmalade pudding left? We'll have some of that, too," the marquess said, and the two of them came to sit opposite where Maximilian was sitting minding his own business in the window.

Delphine had a look of resignation on her face, and she nodded, returning to the kitchen and leaving Maximilian alone with the two aristocrats, both of whom looked at one another and nodded.

"You can't expect her to be interested in you," the earl said, and Maximilian stared at him in surprise.

It was the strangest of things to say, and which Maximilian felt entirely inappropriate.

"Whatever do you mean?" he demanded, fixing the earl with an angry gaze.

"I mean...she won't fall in love with you. She's not interested in men like you," the earl continued, oblivious, it seemed, to the insult he was causing.

Maximilian was not certain what the earl should mean by a "man like him." He was not a man like anyone, or so he hoped. And besides, Maximilian had no intention of wishing Delphine to fall in love with him, even as he knew it would not be beyond the realms of possibility for her to do so. Other women had fallen in love with him, even as he now vowed never to fall in love again.

"Men like me?" he replied, narrowing his eyes.

It was clear the earl was spoiling for a fight, and Maximilian was only too willing to rise to such a challenge.

"Spurned lovers. That's what. It's one thing to charm a lady, but when you come with such a flagrant reputation behind you, well..." the earl said, folding his arms and shaking his head.

Once again, Maximilian could hardly believe what was being said to him. The earl and the marquess knew nothing about him. He had barely spoken to them, and now they had decided to pass judgement on him, and for what? Talking to Delphine?

"Do you intend to insult me, sir?" Maximilian asked, rising to his feet.

"Not at all. I merely speak of the facts of your situation and remind you of the folly which would be yours if you pursued our gracious hostess in matters of love. She's worth far more than the attentions of a spurned lover looking to replace the empty spot in his bed," the earl continued.

Maximilian was astounded by the earl's words. He had never been so insulted in all his life, and now he fixed the two men with a stern gaze.

"Listen to me. I won't sit here and be insulted. But I know all about the two of you and your desperation to gain the favor of our hostess – I've seen it. But she's not interested in either of you. She's not in love with you, and I doubt she ever will be. The sight of the two of you fawning over her…it's pitiful," he said.

Maximilian did not know this for certain, but he guessed by their reaction he was right. The earl and the marquess looked at one another as though it were they who had been insulted, rather than Maximilian.

"We merely wish to defend Delphine's honor," the marquess said, and the earl nodded.

"From men like you, yes, we won't see her hurt. In love, indeed… I've never heard anything so preposterous. But you…yes, we've seen the way you talk to her," he exclaimed.

It was at this point Maximilian decided both the earl and the marquess were quite mad. Their outburst was beyond all reason, and their words so grounded in falsity as to be absurd. Maximilian was not in love with Delphine. How could he be? He had known her for less than a day, and whilst there was no doubting her attractiveness, that fact did not translate into anything more.

"The way I talk to her? I've spoken to her about my luncheon, about the sheets on the bed, and the lack of hot water. That's all," he replied, shaking his head.

"Complaints. Yes…a complaint and then an expectation. You've complained to her and expected her to come running. It's a sure sign – you want her attention," the marquess said, and the earl nodded.

"Yes, precisely. But we won't allow it. Not at all," he said.

Maximilian was about to offer a fresh retort, and he would gladly have challenged the earl and the marquess to a duel if the door to the kitchen had not opened and Delphine herself had not emerged bearing a large platter of mutton chops.

"I'm serving luncheon in the dining room and…oh," she said, staring at the scene before her with surprise.

The earl and the marquess rose to their feet, and the two of them nodded curtly to Maximilian and hurried off into the dining room. Maximilian shook his head and turned to Delphine, who had a worried look on her face, as though she knew very well what had just transpired.

"They're like that with everyone," she said, and Maximilian rolled his eyes.

"What a ridiculous pair," he said, but he was determined not to be intimidated by them.

Maximilian had encountered such men before. There had been an aristocrat – Lord Richmond – who had taken a liking to Lady Frances Stott, back in the days when she had eyes only for Maximilian. Lord Richmond had tried to warn Maximilian off, but Maximilian had paid him no attention and whilst they had avoided a duel, there had been no doubting the force of the angry words exchanged between the two of them.

"They have their eccentric ways," Delphine said, shaking her head.

"I thought I'd never eat again after that magnificent breakfast, but the argument has quite raised my appetite. I'm hungry again," Maximilian said, for he did not want his hostess to think he was angry with her for the behavior of the earl and the marquess.

"Well...do come and eat. I've some potatoes and vegetables to serve, too, and there's bread and butter," Delphine replied.

She led Maximilian into the dining room, where the earl and the marquess were sitting at their usual table. Neither of them looked at Maximilian as he passed, though the earl could be heard to utter an insult over spurned lovers. Maximilian ignored them, even as he decided to have a little fun.

"You look very pretty in your dress," he said, addressing Delphine in a loud voice as she served his lamb cutlets.

Delphine blushed, but she did not seem perturbed by his words – quite the opposite, in fact.

"That's very kind of you to say. I like to dress more formally on a Sunday. My father always used to do the same," she replied.

Maximilian glanced over at the earl and the marquess. He was glad to note his words had given rise to a reaction. Both were scowling at him, and he decided to continue with his fun.

"I think you looked just as pretty yesterday. Is every day your Sunday best?" he asked, and Delphine blushed an even deeper shade of red and served him with another two lamb cutlets.

"Well...when one is hosting guests, it's incumbent on one to look ones' best. Don't you think?" she asked.

Maximilian did think, and whilst he was only having fun, there was no doubt he meant the words he said. Delphine *was* very pretty, and she managed to look so, even whilst serving lamb cutlets.

"I couldn't agree more. The dress suits you very well. Was it a gift from your father?" he asked.

At this point, the earl leaped to his feet, tossed his napkin aside, and stormed across the dining room.

"You can't say that to her. How dare you speak about her father in such a way? Don't you know he's dead?" he exclaimed.

Delphine's eyes grew wide with horror, and she clutched at the earl's arm, even as he was now blue in the face with anger. But Maximilian was unperturbed. He could easily have beaten the earl – and the marquess – in a fight, and he was certain he had said nothing to offend Delphine, who now looked thoroughly embarrassed.

"Isn't a man allowed to ask a question?" he asked.

"I won't hear it. I won't have you upsetting her," the earl exclaimed, but Maximilian merely rolled his eyes and sighed.

"Perhaps you'd care to ask the lady if I've upset her. If I have, I'll apologize immediately, pay my bill, and leave," he said, holding the earl's gaze, as Delphine let go of his arm and stepped between them.

"I'm not upset at all. Why don't you sit down, and I'll bring you some more potatoes," she said, forcing her face into a smile.

The earl backed down and returned to his place, whispering to the marquess and casting murderous glances in Maximilian's direction.

"I'm terribly sorry," Delphine said, but Maximilian merely waved his hand dismissively.

"Think nothing of it. I didn't upset you, did I? I was merely curious. I thought perhaps your father might've bought it for you as a gift," he said, his tone now sympathetic, and Delphine smiled.

"He did buy me it as a gift. On my eighteenth birthday. He bought me a string of pearls, a pair of earrings, and a brooch to match," she said, and her face seemed so radiant with that happy memory that Maximilian could not help but feel glad he had asked the question, despite the earl's reaction.

"That was very kind of him. You must miss him terribly, though you seem more than capable of following in his footsteps," Maximilian said.

If she were her father's daughter, then Maximilian would have been glad to have met the former innkeeper. He had raised a stout young woman, more than capable of dealing with men like the earl and the marquess.

"It's not been easy, I'll admit that much. I miss him terribly and I've a hundred questions every day I want to ask him. But I think…I hope, I'm following in his legacy and running The Seven Bells as he would want me to. I've got Bessie and Alice to help me, too. I couldn't do it without them," Delphine replied warmly.

Maximilian was beginning to realize what an extraordinary woman she was – quite remarkable, in fact. It was not usual to find a woman with such self-assurance, particularly one so young. If her inheritance troubled her, it did not show, and Maximilian might have imagined her to have been the landlady of the inn for years, rather than months. He thought back to his behavior on the day of his arrival at the inn. He had behaved so rudely towards Delphine, and now he could only feel a sense of guilt for his actions. He had not meant to be rude to her, but his anger and sorrow over the loss of Frances had spilled over into a lashing out at the first person or situation that had riled his temper – and that had been Delphine. He wanted to make amends, and now he was determined to do whatever he could to assuage the previous impression of him.

"You do it all very well, I'm sure," he said, still smiling at Delphine as an irritable interruption came from behind.

"More mustard, we must have more mustard," the marquess exclaimed.

"And horseradish. There should be horseradish, too," the earl called out.

Maximilian rolled his eyes. They were behaving like spoiled children, and he had grown tired of them, as, it seemed, had Delphine. She sighed and gave Maximilian a look which said as much, but ever the attentive hostess, she turned and nodded.

"I'll bring a condiment tray out at once. Some mint sauce, too, perhaps?" she inquired. The marquess nodded and thought that would be a very good idea indeed.

When Delphine disappeared into the kitchen, the earl looked smugly across at Maximilian and sneered.

"You upset her with your comments. She won't talk to you again. Not like she talks to us," he said, and Maximilian sighed.

"I don't think the three of us are ever going to see eye to eye on the matter," he replied, turning back to his dish of lamb cutlets.

"She's a good woman, you know. We don't want to see her upset, do we, Jacob?" the earl said, addressing the marquess, who nodded through a mouthful of potato.

"We don't, we certainly don't," he said with a vigorous shake of his head.

But Maximilian had heard enough, and he rose to his feet, intending to return upstairs to his new bedroom and rest. He was tired of the earl and the marquess, tired of their silly games and petty insults. He could not help but feel sorry for Delphine, who was forced to endure their company, whether she liked it or not.

"Then I'm sure I won't remain any longer – to upset our hostess or her unfortunate guests," he replied.

The earl gave him another sneer, just as Delphine returned from the kitchen bearing a tray of condiments. She looked somewhat disappointed to see Maximilian about to leave and glanced at the earl and the marquess, as though she were wondering what they had said.

"Won't you have some pudding?" she asked, but Maximilian shook his head.

"No, thank you...I'm quite full now," he replied.

She smiled at him and nodded.

"Then I wish you a pleasant afternoon," she replied, as the earl rapped his spoon on the table.

"Horseradish!" he exclaimed. Maximilian shook his head and made his way upstairs.

Dreadful fools, he said to himself, but despite his encounters with the earl and the marquess, Maximilian had felt a certain pleasure in his dealings with Delphine and he found himself looking forward to the next time their paths might cross.

Chapter Nine

"He's insufferable," the earl said, after Maximilian left the dining room.

Delphine, who was spooning mustard onto the marquess' cutlets, gave him a withering look.

"And what precisely leads you to that conclusion?" she asked, trying not to lose her temper, as she continued spooning out the mustard.

"The way he talks to you. It's obvious what he's doing. He wants to make you his conquest. It's always the way you know," the earl replied.

The marquess had been listening, rather than watching the serving out of the mustard, and he gave an exasperated cry as he looked down at his plate.

"I can't eat that," he exclaimed.

Delphine, too, had been distracted, and she looked down at the cutlets, which were now entirely covered in the bright yellow mustard.

"Oh..." she said, trying not to laugh.

"You'll have to fetch me another serving," the marques exclaimed.

"It'll scrape off," Delphine replied, not feeling anyway inclined to put herself out for the sake of her annoying guest.

The marquess muttered something, but the earl continued his diatribe against the baron's son.

"You can see it in his eyes. In his mannerisms. In everything he says. You're to be his recompense for a spurned love affair. He wants to assert himself; you see. He wants to make it so it's him, rather than a woman, who makes the decision to break things off. You're a plaything to him. It's wicked," he said, banging his fist on the table.

Delphine sighed. There would be no convincing the earl and the marquess of the opposite. She set down the condiment tray and prepared to retreat to the kitchen. Bessie could see to the guests for the rest of the meal – Delphine had heard enough.

"I'm sure I don't know what you're talking about – either of you," she replied, and the earl looked at her with narrowed eyes.

"You shouldn't encourage him. That's the problem. When a man like that is encouraged, heaven only knows what he'll do," he said, shaking his head.

Delphine rolled her eyes. There was no point in arguing, even as she smiled to herself as she returned to the kitchen. What the earl and the marquess had failed to grasp was that this was all part of her plan. It was not the baron's son who was attempting seduction for his own wicked ends, but instead, it was Delphine's own actions which were leading him on, or so she hoped. She hoped it, because she felt a sense of uncertainty whether something else was going on – what of her own feelings? The baron's son was not the same as he had been when first he had arrived at the inn. Instead, he was becoming...far more affable, far more likable, far more attractive...

"Are those two still at it?" Alice asked, turning from the stove, and giving Delphine an exasperated look.

"When aren't they? They'll sit in the parlor window and pass comment on whatever and whosoever they wish. Then it'll be dinnertime and the whole charade will begin again," Bessie said in annoyance.

The maid had accurately described the behavior of the earl and the marquess, and Delphine sent her out to take the orders for pudding, not wishing for another encounter with them until at least six O'clock.

"Are they satisfied now?" she asked, when Bessie returned a few moments later.

"They both want the currant sponge – with lots of custard, and I'm to tell Alice it's got to be piping hot," she said.

The cook uttered something beneath her breath, but two bowls of pudding were shortly provided, each portion covered in hot, steaming custard. With the luncheon served, and the earl and the marquess temporarily reprieved, Delphine sat down at the kitchen table to take stock of the situation. It was hard to tell if her plan was working, and even if the baron's son was attracted to her, he would be hard pressed to allow such feelings to develop with the earl and the marquess breathing down his neck.

"What of our other guest? Did he enjoy his luncheon?" Alice asked, as she sat down to eat a bowl of soup later that afternoon.

"He enjoyed it very much. He's certainly been a pleasure to talk to. Quite unlike the other night," Delphine replied.

She had put the baron's son's bad mood from the previous few days down to circumstance. If what was said of him by the earl was true, then it was hardly surprising he should be so disposed. For a man to be humiliated by a woman was a dreadful blow, and it was hardly surprising their guest should be licking his wounds and prone to bursts of anger now and again. In fact, Delphine was impressed with the baron's son – he had thus far not allowed the earl's and the marquess' taunts to cause him to lose his temper, and that was an achievement in itself.

"And you're still following your plan?" Bessie asked.

"It's not so much a plan. I doubt it'll come to anything. He's… pleasant enough, though. But he wasn't at first, was he?" Delphine said.

She had imagined her efforts with Maximilian would be in vain. She would attempt any number of pleasantries and he would respond with surly indifference. But that had not been the case at all. Quite the opposite, in fact. For every act she had performed above and beyond what was expected, he had seemed grateful, and had taken considerable pleasure in his new quarters, his large breakfast, the presentation of the periodicals, and everything else Delphine had done for him. It had come as something of a surprise, even as she now wondered how best to proceed.

"You've certainly made an effort with him, ma'am. He's bound to appreciate it," Bessie replied.

"I'm making boiled beef and mustard dumplings for dinner. He's bound to like that," Alice said, rising from the table to continue her preparations for the evening.

"I'm sure he will," Delphine replied, wondering where the evening would lead them and how far she could continue her ploy before it got too serious…

* * *

"We've a full dining room tonight, ma'am. Am I to keep the usual table for the earl and the marquess?" Bessie asked, entering the kitchen, looking flustered.

Delphine was busy polishing cutlery. She looked up and nodded.

"They'll only complain if we don't. I'm surprised they're not here yet. Has Max…the baron's son joined us yet?" she asked, and Bessie nodded.

"He's just come down. I've seated him away from where those two are going to be, though. The last thing he needs is them spoiling his dinner," Bessie replied.

Delphine picked up some of the polished cutlery and followed the maid out into the dining room. There was a lively atmosphere about the place, and the room was full of laughter and chatter. Maximilian was sitting on his own in the far corner, absorbed in a book. Delphine was curious as to what he was reading

Her father had taught her to read. He had once told her he believed in well-educated women, and ever since she was a child, he had told her that one day she would be in charge of the inn. She had not thought about it back then, but everything he had taught her, all she had learned from him, had led to this time when it was she, and not her father, on whom the responsibility of *The Seven Bells* rested.

For business and pleasure, for correspondence and education, he used to tell her. And whenever she had the chance – which was not often, given her responsibilities – Delphine liked to sit with a book in the parlor and read in front of the fire, or outside on the steps of the inn when the sun was shining.

"I trust you had a pleasant afternoon, my Lord. What are you reading?" she asked.

The baron's son looked up at her and smiled.

"It's a volume of poetry. I picked it up this afternoon in a bookshop along the river. I've nothing with me, and found I was rather missing the library I left behind," he said, and Delphine smiled.

"I do like poetry – Shelley, Wordsworth, Coleridge," she said, and Maximilian nodded.

"This is Wordsworth," Maximilian said, holding up the volume for her to see.

"Won't you read me some?" she asked, and the baron's son smiled.

"Very well," he replied, blushing slightly as he thumbed through the pages. "What would you like?"

"Anything at all. I like to hear poetry read out loud," Delphine said, and Maximilian cleared his throat and began to read.

"Earth has not anything to show more fair:

Dull would he be of soul who could pass by
A sight so touching in its majesty:
This City now doth, like a garment, wear
The beauty of the morning: silent, bare,
Ships, towers, domes, theaters, and temples lie
Open unto the fields, and to the sky…"

"Beautiful, I know he's talking about London – it isn't always quite so fair as that. There're times I wish I could escape to the countryside – to see the daffodils in the spring. He wrote about those, too, didn't he?" she asked, and Maximilian nodded.

He was about to reply when an interruption came from behind.

"Miss Delphine, are we to sit in our usual places?" the earl asked, and Delphine turned to find them both looking at her with questioning expressions on their faces.

She sighed and nodded.

"Yes, where you always sit, if you wish," she replied.

She would dearly have liked to remain listening to Maximilian read her poetry. He had a particular way of doing so, pronouncing the words clearly and crisply. She could have happily listened to him all day but was instead brought back to earth with a bump, as the earl and the marquess started making their demands.

"Is it boiled beef tonight? If it's mustard dumplings, I don't want them. I can still taste the mustard on those lamb cutlets from luncheon," the marques said, as Bessie came to pour their wine and bring bread and butter for their table.

"I'll have his dumplings. I've never been so hungry in all my life," the earl said, raising his glass in a toast to the marquess, who clinked his glass with him and grinned.

"I'll tell the cook," Delphine said, but before she could return to the kitchen, the earl – who never seemed to sit still for a moment – had sprung out of his chair and had caught her by the arm.

"We want to make presentation to you. Of gifts, yes, a presentation of gifts," he said, as Delphine looked at him with a confused expression on her face.

"Of gifts? There's really no need," she replied, feeling certain this was yet another bizarre attempt by the two men to curry her favor.

But the earl had now stepped in front of her and the marquess had also risen from his seat and was standing at her side. Both men appeared eager to present whatever gifts they had chosen. The earl rummaged in his pocket and drew out a box, holding it out in front of him with a flourish.

"For you," he declared, removing the lid, and holding up the open box as though he were a waiter bearing a tray with drinks on it.

The rest of the diners were watching this scene with great interest, craning their necks to catch sight of whatever it was that was inside the box. Delphine stared at it in surprise. Inside the box was a paperweight. It was made of pink marble, shaped like a miniature obelisk, and resting on a small red cushion.

"Oh..." Delphine said, somewhat underwhelmed by the sight, which the earl now removed from the box and held out to her.

"For your papers and so forth. It's real marble," he said.

But Delphine had had enough of their games. She did not want a paperweight, and as much as she knew it would offend the earl to refuse it, she pushed it away.

"You really shouldn't have," she said, but the earl insisted.

"I wanted to. I wanted to show you how much I care for you," he exclaimed, as the marquess produced a similar box from his pocket.

"And I, the same," he said, holding it up with a similar flourish to the earl.

Delphine sighed. She wished someone would come to her rescue, but Bessie had disappeared into the kitchen, and the other guests knew well enough not to interfere with the eccentricities of the earl and the marquess.

"I don't want your gifts," Delphine insisted.

"But you haven't even seen mine. Look at it," the marquess

insisted, and he opened the box to reveal a quill and a small ink bottle.

"What am I supposed to do with that?" Delphine asked.

"Write your correspondence, of course. And you can use the paperweight to weigh down the letters you receive," the marquess replied.

Such a set of gifts may have been appropriate for the sort of women with whom the earl and the marquess were better associated with. The sort of women who had correspondence to see to, and who spent their days sending and replying to an endless stream of missives which said little more than trite observations on the weather and recollections of dull social occasions. Delphine was no such woman. She did not have time to send correspondence, and those she received were almost exclusively of a business nature – a bill for this, an enquiry for that.

"I really don't want them You pay your bills, I don't need gifts, thank you. It doesn't feel right to accept them," Delphine replied, forgetting common courtesy for a moment, even as she wondered what her father would say if he could observe the scene now unfolding.

The earl and the marquess looked at one another in surprise. Both – for once – were lost for words. Delphine pushed away the two boxes, which were still being held up in front of her and turned away. Her eyes met with those of Maximilian, who had been watching this charade with amusement. She did not want to accept the gifts, and she did not want Maximilian to think she was interested in the advances of the two men, who now appeared to assert themselves.

"Well...that's a fine thing. We bring you two beautiful gifts and present them to you in such a way, and what do we get in return?" he exclaimed, stuffing the paper weight into his pocket, and tossing the empty box aside.

"I didn't ask you to buy me a gift. I don't need gifts, and

certainly not gifts I'll never use," she said, as the marquess lowered the open box with the quill and ink.

He looked hurt, and Delphine felt a sudden sense of guilt for her reaction. But she was tired of the two men vying for her affections and wearied by their constant demands.

"A fine quill it was, too. Never mind, I'll give it to my niece. Perhaps she might show some gratitude," the marquess said, as he sat back down at the table.

The earl was muttering under his breath, and Delphine sighed and returned to the kitchen empty-handed.

"Whatever was that all about?" Bessie exclaimed, as Delphine sat down heavily at the kitchen table and put her head in her hands.

"A paperweight and a quill pen. They wanted to give me gifts, that's what it was about," she replied. Bessie shook her head as Alice turned from the stove and laughed.

"What use would you have with a paperweight and a quill pen?" she asked, rolling her eyes.

"I'm sure they meant well," Delphine replied, wondering how best to remedy the situation she had created.

It would have been far easier to have accepted the gifts in good grace. But to do so would only serve to encourage the earl and the marquess further in their bizarre behavior. Delphine had no desire to have them believe she was interested in courtship or marriage or whatever else the aristocratic pair had in mind. But what neither of them seemed to realize was that even if she had been interested in one or the other, they could not each possess her. One of them was bound to be disappointed, and on such reasoning, it was better for them both to be.

"Meant well? Meant trouble, more like. Oh…ma'am, why don't you just get rid of them? We've enough business without having to put up with those two all the time. It's a complete nightmare having them here. They make such work for us all. Maybe you did the right thing by refusing them. They might realize the folly of their ways," Alice replied.

Delphine knew the cook had no sympathy for either the earl or the marquess. She would gladly show them out of the inn herself after their many insults to her cooking. But Delphine was always mindful of her father's words.

Always smile, always show hospitality, Delphine, he would say, and Delphine knew she had let him down in that moment – spectacularly so.

And what would the baron's son think of her? He had been watching the proceedings in silence and had not leaped to her defense against the unwanted attentions she had received.

I think I've been rather foolish, she said, as Alice began to serve out the plates of boiled beef and mustard dumplings.

"Let's see what they make of their dinner," she said, as Bessie took up two plates and went out to serve in the dining room.

Delphine did the same, watching the earl and the marquess out of the corner of her eye. They were drinking claret and sitting in silence. They made no acknowledgement of Bessie when she placed their plates in front of them and began to eat with the same steely expressions on their face. Delphine set one of the plates down at the table of an elderly woman eating alone, before taking the next to Maximilian, who had resumed his attentions of the volume of Wordsworth's poetry. He looked up at her and smiled.

"There's never a dull moment here, is there?" he said, and Delphine blushed.

"I'm sorry about earlier, they were...I was..." she began, but Maximilian interrupted her.

"You don't need to apologize. They're both fools. A paperweight and a quill pen? What strange gifts to give. I'd have done precisely the same. Anyway, it made for some good sport," he said, and he winked at her.

Delphine set down his plate. She had added an extra dumpling and a second ladleful of stew. He took up his knife and fork, looking down hungrily at the plate.

"I hope you enjoy it," she said, and he smiled at her and nodded.

"I'm sure I will, and let's hope you have no further disturbances this evening," he replied.

* * *

It seemed the outburst over the paperweight and the quill had subdued the earl and the marquess to an unusual low. They went to bed immediately after they finished their pudding and did not order their customary third bottle of wine or sit up late drinking in the parlor. The inn was quiet – too quiet – and Delphine, Bessie, and Alice found themselves sitting down to their pot of tea long before midnight.

"I've never known it be so quiet, ma'am. Not when those two are here, at least," Bessie said, shaking her head as she poured the tea.

"They might finally have realized what fools they are," Alice said, smiling triumphantly at Delphine, who sighed.

"I don't want them to be offended," she said, but Alice merely waved her hand dismissively.

"Enjoy it while it lasts. They'll come up with something else soon enough. Today it's a paperweight, tomorrow they'll be presenting you with some kind of exotic animal or proposing you runaway together... You wouldn't, would you, ma'am?" Alice asked, fixing Delphine with a searching gaze.

Delphine smiled and shook her head.

"No, Alice, I wouldn't. Besides, I think perhaps they might have realized my attentions are taken by the baron's son," she replied.

Delphine had been glad not to have offended Maximilian by her antics. She had feared he might have thought her a fool or sought to distance himself from her. But it seemed the baron's son had enjoyed the spectacle of the earl's and the marquess' ridicule, even as Delphine felt somewhat guilty for having enacted it.

"Which means they'll leave you alone, ma'am. They can't carry on like this. Not with such foolishness," Alice said, shaking her head.

"But what of the baron's son? What are you going to do about him?" Bessie asked.

Delphine was uncertain. She had not expected her plan to work so readily. It seemed she was having no trouble in attracting Maximilian, and despite what she believed to be her faults – her short temper with the earl and the marquess chief amongst them – there was no doubt as to the growing connection between them.

"Well… I'm not sure, really. I suppose…well, it's not meant to be anything more than a little harmless fun. A man like that doesn't fall in love with the daughter of an innkeeper, does he? If he falls in love with me, then…" she said, her words trailing off as she realized her own feelings for Maximilian were becoming muddled.

When he had read the poem to her, there had been something in his voice, something which had captured her imagination. She could have listened to him all day long, and the thought of his words, his tone, his demeanor…

"Has he fallen in love with you, ma'am?" Bessie asked, and Delphine blushed.

"Well… I don't know about that. We barely know one another. Besides, I doubt he has any interest in women, not after what he's been through. If the rumors are true, he's suffered terribly at the hands of a woman. Would you readily fall in love if you were him?" Delphine asked.

Bessie laughed.

"If I were him, I'd have a grand fortune and a beautiful house in the country. I'd want for nothing. He needs to realize what he's running away from," she said, pouring herself another cup of tea.

But as they sat talking that night, Delphine's thoughts remained with the baron's son. She could not stop thinking about him, and about the cruel hand fate had dealt him. She felt terribly sorry for him, even if the thought of having him fall in love with her remained. If she could make him happy through small gestures of kindness, then so be it. If he fell in love with her...

Well, that's up to him, I suppose, she told herself, as she made her way to bed that night.

Chapter Ten

"The way to a man's heart is through his stomach. That's what my father used to say to my mother, and she was the best cook I know," Alice said, as Delphine sat at the kitchen table the next morning.

During the night, an idea had occurred to Delphine, one she was now fixated on. She was going to cook Maximilian a meal, but not just one meal, three different dishes, served to him at dinner and made by her own fair hands. Alice had thought her quite mad at first, but she had warmed to the idea, and the two women were now discussing the possibilities for what Delphine might cook.

"But why three dishes?" Bessie asked, looking confused.

"Because he's bound to like one of them, isn't he?" Alice said, rolling her eyes.

"Something with chicken?" Delphine said, for despite her enthusiasm, she really knew very little about cooking.

She had often watched Alice at work and marveled at the cook's ability to produce the most delicious of dishes from the most meager of ingredients – even if sometimes things did not go entirely according to plan.

"Not chicken. I don't trust the slaughterhouses with chicken. You'll poison him as soon as he looks at it. No, trout, that's what you want, trout in caper sauce," Alice replied.

Delphine did not care for fish, but she was willing to try if Alice thought the baron's son might like it.

"Yes, trout in caper sauce, and what else?" she asked. Alice and Bessie thought for a moment.

"Stuffed pig's trotters. We used to eat them all the time when I was growing up. "You can eat every part of the pig but the oink, my father used to say. He always raised a pig every year, and the meat would feed us through the winter," Bessie said.

Delphine nodded. It seemed a strange sounding dish, but she was willing to try it.

"And a suet pudding – steak and oyster," Alice said, thus completing the triumvirate.

"Are you making the dishes for the earl and the marquess?" Bessie said, but Delphine shook her head.

"No, they can eat whatever Alice has planned for the menu. These dishes are for the baron's son. He's bound to like one of them and that'll only serve to help my cause, won't it?" she said, smiling at the thought of presenting the three dishes to Maximilian that evening.

"You'll have to go to the market this morning. Go up to Cheapside. You'll get everything you need there," Alice said.

Delphine sat down to write a list of all the things she needed. She used an old quill, which had belonged to her father, and thought with some amusement about the earl and the marquess' gifts from the previous day. Neither of the two men had shown up at breakfast, and it appeared they were hiding from her, as she saw their retreating figures through the parlor window a short while later.

"Have they gone, ma'am?" Bessie asked, but Delphine shook her head.

"Licking their wounds. But they'll be back as soon as their stomachs start rumbling, I'm sure," she replied.

Delphine was not terribly worried about having offended the earl and the marquess. They would soon realize the foolishness of their antics, but there would certainly be more of such gestures to come. Delphine knew the two aristocrats were not finished in their attempts to oust Maximilian from the inn.

But what comes next, I don't know, she thought to herself, as she took up her basket and put on her shawl to go out.

At that moment, Maximilian himself appeared in the parlor. He was dressed for going out, in his overcoat and top hat, and he smiled at her as she nodded to him.

"Are we both going out?" he asked, and Delphine smiled back at him.

"It appears so. I'm going to the market on Cheapside," she replied, though she did not tell him the precise nature of her intentions.

She wanted the evening to be a surprise, and to see the look on his face when she presented the three dishes to him at the table.

"Ah, I'm looking up an old friend in Mayfair. I presume he still lives there. If not, I'm sure whoever does can point me in the right direction. Might I walk with you in that direction? I'll take a carriage once we arrive at Saint Paul's," he said, and to Delphine's immense surprise, he offered her his arm.

She smiled at him and took it, happy to walk with him – delighted, in fact.

"I don't usually have an escort when going to the market," she said, as they stepped out of the door of the inn and made their way along the dock front, past the stables and turning in the direction of Saint Paul's.

Delphine wondered what the earl and the marquess would say if they saw her walking with Maximilian in such an intimate way. But she reminded herself such concerns were not hers to have. It did not matter what the earl or the marquess thought. Delphine was happy, and it surprised her just how happy…

"I must say, this is an interesting part of London to stay in. I've usually taken lodgings in Westminster, but your inn…it's quite a remarkable place," Maximilian said, as they walked along arm in arm.

"It's my father's legacy, I suppose. It would be nothing without him. My grandfather and my great-grandfather before him were innkeepers, too. But it was my father who curated the reputation The Seven Bells enjoys. He had a way about him and a gift for hospitality. I only hope I can emulate him," Delphine replied.

It was her father's legacy she wished to live in, even as she felt she often got things wrong.

"I think you're doing a fine job. I really do. A comfortable inn, good food, satisfied guests," he said making Delphine blush.

"You weren't…entirely enamored of us on your arrival," she reminded him, thinking back to Maximilian's angry outbursts.

He seemed embarrassed.

"Ah…well, I was somewhat…unsettled at that time," he replied.

Delphine had to remind herself that Maximilian himself had told her nothing of his previous circumstances. As far as he was concerned, she knew nothing of his spurning at the hands of the aristocratic woman the earl had spoken of, nor of his flight to London in shame of what had happened. She wondered if he would tell her, or whether this, for him, too, was merely a game – the game the earl and the marquess had warned her of.

"Forgive me, I don't mean to pry," she said, but the baron's son shook his head.

"You've every right to be curious. And you're right, I did come to London in something of a bad mood – a terrible mood, in fact. I was…caught up in some considerable unpleasantness and wanted only to get away from it. I'm glad to say, I have," he replied.

They had reached the steps of Saint Paul's and Maximilian now bid Delphine goodbye. He hailed a carriage and drove off towards

Mayfair, leaving her standing on the steps, lost in thoughts of what might be. Her feelings for him were confused – he was behaving like the perfect gentleman, a complete contrast to his angry outburst of the other evening.

Maybe he really is falling in love with me, she thought to herself, as she wondered as to her own feelings for him.

An organ grinder was playing at the entrance to the market, the music echoing tiny and melodic. Delphine tossed a coin to the man, and he nodded, cranking the shaft a notch faster so that the music became suddenly louder. She stood watching for a moment, her mind on Maximilian and the dishes she would cook for him that evening. Would he enjoy them? What would he think when she presented them to him?

He'll probably think I'm quite mad, she told herself, as she made her way into the maze of stalls which made up the market.

Alice had given her a list of things to buy, and she visited the butcher, the fishmonger, and the grocer, working through her list and filling her basket with all the things she needed to prepare the dishes. The market was a feast for the senses, and everywhere she looked, Delphine saw new sights to tempt her.

"I need two trout," she told the fishmonger, as she approached the stall which was covered with a thick slab of ice, on top of which rested all manner of different fish, their silver scales reflecting the light, their eyes wide and staring at her lifelessly.

"Two trout – straight out of the Thames upstream. They lie in the chalky parts, and I tickle them myself," the fishmonger said, selecting two and wrapping them in brown paper.

"Tickle them?" Delphine replied, for it seemed a strange thing to say.

"Oh, yes, miss. It's an ancient fishing technique for trout. I lie on the riverbank and slip my hands into the water, where it's clear, making sure my shadow doesn't overcast them. Then I wait. The fish come and bask in the sunshine, it makes them docile. Then I start to tickle their underbellies. Just gently, then...wham! I cup my hands and toss them out onto the bank behind," he said.

Delphine laughed at the thought, but the fishmonger was adamant as the effectiveness of his methods, Delphine paid the money for the fish and bid him good day. Having finished her shopping in the market, Delphine returned to the inn alone, and found Bessie busy laying tables for luncheon.

"The earl and the marquess are dining out today, but they'll be back for dinner," Bessie said, with a look of relief on her face.

"A peaceful luncheon service, then," Delphine replied.

She, too, was relieved. The absence of the earl and the marquess would give her ample opportunity to prepare her dishes for the evening, and having helped Bessie finish laying the tables, she returned to the kitchen and put on an apron, hoping Alice would help her.

"Are you sure you want to cook all this yourself, ma'am? I could do it for you, if you wish," Alice said, looking somewhat skeptically at Delphine, who was not noted for her culinary prowess.

"No, I want to do it myself. I want him to be impressed," Delphine replied.

Alice smiled and shook her head.

"You've chosen some difficult dishes, miss. Just ask if you need me to help you," she said, and Delphine nodded.

The table was covered with the ingredients she had brought from the market – pig's trotters, oysters, the two trout – Delphine rolled up her sleeves and set to work. She made the suet pastry for the steamed pudding, mixed the stuffing for the trotters, and made a start on the caper sauce to serve with the trout. The afternoon passed happily by, and Delphine was so engrossed in her work that it was five O'clock before she looked up to find Bessie watching her from across the kitchen table.

"The earl and the marquess are back, and so is the baron's son. They'll all be dining at six O'clock," she said, and Delphine nodded.

"Then I'd better make sure everything's ready by then," she replied.

The suet pudding had been steaming for most of the afternoon, and the pig's trotters were roasting in the oven. Alice had shown her how to use the fish kettle, and the two trout lay side by side on a bed of fennel stalks waiting to be poached.

"Do you need me to help you, ma'am?" Alice asked, but Delphine shook her head.

"No, I think I'm ready. I just hope he likes them," she replied.

She intended to present the three dishes side by side and offer them to Maximilian as a choice, hoping he would like at least one of them. She had made enough for two portions of each – one for her to try to one for her to present.

"You've worked hard all day, ma'am. I'm sure he'll like them," Alice replied.

Delphine went to peer through the kitchen door into the parlor. She could see the earl and the marquess at their usual table in the dining room. They still appeared subdued and were sitting in silence. She knew the presentation of the three dishes to Maximilian would only serve to rub salt into their wounds, but the feelings of the two men were no longer her concern. She was not interested in whether she upset them, but rather on whether Maximilian enjoyed the dishes she had prepared.

"Am I to serve the soup at the same time, ma'am?" Alice said, for the rest of the guests were to dine on the standard fare, rather than anything special.

"Yes, I don't want to make a fuss about things. I'll take the dishes for the baron's son myself, and Bessie can serve the soup. That way, no one need see he's dining on something different," Delphine replied.

She now began to plate up the dishes. The suet pudding was eased out of its basin, and it stood tall and proud on a large blue plate, waiting to be cut into. The stuffed pig's trotters, which had roasted to a golden brown, were placed on a silver platter and garnished with parsley, and the trout were dressed with the caper sauce and presented in a china dish which was decorated with a pattern of flowers.

"They look delicious, ma'am. Are you ready to serve them?" Alice said, and Delphine nodded.

She did not know why she felt so nervous at the prospect of presenting the dishes to Maximilian. She wanted to impress him and make him see the effort she had gone to so that he might enjoy something different to eat. Her heart was beating fast as she placed the threes dishes on a large tray and made her way out of the kitchen, across the parlor and into the dining room. The earl and the marquess were eating their soup in silence and they seemed not to notice as Delphine passed them by and made her way to where Maximilian was sitting at his now usual table. He was reading the volume of poetry he had recited from the previous day, and now he looked up at her and smiled.

"What's all this?" he asked, as she set the tray down before him.

"A beef and oyster suet pudding, stuffed pig's trotters with herbs and breadcrumbs, and trout in caper sauce," Delphine replied.

Maximilian looked down at the three dishes with interest, even as a puzzled expression came over his face.

"It looked like everyone else was dining on soup," he said, and Delphine blushed.

"They are...but I wanted to cook something special for you. A surprise, of sorts. Do say you'll try them," she said, as he grinned at her.

"You've somehow discovered my favorite dishes in all the world. I used to fish for trout as a boy, and the cook always made a caper sauce to go with them. It reminds me of those happy days. Pig's trotters are a delicacy, and these smell divine, and as for a steamed pudding – it's not so much the filling, but the casing. The suet...it melts in one's mouth. I adore it, though I'm not sure where to start. Did you mean all three of them for me?" he asked, and Delphine nodded.

"I wasn't sure which one you'd like the most, though I hoped that at least one of them would be to your liking," she said, as Maximilian took up his knife and fork and looked from one dish to another.

"I like them all. I can't promise to finish them all, but I'll give it a good go. I certainly built up a hearty appetite today," he replied, and Delphine smiled.

She was glad the dishes had been so well received and wondered what she could make next to please the palate of the baron's son.

"I'm glad you like them. I made them specially for you," she said.

He looked up at her, unsure, it seemed, how to respond.

"Won't you...sit down for a moment?" he asked.

Delphine was taken aback. She did not know how to respond, even as she dearly wished to sit with him as he had suggested. But how would it look? And what would happen if the earl and the marquess saw her do so?

"I...well, I can't...not whilst there's still work to do," she said, and it seemed his face fell at these words, making her feel terribly guilty for having led him on.

"Afterwards then. Once you've finished. We could sit in the parlor. I can enjoy these delicious dishes and then you can tell me how you made them," he replied.

Delphine nodded. It was a delightful idea, one she was only too happy to agree to, even as she knew the earl and the marquess would not approve. It angered her to think she was still concerned with what they thought, even as she knew she had every right to determine her own course of action.

"Yes, I'd like that very much," she replied, smiling at him as she returned to the kitchen.

"Did he like the dishes?" Alice asked, as Delphine sat down at the table.

"Oh, yes, they were his favorites," she replied, and the cook smiled.

"Well, you know what they say – the way to a man's heart is through his stomach," she said, and with a shake of her head she turned back to the stove.

Delphine pondered these words for a moment. Had she really found her way to Maximilian's heart? The answered seemed to be yes, even as it seemed he had found his way into hers, quite unexpectedly...

Chapter Eleven

"Soup? Is that all we get? *He* got a steamed pudding – I saw it," the earl exclaimed, pushing aside his bowl as Delphine cleared the table.

"And trout, and stuff pig's trotters. We could smell them. Why don't we get those things? We've paid the same as him," the marquess said, fixing Delphine with an angry expression.

"Because...he just does," Delphine replied.

She could not summon the strength for an argument. There was no rational reason why Maximilian should have been treated in such a way. It was favoritism, a special privilege, one which Delphine had no intention of extending.

"That's not good enough. You've treated us terribly these past few days. And why?" the earl demanded.

To this, Delphine had no answer. Or rather, the answer she wanted to give would have caused such offence as to be better left unsaid. She merely shrugged and cleared away the half-eaten bowls of soup which the earl and the marquess had pushed away. Maximilian was still sitting in the corner reading his book. He had done ample justice to the dishes set before him, and the plates were clean, save for the detritus of fish bones and the remnants of the trotters.

"I hope you enjoyed it," Delphine said, as she stacked the crockery.

"It was all delicious. Am I to get used to such fare?" he asked, smiling at her.

Delphine blushed. She would not be able to match her culinary achievements each night, but she would certainly be willing to present further dishes to him if it pleased him. Once again, she found herself taking the idea of her game rather more seriously than she had intended. She had wanted Maximilian to fall in love with her, but instead, she was beginning to fall in love with him, as strange as that seemed.

"Well...you need only ask if there's a particular dish you favor," Delphine replied.

"I'm rather partial to something sweet," he said, holding her gaze as Delphine blushed even further.

She took the empty plates and dishes back to the kitchen. Bessie was scrubbing the kitchen table, and she looked up inquisitively at Delphine, who now put down the plates and sighed.

"Is everything all right, ma'am?" she asked.

"He's asked me to sit with him this evening. I can hardly refuse, can I?" she replied.

"It would be rude to do so, ma'am. But forgive me...isn't this what you wanted?" Bessie asked.

Delphine smiled. It *was* what she had wanted, at least from Maximilian. But she had not expected her own feelings on the matter to be so confused. She had long vowed not to fall in love, and she had thought herself more than capable of resisting, even as she found herself wondering if she had truly managed to do so.

"It is, but...well, I rather like him. He's nothing like we thought him to be at first," Delphine admitted.

First impressions have a nasty habit of remaining the de facto truth in one's dealings with others. A first impression can make or break what comes next, but whilst Delphine's first impressions of the baron's son had been far from favorable, those now given were quite different.

"Then why not sit with him for the evening, ma'am. Alice and I can manage here. We've served the soup, and if the earl and the marquess go off to bed like they did last night, we'll have a quiet evening ahead of us," Bessie replied.

Delphine was grateful to them both, and taking a deep breath, she decided she *would* spend the evening in the company of Maximilian. She was curious about him, and whilst it was her own actions which had led him to ask her, she knew her feelings desired this, too.

"Shall we sit in the parlor?" she asked, after she had returned to the dining room and approached Maximilian, who was still reading at the table in the corner.

He nodded and smiled at her. He had a pleasant smile, the sort that lights up a person's face, and is only given truthfully and with sincerity.

"I'd like that. Would you…care to hear some more poetry?" he asked. Delphine nodded.

"I'd like that very much," she replied, as Maximilian rose to his feet, and followed her towards the parlor.

They had to pass the table at which the earl and the marquess were still sitting, each nursing a large glass of brandy.

"I hope it won't just be soup for dinner tomorrow," the earl said, and Delphine rolled her eyes.

"Didn't you enjoy it?" she asked, and the earl shook his head.

"Not when I could see a magnificent, steamed pudding brought to another table," he replied, glancing at Maximilian and scowling.

The baron's son laughed.

"I'm sure you could've asked for the same," he replied.

"No, we couldn't. *You* got special treatment," the marquess exclaimed petulantly.

"Nonsense. I received a kindness, that's all," Maximilian retorted.

He was clearly unperturbed by the earl and the marquess, and Delphine was relieved that thus far, her two aristocratic guests had failed to oust the baron's son from the inn, as they had done with so many others before him. But Maximilian was different, for not only had he taken a liking to Delphine, but she had also taken a liking to him...

"A kindness you didn't refuse," the marquess said, and Maximilian rolled his eyes.

"Why would I refuse? What possible reason could there be for doing so? I was only too glad to receive such kindness. But I'm going to sit in the parlor now. Good evening, gentlemen," he said, and without waiting for a response, he removed himself to the parlor, leaving Delphine to smile and shrug.

"Be careful, Miss Delphine. You don't know him at all. He could be dangerous," the earl exclaimed.

"He's not dangerous. Why would he be dangerous?" Delphine exclaimed, as the earl and the marquess exchanged knowing glances.

"Don't you think it's strange? A man arrives at the inn out of nowhere, a spurned lover...he's out for revenge on the fairer sex. You can see it in his eyes," the marquess said.

At these words, Delphine could not help but laugh. She had seen nothing in Maximilian's eyes but kindness – and perhaps exasperation at the antics of the earl and the marquess.

"What nonsense. Why would he go to such trouble just for revenge? If he truly hated women, why didn't he just... I don't know, take revenge on the one who spurned him? I hardly think he intends to make me a second Eve and place on me the guilt of generations. That first night, he was angry, but he's different now," Delphine replied.

"You'd be surprised at what these men are capable of. Take

care, Miss Delphine, take good care," the earl implored her, and he took her hand in his and brought it to his lips.

Delphine humored him for a moment. He exasperated her, but she could not be angry with him for long. His antics were like those of a child – as were those of the marquess. Somehow, neither of them seemed to understand the proper way to behave towards women, nor did they appear capable of understanding the ways of their own sex, either.

"I'm sure it won't come to anything more than the sharing of my company," Delphine said, extracting her hand from that of the marquess and nodding to them both.

"Thank goodness you have us here to watch over you," the marquess said, as Delphine retreated to the parlor.

Maximilian was sitting in a chair by the window. It was growing dark now and Bessie had lit candles around the room and stoked up the fire.

"Shall I get you a drink?" Delphine asked, and the baron's son nodded.

"Wine, perhaps – a bottle for us to share," he replied, and Delphine smiled.

Her father had always prided himself on the excellence of his cellar. He knew everything there was to know about wine – at least as far as an Englishman might be said to know about wine – and had passed some of his knowledge on to Delphine.

"A red wine, perhaps?" she asked, chastising herself for not having offered Maximilian a bottle with his dinner.

"Red, yes. If you'd like that," he replied.

"Oh, it rather goes to my head. But a small glass, perhaps, I'll fetch something from the cellar," she replied.

The door to the cellar lay in the corner of the dining room, next to a large wine rack covered in dusty bottles. The key to the door was in Delphine's pocket and she unlocked it, taking up a candle and making her way down a narrow flight of stairs to the cellar below. The walls were lined with racks, and she knew some of the vintages to be ancient – bought by her great-grandfather when he had first acquired the inn all those years ago.

"*This'll do,*" she said to herself, selecting a bottle from a nearby rack and holding it up to the light of the candle.

It was an 1805, a vintage from Burgundy, and one she remembered her father speaking highly of. She dusted it off and returned up the narrow stairs to the dining room. The earl and the marquess had gone to bed and only a few guests remained sitting at the tables. Delphine took a bottle opener and two glasses and returned to the parlor, where the baron's son was waiting.

"As the fresh wine the poet pours, what asks he, Phoebus, what implores?" Maximilian said, reading from his volume of poetry.

"Wordsworth again?" Delphine asked, as she deftly uncorked the bottle and poured the wine into one of the two glasses, a splash at first, which she swirled around and sniffed.

"Wordsworth's *Ode to Apollo*. It's one of my favorites. How's the wine?" he asked, and Delphine nodded as she poured out a second glass.

"It's excellent. It's one my father used to recommend. He bought several cases of it a few years ago. The taste reminds me of him," she said, sitting down opposite Maximilian, who raised his glass to her in a toast.

"To your father, and his memory," he said, and Delphine returned the gesture.

"That's very kind of you. He'd be pleased to know his wine was being drank by one who appreciated it," she replied.

"I certainly appreciate it. You've a well-stocked cellar, I presume?" he asked, and Delphine nodded.

"My father made sure of it. He was something of a connoisseur, and he liked nothing better than seeing others enjoying the wine he served them," Delphine replied.

She felt relaxed in the company of Maximilian, and the thought of his behaving as the earl had suggested seemed ridiculous. He was not out to take revenge on the fairer sex. The idea was complete nonsense. He had been hurt, and perhaps he was cautious with his feelings, too. Once again, Delphine felt a sense of guilt at having set out to play a game with him, even if now those feelings seemed very real.

"And now you feel the same, I presume?" he asked, taking a sip of wine, and sitting back in his chair.

"I'm glad to see my hospitality enjoyed. But I've still so much to learn. I don't know a great deal about wine or how to tell what's good and what isn't. And that's only the beginning… I've still got so much to learn, as I told you," Delphine replied, but Maximilian shook his head.

"You mustn't compare yourself to your father. When we compare ourselves to others, we naturally find our abilities lacking. But you've your own talents, Delphine. You can offer so much. You're your father's daughter, but you're you own person, too. Run this inn as you see fit and make it your own. We don't always have to live with legacies," he replied.

Delphine thought about this for a moment. She had never considered running the inn in anything but her father's legacy. She wanted everything to be just the same as it had been when he was alive. But Maximilian was right. It could not be the same, it had to change. Delphine could not live in her father's shadow for the rest of her life, and neither would he want her to. His death had been a bitter blow, but it was also a new beginning, one in which Delphine would be forced to forge her own path for the good of herself.

"You're right, and I wouldn't want to, though it can be daunting to think of the responsibility that's mine," she replied.

He smiled at her and took another sip of wine.

"I think you're doing a fine job of running this inn. You've certainly looked after me very well, and I've heard no complaints from the other guests. Well…apart from the earl and the marquess. But I think you could place them on a gilded lily, and they'd still find something to complain about," Maximilian replied, shaking his head with a wry smile.

Delphine agreed. She had tried her best to run the inn as her father would have wanted it, and she had tried not to take to heart the complaints of the earl and the marquess. They could be kind at times, but they could also be cruel. She thought back to Maximilian's arrival. He *had* made his complaints very clear at that time, but in the days gone by he had mellowed, no doubt, in part, thanks to Delphine's efforts at winning him over.

"You're right. I just... I want everything to be just so. I hate to think of anyone complaining," she replied.

She had taken several sips from her own glass and was already feeling somewhat emboldened. Liquor did not agree with her, even in small quantities. It made her giddy and loosened her tongue.

"It doesn't matter if they do. You know you've tried your best. I must say... I'm glad of this place as a refuge," he replied.

Delphine knew she was about to ask the wrong question, but she could not help herself, and she blurted it out without pausing to consider the consequences.

"Why did you come here? Were you running away from something?" she asked.

Maximilian looked uncomfortable, and he took a larger sip of wine, considering his response before he spoke.

"I was...spurned. I was in love with a woman named Frances Stott. I thought she loved me, too. We were to be married; you see. It was all arranged. We had our whole lives ahead of us. But..." he said, and his words trailed off.

"She wasn't the one for you?" Delphine asked, gazing at him sorrowfully.

"It turned out I wasn't the one for her. She chose to marry another man. A man I knew nothing of. They'd been meeting secretly – an affair, I suppose you'd call it. She broke my heart, even though I knew I'd been a fool to allow myself to get caught up in the possibility of what might be. Love does foolish things to us, doesn't it?" he said.

Delphine had no real experience of love – the love between a man and a woman, at least. She knew of parental love, and the love of friendship, but as for romantic love...

"I suppose it does. But...did she ever give you a reason why she behaved so cruelly?" Delphine asked.

Maximilian shook his head. I didn't give her the chance. I didn't speak to her again. I fled, like a coward," he replied, shaking his head and sighing.

Delphine leaned over to pour him another glass of wine. He seemed less affected than she by the liquor, and despite having only drank a small amount from her own glass, she was feeling decidedly drowsy.

"But you were humiliated. It's she who's the coward. Didn't she give you any kind of explanation for her actions?" Delphine asked, but Maximilian shook his head again.

"None. She didn't even have the decency to tell me to my face. I found out by hearsay. But she knew what she was doing. She wanted me to suffer. I know she did," he said, and there was a bitterness in his voice, which made Delphine almost fear him.

What did he intend to do in response to the cruelty inflicted by Lady Frances Stott? Perhaps the earl was right...

"And so, you had no choice but to flee?" Delphine said.

"I could've stayed. But imagine it – the subject of endless gossip and seeing her and her lover riding in her carriage each day. I couldn't possibly have countenanced it. The thought is...too distressing," he replied.

Delphine could only imagine such a humiliation. She had heard such stories before – an inn is full of stories, and she had known of spurned lovers and broken hearts. But to hear such a story from a man was different. It was men who spurned women, men who rode roughshod over emotions, men who broke hearts... to see a man subjected to such cruelty was astonishing. It showed a vulnerability not usually noted the opposite sex, but one which Delphine found…attractive. Maximilian did not need to tell her the truth, but he had trusted her enough to do so, and for that, Delphine was grateful.

"I'm so sorry," she said, taking a sip of wine, even as she knew it had already gone to her head.

"I may well have had a lucky escape. Imagined if we'd married. It fills me with dread to think of it. One can break off an engagement with ease – and I shall certainly make it known it was she and not I who caused the break. But after marriage…no, it's almost impossible," he said, and Delphine nodded.

"I understand. But still…it must be very hard for you. I'm sorry you had to endure it. But what will you do now?" she asked.

This was the second question she had so wanted to ask. But she had felt it was not her place to do so, even as curiosity now got the better of her. He shrugged his shoulders and sighed.

"I left Berkshire not knowing where I'd go – apart from here. I had a vague notion of fleeing to the continent. But what does one do there? I could wander the classical ruins of the Italian peninsula, but like the glories of Rome, I'd feel myself fading, too. I've nothing left to offer. That's how it seems, at least," he replied.

His tone was pitiful. He was like a sheep without a shepherd, a lost soul whose whole world had been turned upside down.

"You must find it hard to trust anyone," Delphine said.

Maximilian looked up, fixing his gaze on hers, and nodded.

"That's precisely how I feel," he replied, and it was as though an understanding now existed between them, one which Delphine wished only to deepen.

She wanted to tell him about herself – about the loss of her father and how difficult she had found the past few months. She wanted someone – him – to know the struggles she had faced, for it seemed he would understand.

"I…" she began, but at that moment, the kitchen door banged open, and Bessie appeared, looking flustered.

"Oh, Miss Delphine, I'm sorry to disturb you, but it's the oven door, it won't close. You fixed it the other day, but neither Alice nor I can do it," she said.

Delphine smiled and rose to her feet.

"Will you excuse me a moment?" Delphine said, and the baron's son rose respectfully from his chair.

"Please, I'm taking up far too much of your time," he replied, but Delphine shook her head.

"I'm only too happy to have it taken up," she replied, smiling at him, before following Bessie back to the kitchen and the problem of the oven door.

Chapter Twelve

Maximilian had surprised himself by asking Delphine to sit with him that evening and share a bottle of wine. It had been an excellent claret, one of the best he had ever tasted, and he was surprised by the fact he had discovered such a vintage here at the inn. But his surprise had not stopped at the wine. Maximilian was surprised by his feelings for Delphine.

They had come on him unexpectedly. He had not intended to allow himself such indulgences. On the ride to London, Maximilian had vowed never to trust any woman ever again. But Delphine was different – at least, she appeared so. She listened to him. She had been kind to him. She had gone above and beyond any expectations he had of her.

But that's her job. She's meant to listen to endless stories from people she couldn't care less about. She meant to be kind and hospitable. She's meant to go beyond the expectations of her guests, he said to himself.

But despite these thoughts, Maximilian could not help but wonder – hope – that Delphine's motivations were different. He did not want to fall in love, but he knew such a want was not always possible. Love found the individual. Maximilian had not expected to fall in love with Frances Stott, and with the gift of hindsight, he wished he had not done so.

Which is why you need to be careful, he told himself.

It would be all too easy to allow his feelings to run away with themselves. That had been Maximilian's mistake before. He had fallen in love and falling out of love was far harder than falling into it. If the experience with Lady Frances had taught him anything, it was caution. Maximilian had no intention of making the same mistake twice. He had only one heart, and it had already been broken once, so he could not afford to have it broken again.

Yes, steady and certain. That's the only way, he thought to himself, reaching out for the wine bottle, and topping up his glass.

At that moment, footsteps on the stairs caused him to look up. The earl and the marquess were there, each dressed in their nightgowns, wrapped in matching robes, and with nightcaps on their heads.

"We can't sleep. There's far too much noise coming from down here," the earl exclaimed, and Maximilian raised his eyebrows.

There was no noise coming from the parlor, and only one table in the dining room was still occupied by a large gentleman nodding off to sleep, while his wife sat next to him with a bored expression on her face nursing a glass of sherry.

"I've not been disturbed myself," Maximilian replied.

"I require absolute silence when I'm going to sleep," the earl said, fixing Maximilian with an imperious look.

"I see," Maximilian said, hoping the two aristocrats would soon return upstairs.

But instead, they came and sat next to him, and Maximilian could smell the real reason for their restlessness. They had been drinking brandy, and the manner in which the marquess swayed as he sat down heavily appeared to confirm their present state.

"You don't see. It's most distressing," the earl replied, and he sighed deeply.

"One *should* be able to sleep soundly. Don't you think?" the marquess asked.

"It's all right for him. He's been put up in the roof. He'll sleep like a baby in those lodgings. Ah, yes, don't think we don't know. She moved you, didn't she?" the earl said, pointing at Maximilian, who rolled his eyes.

"Yes, she's never put either of us up there. We've never been moved. Take the higher place, *she* says, and you jumped at the chance, didn't you?" the marquess said, joining the earl in pointing an accusing finger at Maximilian.

There was both annoying exasperation and comedic pleasure to be derived from the company of the two men. Maximilian found it quite extraordinary how they behaved. It was as though they were determined to find any means possible to insult him, but did so only at their own expense, making themselves appear more and more ridiculous with every word they uttered.

"I didn't ask for it. I didn't even know the lodgings existed," Maximilian pointed out.

"Nonsense. You must've done. You came here with the express intention of securing Delphine's affections. That's the only reason, isn't it?" the earl said. At this Maximilian had to laugh.

He threw his head back and laughed so loudly that the man asleep in the dining room awoke with a start. The earl and the marquess looked at one another in surprise.

"You really are the most ridiculous individuals, aren't you?" he said.

"We're only trying to protect Delphine. She's…like family to us to us," the earl replied.

"Then why did she reject your gifts?" Maximilian replied.

He had decided to speak his mind, rather than be the butt of the two men's insults. By the looks on their faces, Maximilian knew he had struck a chord.

"Well… I suppose…she…" the earl stammered.

"We presented them at the wrong time," the marquess said,

and Maximilian smiled and shook his head.

"I rather think you could've presented them at any time and they'd still have been rejected. A paperweight and a quill pen – given your obvious wealth, are hardly generous gifts. What did you expect to achieve by them?" he asked, knowing he was twisting the knife, but rather enjoying seeing the two men squirm.

"It's not the object itself...it's the thought of the gift. What have you done for her? Nothing," the earl exclaimed, quickly regaining his composure.

"Listened to her, which is more than can be said for either of you," Maximilian replied.

Once again, his words appeared to cut to the quick, and both men looked at one another with expressions which suggested Maximilian was speaking the truth. But his words came only from observation. The earl and the marquess spoke *at* Delphine. They did not listen to her. They imparted their opinions, they aired their views, and they believed they held a particular place in her affections.

"We speak with her every day," the marquess retorted smugly, but this was not what Maximilian had meant, and all of them knew it.

"Everything was fine until you arrived. You came here to seduce her. She'd have been delighted with our gifts if you hadn't poisoned her mind against us. You've made up all sorts of stories about us, I'm sure. Listening to her? You only want to seduce her!" the earl exclaimed. He banged his fist down hard on the table so that the half empty wine bottle rocked from side to side.

Maximilian had never heard anything so ridiculous in all his life. He had no intention of seducing Delphine, nor had he come to the inn to do so. He had never heard of Delphine until a couple of days ago, and the suggestion he had arrives with a grand plan for seduction was so ridiculous as to be laughable.

"You're drunk and making a fool of yourself. As for seducing Delphine – I'd never be so impertinent as to assume I could. If she wanted to be seduced, then why haven't either of you managed it yet?" Maximilian asked.

He really was tired of being spoken to in this manner and wished the two men would leave him alone. He had no alternative agenda in relation to Delphine. She was kind, witty, charming, and a delight to be with. There was no doubting his feelings for her, even as he knew those feelings should remain hidden – if only for his own sake.

"You insult us by such insinuations," the marquess exclaimed, rising unsteadily to his feet.

"And you insult me with yours, sir. Can't a man enjoy the company of a woman without the suggestion of something more? Delphine and I... Miss Delphine and I are friends. Nothing more. Yes, she's been very kind to me since my arrival – an excellent host, just as she would be to you, if only you'd both stop behaving in such a ridiculous manner," Maximilian replied, shaking his head.

The earl and the marquess looked at one another. The marquess sat down again and sighed.

"Well...we don't like the way you're behaving towards her," the earl said.

It was the same words, spoken differently every time. They had nothing new to say. The same insults, the same accusations, the same false beliefs. None of it was true – Maximilian had not come to The Seven Bells = to seduce Delphine, nor with the intention of doing so to any woman. He was simply not interested in romance, even as his feelings for Delphine were growing stronger.

"And I don't think she likes the way you're behaving towards her either. If you want to be her friends, then why not start acting like it? These foolish gestures, these diatribes...they're worth nothing. You're sitting here insulting her, insulting me, and for what?" Maximilian demanded.

"I've heard enough. Bessie!? Bessie!? Where are you, girl?" the earl called out, and the kitchen door opened, revealing a flustered looking Bessie, whose apron was covered in black soot.

"Yes, my Lord?" she asked.

"Wine, we must have wine," the earl exclaimed, and Bessie nodded.

"At such a late hour…" she began, but the earl banged his fist on the table and gave an angry exclamation.

"Yes, at whatever hour we choose. Fetch a bottle of claret from the cellar and *two* glasses," he said, glancing at Maximilian with a sneer.

Maximilian reached out to pour himself a glass from his own bottle. The earl and the marquess could please themselves. Maximilian had no wish for their company any longer, but he was determined not to leave Delphine at their mercies. He would remain in the parlor until it was time for the inn to close, and he would be sure to defend Delphine's honor whilst doing so.

"Yes, my Lord. I'll fetch it at once," Bessie said, glancing at Maximilian with an apologetic expression on her face.

"That's better," the earl muttered, sitting back in his chair, caring not, it seemed, for the fact he was dressed in his nightgown and had just summoned the maid to fetch him a drink.

"Are you staying up?" the marquess asked Maximilian.

The question appeared as a challenge, as though the two aristocrats were playing a game – which they most certainly were.

"I'm enjoying this excellent claret. Delphine said she'd only be a few moments," Maximilian replied.

He wished Delphine would return, though for her own sake, it was perhaps better if she remained in the relative safety of the kitchen. The earl and the marquess would only cause further chaos, and with the wine brought, it seemed they had no intention of returning upstairs anytime soon.

"Then we'll all wait for her," the earl declared, as Bessie poured a glass of wine for him.

"Yes, we can all wait," Maximilian replied, raising his glass in a toast – a toast which was not returned.

Chapter Thirteen

"You have to lift it just so. The handle won't turn otherwise. You see...just like this. Lift, turn, push, then it's secure," Delphine said, as the oven door closed.

"I just don't understand it. Sometimes it does, sometimes it doesn't," Alice said, straightening up and shaking her head.

"These things are temperamental. Don't worry, it's fixed now," Delphine replied.

She was covered in soot, and dusted herself off as best she could, just as Bessie entered the kitchen.

"They wanted wine – at this hour, they wanted *wine*. I hate going down to that cellar. It's always so dark and there're cobwebs everywhere. I remember your father – God rest his soul – used to say, *Bessie, if a wine cellar's not full of cobwebs, it's not a wine cellar*. But I'd prefer a few less. They get in my hair," the maid said, shaking her head.

Delphine smiled, though she felt a sense of exasperation, too, at hearing the demands of the earl and the marquess. It was almost midnight, and she had hoped they could soon be cleared up and close the inn for the night.

"I thought they had gone to bed earlier on," she said, but Bessie shook her head.

"Apparently, it was too noisy. They couldn't sleep," she replied.

"So, they came downstairs to make their own noise, did they?" Alice replied.

Delphine suddenly remembered Maximilian. The earl and the marquess were certain to be causing him trouble, and she dusted the last of the soot of her dress and hurried out of the kitchen into the parlor. The earl and the marquess were sitting across from Maximilian, who had drained the dregs of his own wine bottle and was sitting facing the two aristocrats with a defiant expression on his face. The earl and the marquess looked up as Delphine emerged from the kitchen. The earl beckoned her over.

"A fine vintage, the ninety-two. Yes, excellent," he said, raising his glass.

Delphine knew what was coming next. The earl and the marquess liked to think of themselves as connoisseurs of wine. They used to behave in just the same way with Delphine's father, who had often privately remarked that neither of the two would know a good claret from a bowl of dishwater.

"Yes, a delightful bouquet. The scent is…of the sun kissed slopes of the southern climes. One can almost picture the vineyards," the marquess said, swirling the wine in his glass and breathing in the aroma.

Delphine glanced at Maximilian, who had a bemused expression on his face, and she, too, had to bite her lip to stop herself from laughing. Neither the earl nor the marquess knew what they were saying. It was nonsense, especially as Delphine knew there were no cases of the ninety-two in the cellar. It had been a bad year for wine, and she remembered her father telling her he had received nothing of any quality from the continent during that vintage.

"I'm glad you like it," Delphine replied.

"I always used to say to your father, it's a particular sort of gentleman who knows the quality of wine. We drink too much sherry in this country. The fortified stuff that makes little impact on the palette. But these vintages…ah, yes, excellent. Simply excellent," the earl said, raising his glass to the lamplight with a swirl as though he was examining the contents for some unseen quality.

"Are you that sort of gentleman?" Maximilian asked.

His voice was the pitch of innocence, even as Delphine knew precisely what he was doing. She smiled and sat down next to him, knowing this would further irritate the earl and the marquess, who glanced at one another and scowled.

"I know more about wine than any man in England. I could write a book on it, several, in fact. I might do it. I *could*, you know," the earl replied.

"So could I. We might write a joint book and tour the continental vineyards," the marquess interjected.

"I confess to knowing little about wine, save for the taste. I know what I like, and that's the limit of my expertise," Maximilian replied.

The earl gave him a withering look and swirled the wine around in the glass.

"It's not something one can simply learn. You've got to have a nose for it and a palette, too. Scent and taste. That's what matters in a wine. Take this ninety-two vintage, for example. The scent is a perfume of different sensations, and the taste…ah, *exquisite*. Like… cherries, strawberries, damsons. There's a richness to it," he said, raising his eyes as though to some unseen divinity.

"We drink only the finest wines," the marquess said, reaching out to pour himself a second glass.

"You are both quite the experts, it seems," Maximilian said. The earl smiled smugly.

"Ah, yes, we are," he replied, clearly enjoying the flattery.

"And the cellar here is so well stocked, thanks to your father, Delphine," the earl said, glancing at Delphine and raising his glass to her.

Delphine could not dispute his point. The earl was right. Her father had ensured the cellars at *The Seven Bells* were amongst the finest in all of England, rivaling those of the royal palaces. If anyone should have written a book on wine, it would have been her father.

"He was a connoisseur himself," Delphine said, thinking fondly of her father and the many times he had taken her down to the cellar with a candle in hand and shown her the rows of bottles.

Everyone is different, Delphine. There's an art to winemaking. A very special art, he would say, and Delphine would be fascinated by the sight of the bottles, with their ancient labels, all covered in dust.

"He was, and we were able to teach him much about the art of the vintner," the earl replied.

Delphine knew there was little point in arguing. The earl and the marquess were merry, and if she wished to sit with Maximilian – which she did – she knew she would have to ensure their company for as long as it took them to tire. But she endured it only for Maximilian's sake, and not for theirs. She had very much enjoyed their conversation earlier that evening and wanted only to continue it – alone.

"I'm sure you taught him *everything* you know," Maximilian said, and it seemed he was enjoying teasing the earl and the marquess without their realizing it.

"Oh, yes, he was most grateful for our advice. We encouraged him to consider wines from the Germanic states, and it certainly changed his mind about the French," the earl said.

Delphine smiled. She remembered the day the earl and the marquess had lectured her father on the virtues of an obscure wine from Bavaria. He had listened patiently – as was always his way – and thanked them for their recommendation. But the wine had proved...elusive to find, or so he had told the two aristocrats, whilst secretly confiding in Delphine, that the bottle he had procured from a merchant had been corked and tasted foul.

"Well… I really don't know about such things. But I'll take your word for it," Maximilian said.

"You should do. We can tell you a great deal about wine. I could speak all night on the subject. I could tell you anything you wanted to know. I've even begun an experiment on my own estate in Oxfordshire. We're growing vines in the kitchen garden. It has a high redbrick wall and faces south. It always feels warm there, and I think the vines will flourish," the earl said, looking proudly at Maximilian, who smiled.

"Your own vintage? Will we be permitted to sample some?" he asked.

The earl narrowed his eyes.

"Miss Delphine will be presented with the very first bottle. If she's willing to accept a gift from me, that is," he said, turning to Delphine, who sighed.

She knew neither of the two men would ever allow her to forget the refusal of the gifts. It had been a churlish thing to refuse them, even as she had known she was making a point in doing so.

"I won't refuse. Though a few vines won't produce many bottles, will they?" she replied.

The earl looked hurt by this remark.

"Producing a wine in England is nigh on impossible. The fact I'm to be the first to do so must have some merit to it," he said.

"Every merit," the marquess assured him, as he poured the earl another glass of wine.

The conversation continued in this way for some time, and Delphine was growing increasingly weary. She wanted to go to bed, but she did not wish to leave Maximilian in the company of the earl and the marquess, whose insults were bound to be magnified if she left the three men alone.

"Another drink?" she asked, turning to Maximilian, who smiled and shook his head.

"No, I think not. I'm going to go to bed," he replied, and Delphine breathed a sigh of relief.

"Then I'll...see you in the morning," she replied.

"Aren't you going to stay with us?" the earl demanded, but Delphine shook her head.

"I think not – not tonight, at least. Goodnight," she said, glancing back at Maximilian, who had risen from his place.

The earl and the marquess seemed perturbed. Perhaps they suspected illicit intimacy, and now they, too, rose. All thoughts of wine apparently discarded.

"We'll go, too," they said.

Delphine nodded. She had no intention of following Maximilian upstairs, as much as she had enjoyed his company. She wondered when next the opportunity might arise for the two of them to spend time together, even as she knew her feelings for Maximilian were getting the better of her.

"I hope you sleep well, and there's no further noise," she replied, still smiling at Maximilian, as she returned to the kitchen.

"Have they gone to bed yet?" Alice asked, as the kitchen door banged shut.

"Yes, they've all gone. But you didn't need to wait up," Delphine replied, seeing how tired both Bessie and Alice looked.

"And leave you at the mercy of the earl and the marquess? Oh, no, ma'am. We're in this together," Alice replied, as Bessie brought a pot of tea to the table, and the three women finally sat down to their refreshment.

* * *

"The privileged right turn," the earl said, as Maximilian turned at the top of the stairs towards the narrower staircase leading to his own quarters.

"I don't know what you're talking about," Maximilian replied.

"Your lodgings in the roof, that's what. She's put you up there to laud it over the rest of us," the earl said, as the marquess nodded in vigorous agreement.

"You'll be pacing up and down, creaking the floorboards. It's no wonder we can't sleep. You make enough noise to wake the dead," the marquess said, and Maximilian rolled his eyes.

Arguing with a drunk man was never wise. There could be no reasoning with two men who had consumed an inordinate amount of brandy, followed by a bottle of wine. Not to mention the two bottles they had drank with dinner.

"If you say so," Maximilian replied.

"We do say so, and what's more, you need to be careful," the earl continued.

"Careful of what? Careful of the two of you. Yes, excellent advice, Goodnight," Maximilian said, turning on his heels and making for the staircase up to his room.

He was longing for some peace and quiet, and far from intending to make a noise, he wanted only to be left alone.

"Careful of falling in love with her. That's what," the earl said.

Maximilian stopped dead in his tracks. Now it was the earl's turn to have hit a nerve. But love and affection were two different things. The earl had made such comments before – entirely baseless in the moment – but now...

"I'm...not falling in love with her," Maximilian replied, turning to face the earl and the marquess along the dimly lit corridor, where only a single candle burned in a sconce. The silvery light of the moon came through a distant window.

"Then what would you call it?" the marquess retorted.

"Friendship...companionship, mutual enjoyment of one another's company. Can't a man and woman be friends?" he asked.

The earl shook his head.

"It's not appropriate. She just lost her father. You're taking advantage of her emotions. We've been watching you," he declared, but Maximilian had heard enough, and he refused to engage any further.

"Goodnight," he replied, and turning he marched up the stairs and slammed the door of his lodgings behind him.

He purposefully paced up and down the length of the roof space, enjoying the sound of the creaking floorboards and knowing how much it would irritate the earl and the marquess below. It was a ridiculous assertion – he was not in love with Delphine. He barely knew her, but...

I feel...torn. My head and my heart. I can't... I can't fall in love with her. Or with any woman, he told himself, pacing up and down his lodgings.

He paused and put his head in his hands. The memory of Frances...everything that had happened to him in those weeks and months gone by.

We were so happy, he told himself, and now he knew why he felt such fear at the prospect of allowing himself to fall in love once again.

Delphine was not like those women he had known in his youth – the silly, giggling daughters of aristocrats, who flocked to balls and soirees in flocks and sat tittering with one another behind their fans. It was a woman like that whom Maximilian had been expected to marry. The son of a baron would marry the daughter of nobility. That was how it was meant to be. It did not particularly matter what that daughter was like, so long as she was of a particular social standing.

Maximilian had resigned himself to such a lot, even as he had begun to despair of ever encountering a woman who broke the mold just a little. It was in this moment of despair he had met Frances. She had not been like the others. She had passion, flair, and an attraction which had seemed overwhelming to the young Maximilian. He had fallen in love with her the moment he had lain eyes on her, and that had been his downfall. It was a mistake he had no intention of making again, even as he knew he might have no choice.

I can't help it if I fall in love with her. But I can stop myself from making another foolish mistake. I might love her, but I can resist her.

Surely, I can resist her? He thought to himself, even as the idea appeared absurd.

But there was something about Delphine – just as there had been something about Frances. It was impossible to say what it was, and certainly Delphine was very different from any of the women whom Maximilian might have been expected to marry. But that was part of her allure, her charm, her delight… Maximilian knew the earl was right, even as he resented the fact of it having been recognized.

But I won't let my heart be broken. I won't… he told himself.

He had begun to pace again, and a sudden banging on the ceiling below caused him to stop.

"Enough!" came the marquess' voice from below, and Maximilian smiled at the thought of the aristocrat balancing precariously on his washstand in order to bang on the ceiling.

He made a deliberate jump, so that the whole room shook and another angry exclamation – this time from earl – came from below.

"We'll have you thrown out," he called out.

Maximilian smiled to himself as he climbed into bed that night and pulled the blankets up over himself. Delphine would not throw him out, of that, he was certain. But was he really in love with her…and what of her feelings for him?

Don't think too much about it, he told himself, but as he fell asleep that night, Maximilian's thoughts were on one person, and one person only – Delphine, and the fact he *had* in fact fallen in love with her.

Chapter Fourteen

Maximilian awoke with a dry mouth. The dinner had been salty, and after consuming most of the bottle of wine he had shared with Delphine, his thirst was raging. There was nothing to drink in his lodgings at the top of the inn, and he cursed himself for not having brought a drink with him to bed – a glass of milk mixed with honey was his favorite.

It must still be late, or early, or some ungodly hour, Maximilian thought to himself, and he rolled over and pulled back the blankets.

It was dark outside, and through the floorboards, Maximilian could hear either the earl or the marquess snoring loudly. If he had wanted to be mischievous, Maximilian knew he could leap from the bed and dance across the creaking floorboard. But as much as such a desire had its appeal, he knew, too, the wrath he would engender in doing so.

It's not worth it, he told himself, and he cautiously got up, trying to avoid the creakiest of the floorboards, as he fumbled his way to the door.

He intended to go downstairs and see if he could find some

milk in the kitchen larder. He would tell Delphine the next day and compensate her. His mouth was so dry he knew he could never get back to sleep without a drink, and the thought of a cold cup of milk was ever so appealing.

I'll be back in bed soon enough, he said to himself, yawning, for he knew he had only slept a few hours at the most.

Apart from the distant sounds of snoring, the inn was quiet, and Maximilian made his way slowly down the stairs to the landing. A single candle was guttering in a sconce at the far end by the staircase leading down to the parlor below, but it gave little light, and Maximilian collided with a table on the landing as he felt his way along.

"Ow!" he exclaimed, stubbing his toe on the table leg.

He paused for a moment, listening for the sound of aristocratic snoring. It was still there, rhythmic and unbroken. With greater care, Maximilian now made his way to the stairs leading down to the parlor. He was surprised to see a flicker of light coming from below, and for a moment, he feared the inn had been broken into. But there was no sound, and he wondered if perhaps the maid or the cook were still up.

I'll try not to startle them, he thought to himself, as he made his way down the stairs.

To his surprise, he found Delphine there. She was standing at one of the tables in the dining room polishing cutlery. Maximilian could see her through the door from the parlor. She looked up at him in surprise, embarrassed, it seemed, to be caught at her work at such a late hour.

"Oh, I'm sorry...it's still a while until breakfast. Alice won't be up for a few hours yet," Delphine said, glancing at the ticking grandfather clock which stood against the far wall of the dining room, and which told Maximilian it was two o'clock in the morning.

He shook his head and smiled.

"Forgive me. I'm not seeking breakfast at some ungodly hour. I thought I might get myself a drink of milk. If you don't mind, that is. My mouth feels terribly dry. I could drink a gallon, I feel," he said, and Delphine nodded.

"Certainly. I'll fetch you some. It'll be nice and cold straight from the larder," she said.

Maximilian was curious as to why Delphine was still awake at such an hour. He had thought she would go to bed shortly after he and the others had done, but it seemed she had been awake the whole time. A moment later, Delphine returned from the kitchen with a cup of milk which she handed to Maximilian, who thanked her.

"You're very kind. I'm sorry to disturb you. I didn't realize you'd still be awake and working at this time," Maximilian replied.

He looked around the dining room. The tables were half set, and a mound of cutlery remained on the table, to which Delphine now returned.

"I'm awake at this time every night. There's always something to do. I can't expect Bessie and Alice to stay up, too. I always like to have the tables laid and ready for the next morning. But when you have the likes of the earl and the marquess staying up until midnight, there's no chance to do so before now," she said, taking up a knife and a cloth and beginning to polish.

Maximilian felt a sense of guilt at having played his own part in this late hour.

"I'm sorry. I didn't realize. I'd have gone to bed much earlier…" he began, but Delphine interrupted him.

"I didn't mean you, I'm sorry… I shouldn't complain. I'm glad to have so many guests and for *The Seven Bells* to be such a lively place. But it's relentless, too. I don't know how my father managed it all these years," she said, shaking her head.

"You're doing a marvelous job. Here…let me help you. I could polish the forks if you'd like," Maximilian said, taking a sip of milk and stepping forward.

Delphine looked embarrassed – though not displeased – at the thought.

"But you're a guest. I can't expect you to..." she began, but Maximilian had already set down his cup and taken a pile of forks and was beginning to polish them vigorously.

"It's quite all right. I'm only too happy to help. Besides, if I go back upstairs, I risk the wrath of the earl and the marquess if put so much as a foot on a creaking floorboard," Maximilian replied, smiling at her.

Delphine shook her head and rolled her eyes.

"I'm sorry about them. They're behaving like two schoolboys. I'm sure they weren't like this for my father," she said.

"They probably didn't think they could get away with it. I'm sure they couldn't. But don't worry about them. They'll not keep it up, and they've certainly had a lot to drink this evening," Maximilian replied.

Delphine laughed, and she turned to Maximilian with a smile on her face.

"They certainly had. All those claims to know everything there is to know about wine. It's nonsense, of course. They don't know anything about wine. We don't even have a ninety-two vintage. My father poured the few bottles we had of it away. It was of a terrible quality," Delphine confided.

Maximilian laughed to hear this. The earl had spoken with such authority, but in truth, he had been speaking nonsense.

"It just goes to show, doesn't it? One can appear so very right, but be so very wrong," he replied.

Delphine sighed.

"That's just what they're like. Experts in everything. My father never seemed perturbed by them, though. He allowed their nonsense to wash over him. I wish I could be so...unaffected by them. I try not to say anything, I try not to get angry...but when they're drunk, it's even worse. I'm sorry you've had to put up with them. You've done so with such grace and charm. I don't know how you manage it," she replied.

"By delighting in the fact I've discovered they're wrong. I suspected as much, but I really know nothing about wine. My parents kept only a moderately stocked cellar. A sherry before dinner was as much difference as we ever had. We'd drink claret sometimes, and the occasional bottle of champagne. But that was it. Your father, on the other hand, seemed quite the connoisseur," Maximilian said.

He did not want to upset Delphine by talking about her father, but it seemed she did not mind being reminded of her memories, and she paused, putting down the piece of cutlery she was polishing and nodding.

"He knew all there was to know, but he wasn't boastful in it. Not like the earl. He enjoyed seeing others enjoying what he provided," she replied.

"Did he have a favorite? A favorite wine, I mean?" Maximilian asked.

He was interested in hearing more about Delphine's father. She imagined them to be of much the same temperament, and if that had been the case, then he was certain he would have enjoyed the man's company, just as he enjoyed that of Delphine.

"Oh, yes, he did. There was one particular year, one particular vintage, he favored above all others. I've only got two bottles left. I'll keep one in perpetuity. I won't open it. Not ever," Delphine said, glancing at the cellar door as she spoke.

"And the other?" Maximilian asked.

His interest was roused, and he wondered what the wine was like. Why that bottle? What did it taste like? What set it apart?

"I'd save for a special occasion. I'd want whoever drank it to share it with me, to savor it. I dare not mention it to the earl and the marquess. They'd buy it and open it, and I'd have to listen to them extol its virtues. As I told you, I don't drink a great deal of wine. It goes to my head so quickly. But I'd like to drink this one, and be reminded of my father, if only fleetingly," Delphine replied.

Maximilian thought for a moment. He knew what he was about to say was a risk, and he thought back to the battle of his head over his heart. But something drew him on, a desire to make Delphine happy and to share in the memories of her father.

"How would it be if I bought the bottle and we shared it together?" he asked.

Delphine stared at him in amazement, and for a moment, Maximilian thought he had overstepped.

"Would you really do that? Would you share it with me?" she asked, and Maximilian nodded.

"Gladly so. I'd be only too pleased to. We could drink it together tomorrow – privately," he said, and Delphine smiled.

"I'd like that. I'd like it a lot. Shall I fetch it?" she asked.

"Please do," Maximilian replied.

He watched as she lit a candle and made her way over to the cellar door. The hinges creaked as she opened it and she disappeared into the black void beyond, the flicker of the candle hardly dispelling the darkness which engulfed her. A moment later, Delphine returned, holding a bottle in her hand. It was very dusty and covered in cobwebs.

"Here we are. The eight hundred. It's a claret. Mt father's favorite. He had two cases, but this and the final bottle are all that's left. It makes me think about him. It makes me miss him even more to hold it in my hand," she said, looking down at the dusty bottle. A tiny sigh escaped her lips.

Again, Maximilian wondered if he was doing the right thing.

"I...are you sure you don't mind opening it? I don't want to upset you," he said.

"Oh, but you won't be. What's the point of having wine if it lies dusty in a cellar? It's got to be drunk. It's full of memories. It's a memory in itself. No, I'm only too happy to share it with you. I *want* to share it with you," she replied, smiling at Maximilian, who blushed.

He knew he had overstepped yet another mark he had vowed to avoid. But Delphine had been so kind, and he was only too glad to have been able to do something in return. He had marveled at how open he had been in sharing his story with her. Maximilian had come to London in the hope of escaping his past, but he had realized he needed someone to confide in, someone who would understand the injustice he had experienced, and that person had been Delphine.

"Then we'll open it tomorrow, and drink a toast to your father, shall we?" he asked.

"I think that's an excellent idea. But I'll hide it from the earl and the marquess. We'll wait until they go to bed – even if we have to stay up all night," Delphine replied with a twinkle in her eyes.

They finished polishing the cutlery and laid the tables for breakfast the next morning. Maximilian moved some chairs for Delphine and helped her carry two of the tables through from the parlor.

"I hope you didn't mind me helping you," he said, when everything was in its place for the following day.

"Mind? No, it's been done in half the time, and I've enjoyed your company. Truly, I have," she said.

Maximilian bid Delphine goodnight and returned upstairs with the half-finished cup of milk in his hand. He did not think about the creaking floorboards, so preoccupied was he with thoughts of Delphine and the bottle of wine they would share together the next day.

I know I shouldn't feel like this. I know I shouldn't get carried away with romantic notions, he told himself, but a part of him could not help but wonder what would be if he allowed his heart to rule his head and see where such a risk would take him…

Chapter Fifteen

Delphine checked the bolt on the main door of the inn for the last time. It was a ritual for her – the same ritual she had observed her father enacting every night since she could remember.

"When the bolt's across, that's when we're safe," he would say, before taking her up to bed.

The bolt was always the last thing Delphine checked. A sign the day was over, even as the new one was not long to come. It was after two O'clock when she made her way up to bed. She could hear the earl and the marquess snoring as she crept past their bedrooms and up a short flight of stairs to the servant's landing. Her own bedroom was modest, simply furnished, with a window looking out over the stable yard.

What a long day, Delphine thought to herself, as she climbed into bed and yawned.

Alice would rouse her at six O'clock, though she was usually awake at five O'clock when she would hear Bessie emerging from her bedroom to begin her work. It was the maid's job to light the fires first thing in the morning, so that the kitchen was ready for

Alice to cook the breakfast in, and the dining room and parlor were warmed through for the guests. Next would come the heating of the hot water, and Bessie would take in jugs to the bedrooms, and breakfast would then be served.

It's hardly worth going to sleep, Delphine thought to herself, even as she gave a loud yawn and rolled onto her side.

She was pleased at the thought of sharing her father's favorite bottle of wine with the baron's son. What a contrast his demeanor was now from that of the angry man who had first arrived at *The Seven Bells*. Delphine closed her eyes, allowing sleep to wash over her. She was back in her childhood, her father was there, he was telling her about the wine.

* * *

"Ah, look, Delphine. We have the finest bottles in all the world laid up here in this cellar," Delphine's father said, carrying her in his arms as he spoke.

Delphine did not like the cellar with its dust and cobwebs. It was dark there, and only the light of candles burning in sconces on the walls illuminated it, the flames flickering to reveal the arches and rows of bottles lining each wall. There were hundreds there, and Delphine – even at such a tender age – knew they were her father's pride and joy.

"Why are they so special, father?" she asked, as her father reached down and pulled out one of the bottles to examine.

"Because they bring joy and happiness. Think of the stories we hear about wine. Didn't we hear one in church just last Sunday? The story of the wedding feast at Cana, when Jesus turned water into wine? It was a miracle which showed joy. Wine brings joy, it makes men merry – sometimes too merry – but always joyful. That's why we drink wine, and that's why our guests deserve such a choice of wine to enjoy with their food," Delphine's father replied.

They made their way back up the stairs into the dining room. Delphine loved it when her father carried her in his arms, though he had *warned her she was getting far too big to be carried. She was seven years old, and her father was her world. The dining room was busy, and Delphine's father set her down, and she followed him to a table where a couple were dining on lamb and new potatoes.*

"Ah, the claret," the gentleman said, as Delphine's father uncorked the bottle.

"The finest of vintages, my Lord. I think you'll enjoy this. Full-bodied and robust. The perfect accompaniment to your lamb," Delphine's father replied.

"I'll say it again, William, there's not a finer place to dine in all of London, than The Seven Bells," the man said, smiling at Delphine as her father poured two glasses of wine.

"I'm pleased you like it here, my Lord. I try to make every guest feel welcome," he said.

"And you certainly do. Your dining room's full, your food is excellent, and you've a remarkable cellar. What more can a man want?" the man replied, raising his glass in a toast.

"What more, indeed?" Delphine's father replied.

Delphine was about to say something, but as she looked up proudly at her father, filled with love and admiration for him, the sound of a gentle tapping disturbed her.

"Ma'am? It's Alice, it's time to get up, I'm afraid," Alice was saying, and Delphine was returned to waking life, after the pleasant memories of her dream…

* * *

Maximilian had tried to sleep. He was no longer thirsty, but his mind was filled with thoughts of Delphine. He had enjoyed their unexpected liaison in the dining room, and it amused him as he wondered what the earl and the marquess might have said if they had witnessed the scene.

They'd have played merry hell over it, he thought to himself, as he lay on his back on his bed, listening to the sounds of snoring coming from below.

He yawned, but he was not really tired. He thought about Delphine and her father's wine. He was looking forward to drinking it the following day and allowing Delphine to speak of her past. It was not the wine that mattered, but what it evoked. Maximilian knew how important it was to Delphine, and that was why it was important to Maximilian, too.

He was not sure what had compelled him to ask that she share the wine with him, and he had wondered immediately if Delphine might refuse. But she had seemed only too glad to accept his offer, not only of the wine, but of his company, too. And it was her company Maximilian was most looking forward to, even as he knew the danger involved.

You've already fallen in love with her. Admit it. It happens so quickly. You can't help yourself. It's your Achilles heel, Maximilian told himself.

That much was true. He did not find falling in love difficult. Women could so easily captivate his heart. He was a romantic at heart, a man who believed in true love, even as it had so far eluded him. But what he had realized – to his detriment – was that love required the entwining of two hearts, rather than the folly of one. To fall in love was a beautiful thing, but only if that love was reciprocated. Otherwise, pain and heartbreak were inevitable.

But the earl was right, wasn't he? I have fallen in love with her, he said to himself, even as he would never publicly admit it.

Whether he was in love with Delphine or not made no difference. In the past, Maximilian would have readily declared such love. He would have shouted it from the rooftops so that everyone knew. But not now. Love had humiliated him, it had broken his heart, and he was uncertain he could afford such a risk again. He did not want to be hurt – whether deliberately or unintentionally. Love was not something to be controlled, he knew that, but how he wished he might have certainty as to who its declaration would be received.

I can't just tell her, he told himself, rolling onto his side and sighing.

But his mind was too restless to sleep, and he got up and sat on the side of his bed with his head in his hands. He felt a sense of inevitable despair, as though he was careening down a hill in a carriage without a horse. It had been just the same with Frances, though with her, Maximilian had done nothing to prevent himself from falling.

This would be different.

Put her out of your mind. Forget all about her. Share the bottle of wine and be done with it, he said to himself.

But Maximilian knew his folly too well. He tended to act on impulse, rarely thinking of the consequences. He had fled Berkshire on a whim, without a thought of what was to be, and now he had allowed his feelings to run away with him again, and *this* was the consequence. Women were his weakness, as well as his delight.

I shan't see her tomorrow, he told himself, rising from his bed and beginning to dress.

Dawn was coming, and Maximilian was due at a reunion with his Oxford friends that day. He had met one of them by chance on a walk the previous day and been invited to join them at the home of Sir William Blake, a member of parliament with whom Maximilian had shared a staircase at Magdalen. He was looking forward to seeing his old friends again, even as they would all, by now, know of his humiliation. But the camaraderie of the companions would be such as to support him, rather than mock him, and there was no doubt in Maximilian's mind that no one present would have a good word to say about Lady Frances Stott.

I'll leave now, then I won't be...tempted, Maximilian said to himself, thinking of Delphine and pulling on his shirt and breeches, before slipping out of the inn.

Chapter Sixteen

"Sausages, bacon, black pudding, fried eggs, fried potatoes, mushrooms, and tomatoes," Delphine said, pointing to the large frying pan sizzling on the grate above the stove.

Alice was slicing a large loaf of freshly baked bread, and Delphine had prepared a tray with butter, preserves, and a pot of fresh coffee. She was planning to present Maximilian with another impressive breakfast, and now she took the frying pan from the flames, ready to carry it into the dining room.

"Tell Bessie to come for the tray, ma'am," Alice said, as she placed a jar of marmalade next to the pat of butter, along with several spoons and knives.

"I hope he'll enjoy it," Delphine said, and the cook smiled.

"The way to a man's heart, ma'am…it might not only be through his stomach, but there's no harm in trying," the cook said, as Delphine made her way out into the dining room.

She had expected to find Maximilian sitting in his usual place. But the table was empty. She looked around her for Bessie, who was busy laying the tables by the window.

"Where's the Baron's son?" she asked, feeling disappointed that her grand entrance had no one to receive it.

"Oh, he went out very early, ma'am. I was raking out the fires and I heard footsteps and looked up. He was hurrying out looking very smart," Bessie said.

Delphine's face fell. She had been looking forward to seeing Maximilian that morning, and he had mentioned nothing about going out, even as she reminded herself he was under no obligation to do so. What her guests did, where they went, and whose company they kept was none of her business. But despite this fact, Delphine could not help but feel a little hurt that her gesture had come to nothing.

"Oh…did he say where he was going?" she asked, and the maid shook her head.

"No, ma'am. I didn't speak to him. He was gone before I could speak to him. I don't know when he'll be back."

Delphine nodded. It would not do to show her disappointment. Maximilian could do as he pleased. He was under no obligation to her. She was about to return to the kitchen, still holding the enormous frying pan in her hand, when a clattering on the stairs announced the arrival of the earl and the marquess. They appeared in the dining room, smartly dressed, and smelling of rosewater, as though they, too, intended on being out that day.

"Oh, how wonderful, look at that breakfast, two of everything for me," the earl said, sitting down at his usual place.

The marquess said the same, and Delphine had no choice but to serve Maximilian's breakfast to them instead.

"Bessie, are you coming to collect this tray or not? Oh…" Alice said, appearing from the kitchen with the tray of bread, butter, preserves, and coffee.

"And all the accouterments, how splendid," the earl said gleefully, beckoning to Alice, who reluctantly stepped forward with the tray.

It was thus the earl and the marquess who enjoyed the excellent breakfast that morning, remarking on how pleased they were to be treated in such a kind and considerate manner.

"And on the very day we go to the Mansion House for luncheon with the Lord Mayor. What a perfect start to the day," the marquess said, as Delphine cleared the plates a short while later.

"You're both out for the day?" she asked, hope for a silver lining to the otherwise gray cloud.

Both men nodded.

"Yes, a very important luncheon. We're to be personal guests of the Lord Mayor himself at a gathering of the city guilds," the earl said, in a pompous and self-important tone.

Delphine cared little for the details, but she was pleased to know the two aristocrats would not be bothering her that day, even as she was sad to think she would spend it alone. The bottle of wine stood waiting on the table by the cellar door, and Delphine was looking forward to sharing it with Maximilian later that evening.

"Will you be...late?" she asked.

"Oh, we'll probably be invited to stay on. You know how these sorts of things go. A bottle or two of claret, a long luncheon, brandies in the afternoon. It usually turns into dinner and by the time you realize where you're at, it's gone midnight," the earl replied.

Delphine did not know what it was like, but the thought of the earl and the marquess being out of the inn and out from under her feet for a whole day was a most appealing prospect. She never knew quite how long they intended to stay, or what their plans were. They came as a pair, stayed as a pair, and left as a pair. One was never without the other, and when they eventually left, it would not be long before they returned. What they did in between times was anyone's guess, though Delphine could only imagine it involved mischief of some kind.

"Well... I hope you enjoy your day," she said, and the earl smiled at her.

"And what of you, my dear? You'll be busy, no doubt. I see our friend isn't down yet," he said, nodding to Maximilian's empty place.

"He…went out, or so I believe," Delphine replied.

The earl and the marquess glanced at one another.

"I heard him pacing up and down last night. You shouldn't allow him to pace up and down like that – the floorboards creak terribly and I had to bang on the ceiling to make him quiet down," the marquess said, tutting and shaking his head.

Delphine tried not to smile at these words. She could imagine Maximilian's delight in causing the earl and the marquess a restless night.

"I'm sure he didn't mean it," she said, but the earl waved his hand in an angry gesture and snorted.

"Bah! He meant it, all right. The man's a menace. He's turned this place upside down. An uproar, that's what he wants to cause," he said, as Delphine rolled her eyes.

"He's just a guest here," she replied.

"And a troublemaker, too," the marquess said, nodding to the earl, who nodded back.

"Precisely, Jacob," he said.

Delphine was not about to argue with them. If that was what they wanted to believe, then so be it – she knew who the real troublemakers were.

"Are they going out today?" Alice asked, when Delphine returned to the kitchen with the empty plates.

"All day, or so they say," Delphine replied, and the cook clapped her hands together with glee.

"I'll have a spring in my step all day, ma'am. No demands at luncheon, no sending back the dishes a dozen times to correct the smallest things. Will they dine tonight?" she asked, and Delphine shook her head.

"I don't think so, no," she replied.

But her thoughts were elsewhere, even as she tried to put them aside. She was thinking about Maximilian, and wondering if he would return for luncheon, or dinner, or indeed to share the bottle of wine which was promised. She knew it was foolish to feel disappointment in his absence. He owed her nothing, they were merely on friendly terms, and for Maximilian to absent himself for a day was hardly grounds for getting upset.

"Excellent. I won't have any complaints about my sauces, or the cooking of the meat...oh, those two," Alice said, shaking her head.

She was kneading dough on the kitchen table, and she struck it with such force as to make the whole kitchen shake. Delphine set down the empty plates and sighed. She felt foolish at having allowed her feelings to get the better of her. This was not how it should have been. When Delphine had decided on her plan, she had intended to show Maximilian that all women were not like the one who had spurned him. She had wanted to change his mind about women, not fall in love with him! She had thought him cold, distant, and angry, but now that she knew him better, she had discovered the opposite was true.

"I'm going to clean up in the dining room," Delphine said, wanting to be on her own.

"Oh, I'm quite happy here, ma'am – with those two gone, I'll be happy all day," Alice replied.

The earl and the marquess had now left, and the dining room was empty. Bessie had gone upstairs to see to her chores, and Delphine began to straighten the chairs and scrub the tables. She kept glancing at the bottle of wine standing on the table next to the cellar door. She thought back to her dream from the previous night, of her father carrying her down to the cellar and proudly showing her the wines.

What would you say if you were here now, Father? Am I a fool? she asked herself, even as she was fairly certain of the answer.

To fall in love was not what she had intended. Nor was this how she had ever imagined she *would* fall in love. Falling in love was a matter of intention, of courtship, of being the object of a man's affections, or so she believed. Delphine had never intended to fall in love like this – or ever. Her lot was to be the innkeeper of The Seven Bells and live out her father's legacy. But despite this knowledge, Delphine could not help but feel a sense of loneliness in that task, and a desire to share it with another.

But you're being foolish. He's the son of a baron, an aristocrat. He'll inherit a title, he'll return to Berkshire, you're not the same – he's proved that today. Wherever he's gone, it's not a place for you. It's impossible, she told herself, even as her mind wandered to the possibility of what might be.

With a sigh, Delphine looked around the dining room. All was neat, all was orderly, all was ready for the next performance. That was what her life suddenly felt like – a performance, an act put on for others. She was expected to be all things to all people, but inside, Delphine was hurting. She missed her father terribly, she was unsure of the future, and now her feelings for Maximilian were confused.

I can't go on like this, she said to herself, glancing again at the dusty bottle of wine on the table by the cellar door.

But go on was just what she had to do – not only for her sake, but for those who depended on her, too.

Chapter Seventeen

Maximilian had spent the better part of the morning at the pleasure gardens in Vauxhall. He had arrived there early, just as the debaucheries of the previous night had ended. Elegantly dressed ladies and fashionably dressed young men were leaving arm in arm, whilst others slept amidst the pavilions and the secluded groves of the gardens.

It was a strange place, one which Maximilian had not visited in many years. A place where the upper classes could play out their delights amidst all manner of entertainments, which lasted long into the night. But now, with the breaking of the dawn, it was quiet, and Maximilian ambled past the flower beds, pausing to admire the vista across the borders, where tall trees grew up around a pavilion which housed a ballroom and salon.

What am I doing here? he asked himself, as a couple emerged from the shrubbery hand in hand, giggling to one another.

He took some refreshment in the coffeehouse, thinking back to the previous evening. His feelings were confused – especially when it came to Delphine. Maximilian had come to London with an express hatred for the fairer sex. He had wanted nothing to do with them and wished only to forget his ordeal at the hands of Frances by building a barrier between his heart and anything which might have the potential to break it. But meeting Delphine had changed that.

She was unlike other women, and she was certainly not like Frances. In Delphine, Maximilian sensed no guile, even as he was aware of his own weaknesses surrounding women. He knew he fell in love far too easily and could not be trusted with his own judgement. His heart was still broken, he was vulnerable to the charms of seduction, and he knew how easily he could be hurt.

Then don't allow yourself to be, he said to himself, as he finished his coffee and left the pleasure gardens.

The home of Sir William Blake was a fashionable townhouse in Mayfair, and Maximilian took a carriage there, arriving shortly before noon. The reunion was to be a luncheon party, followed by an afternoon of drinking. At Oxford, this was how Maximilian and his friends had passed much of their time, and he was looking forward to seeing his old companions from Magdalen.

"Max! How splendid to see you," Sir William exclaimed, as Maximilian was shown into the drawing room after his arrival.

The others were already gathered there – the friend he had met by chance, Sebastian Grayson, the one who had invited him to the gathering, along with Charles White, Theodore Stapleton, and Rupert Davis. Their wives were there, too, and amongst them Maximilian recognized Annabella Stapleton, Theodore's wife and a close friend of Frances. He had assumed only the men would be present, and his heart fell as her eyes met with his and she gave him a curt nod.

Every tale had its opposite, and Maximilian could only guess as to what Frances had told Annabella of her reasons for breaking off the engagement. Had she made up falsities about him? Perhaps she had laid the blame entirely on his shoulders and made it out to seem as though it were he who was in the wrong. Frances was like that. Maximilian had come to see her faults in the aftermath of their separation, faults he had blinded himself to during his infatuation.

"And I'm pleased to see you, too – all of you," Maximilian said, nodding to each of his friends.

The ten years which had passed since they had left Oxford had seen each of their lives taking quite different courses. Sir William was a member of parliament, Sebastian owned sugar plantations in the colonies, Charles had recently inherited his father's title and was now the Earl of Carlisle, Theodore had inherited a barony in Norfolk, and Rupert was shortly to take up a diplomatic post in Florence. They were married, successful, and prosperous. Maximilian felt somewhat out of place, even as he was glad to be in the company of those men who had known him the longest.

"Come and sit down, we were just talking about you," Sir William said, signaling to a footman to bring Maximilian a glass of sherry.

"I see..." Maximilian said, glancing again at Annabella, and wondering what her true opinion might be.

The matter was complicated by the fact that he and Annabella had once shared a fleeting romance, one which Theodore was unaware of.

"Yes, a terrible business with Lady Frances. You've not had much luck with women, have you?" Sir William said, and the others laughed.

"Or they've not had much luck with me, I suppose," Maximilian replied, taking a sip of sherry as he sat down on a chair by the hearth.

The drawing room was comfortably furnished, and he looked around at each of his friends in turn, imagining what each might have said. Their features were the same, but each of them had grown older. Sir William's hair was graying, Sebastian was tanned from the colonial sun, though his face looked older, Charles had lost most of his hair and now wore a wig, Theodore's face was pinched, and he had the look of one for whom illness is not far, and

Rupert's chin was marred by a scar, the result of a brawl with a foreigner some years previously. Maximilian knew he, too, had changed – they were the same men, but very different, nonetheless.

"Frances was upset," Annabella said, fixing Maximilian with a stern gaze.

"Is that so? I'm sure she has her consolation," Maximilian replied.

He was not about to let Annabella dictate the narrative. Their own romance had been fleeting and had ended agreeably, even as Maximilian had known Annabella wanted more. Theodore had been her consolation prize. She was an ambitious woman, and to be the wife of an aristocrat had been a long-held ambition for her – it did not particularly matter who it was.

"That may be but…" Annabella continued, but Maximilian cut her off.

"I don't want to talk about her, Annabella. I've put her behind me. It was she who dissolved the engagement. She's already married to *that* man. I don't need to be reminded of it," he said, turning back to his host and taking a sip of sherry.

An awkward silence fell on the room.

"Where are you staying whilst you're in London?" Rupert asked, clearing his throat, and sitting up in his chair.

His wife – a pretty young woman called Lucy – was sitting next to him, and she smiled encouragingly at Maximilian, who was relieved to have something else to talk about.

"An inn called The Seven Bells. It's not far from Saint Paul's. It's an excellent place. Very hospitable," he said.

"Ah, I know it well," Charles said, and Sir William nodded, too.

"Yes, I do, too. But didn't the landlord die recently? That's what I heard, at least," he said.

"Yes, but it's been taken over by his daughter, Miss Delphine. She's running the place, very well, I must say," Maximilian replied.

"I don't like inns. Why stay at an inn when you can have a townhouse?" Sebastian said.

He had always had more money than sense, and it would never have occurred to him to consider economy over comfort.

"We don't all have the means to such ends," Maximilian replied.

He was beginning to realize the gulf which now existed between him and his friends from Oxford. Back at college, their lives had seemed open to possibility. They could be whatever they wanted to be, or so it had seemed. But the passing of time had molded them into what they now were – establishment figures, set on a particular course of life. Maximilian was pleased to see them, but he was glad not to be like them. Had he married Frances, then this would have been his lot. They were all the same – of the same opinions, same tastes, same dispositions.

"I suppose not," Sebastian replied, just as a gong sounded in another part of the house.

"Ah, that's luncheon served. Shall we go through?" Sir William asked, rising to his feet.

Maximilian was glad of the interruption, and he rose to his feet, offering Lucy his arm as they walked towards the dining room, whilst Rupert walked with Sir William, whose wife was staying with a cousin who was having a baby.

"I don't believe we've met. You married Rupert rather hastily, didn't you?" Maximilian said, and Lucy blushed.

"We were in love. We didn't want to wait. And I love him just as much today as I did then – even more so," she said, glancing at Rupert, who turned to her and smiled.

"He's a very lucky man," Maximilian replied.

At these words, she blushed. She was a pretty creature, but it was not only her looks that were attractive. She had a wit and a charm about her which Maximilian could not help but find endearing.

"Rupert told me what happened to you. For what it's worth, we both believe you to be the wronged party. What Frances did to you was terrible. You must find the thought of trusting any woman ever again terribly difficult," she said, and Maximilian nodded.

It was not something he had readily admitted, but Lucy – despite having known him for all of half an hour – had discerned the truth perfectly. Trust was the key, and Maximilian felt entirely devoid of trust in women. It was for this reason he held back when it came to Delphine. He could not bring himself to trust her intentions or to believe she was sincere in her actions. He wanted to, but his reason would not allow it, even as his heart suggested otherwise.

"You're right. I do find it difficult. I was in love with Frances – deeply so. I thought we'd spend the rest of our lives together, just like you and Rupert, or any of the others here. It's very hard when one's hopes are dashed, and in such a cruel manner," he replied.

Lucy nodded and patted his arm.

"It'll be all right. Not all women are like that," she replied, as they came to the dining room.

To Maximilian's relief, Sir William had seated him as far away from Annabella as possible. He was sitting between Rupert and his host, and the conversation over luncheon was congenial. The soup was delicious – a lobster Thermidor – and rack of lamb followed it, served with new potatoes and vegetables. The meal concluded with a Charlotte Russe, followed by coffee and candied fruits. The ladies did not leave the table as was the usual custom, but remained so that the conversation might continue between the couples.

"I was at matins the other day at Saint Paul's," Sir William said, as he and Maximilian sat in conversation over their glasses of brandy, the table having somewhat divided itself into smaller groups engaged in conversation together.

"I can't abide the choir these days. All shrill anthems, nothing of tradition," Rupert said, shaking his head.

"I like the choir, but the sermon was interrupted by the most outrageous display of nonsense – two men whispering throughout the whole thing, and then challenging the preacher in the pulpit," Sir William said, shaking his head.

Maximilian smiled wryly. He could imagine who those two men might be.

"An earl and a marquess?" he asked, and Sir William nodded.

"The very same. I was astonished to discover it. Do you know them?" he asked, and Maximilian nodded.

"I've made their acquaintance. They're staying at The Seven Bells. A rather strange pair. Do you know anything about them?" he asked, wondering if there might be some scandal to report back to Delphine.

Sir William shook his head.

"Robert Grantham, the Earl of Paxton and Jacob Rollins, the Marquess of Renfrew. There's nothing more to say about them. Obscure aristocrats who appear to make a habit of forcefully displaying their eccentricities. Have they spoken to you?" he asked.

"On more than one occasion," Maximilian replied wryly.

Despite their many annoyances, he knew the earl and the marquess were, at heart, a harmless pair. They wanted what was best for Delphine, even as they had a strange way of going about it. Maximilian had come to realize it was best to allow their presence to simply wash over him, rather than try to fight against their tide.

"Well, I can't see them being welcome at Saint Paul's again. I'm surprised the good canon maintained a Christian attitude towards them. I'd have given them what for," Sir William replied.

The conversation now turned to other matters before the party rose to take further refreshments in the drawing room. Maximilian once again escorted Lucy, who looked at him with a concerned expression on her face as he declared his intention to leave.

"So soon? We were going to play quadrille," she said, as Charles and Theodore began to set up Sir William's card table.

"I can't abide the game – nor any other. I'm terrible at them.

They're always so confusing. Besides... I'm not the best of company at the moment," Maximilian replied, blushing as he spoke.

He knew he was being rude, but the gathering had reminded him just how different he was from his friends. Their lives were settled, their futures assured, and they had everything they had ever wanted – or so it seemed. But Maximilian was different. He had been so close to this, even as *this* now seemed eminently unappealing. He did not want what his friends had, but nor was he certain of what he did want, either.

"I hope you find what you're looking for," Lucy said, and Maximilian smiled at her.

"I hope so, too, but I can hardly be sure of it," he replied.

"Are you leaving us, Max? So soon?" Sir William inquired, as Maximilian thanked him for his hospitality.

"I'm grateful to you for your kindness. It's been...a very pleasant occasion," he said, glancing at Annabella, who narrowed her eyes at him.

"Shall I tell Frances you send your regards?" she asked, but Maximilian shook his head.

"I think she knows well enough what I send her. Good day to you all," he replied, and with that, he took his leave of them.

Maximilian was relieved to step out of Sir William's townhouse and onto the street. He breathed a sigh of relief at once again being alone. This was why he had fled from Berkshire – the inevitable questions, the scrutiny, the well-meant remarks. It had been pleasant enough to see his friends, and Lucy had been charming, but he was tired of company. As he walked aimlessly through a nearby park, his mind fixated on one thing alone.

Delphine...why does her very name so captivate me? he asked himself, astonished at the force of his feelings.

He had fallen completely in love with her. There could be no denying it. All it had taken was a few short days, a kind word and gesture. He was hers. The thought was both fascinating and terrifying. This was precisely how he had felt about Frances. He had fallen in love with her in but a few days, and pledged his heart to her within a month. It was no wonder she had used that fact to play him. He had been blind to her actions, failed to recognize the signs of her infidelity, so smitten had he been.

And now it's just the same and your heart waits to break once again, he told himself.

That was the inevitability. Women could not be trusted. That much was certain. They were all the same – like wolves in sheep's clothing. He sighed to himself and paused, looking around him as though he expected to find the answers to his dilemma in the flower borders or on the boating lake to his right, where young couples frolicked on the waters in little boats, laughing and calling to one another without a care in the world.

But you don't want that. You don't know what you want, he told himself, angry at the lack of certainty, both in himself and what was to come. He had no plans for the future, no certainty like that of his friends. He both desired it and feared it. Commitment to a woman came with risk – he knew that all too well, but his heart was far beyond the reasoning of his mind.

It's only a bottle of wine and a conversation, he told himself, as he began walking back to The Seven Bells.

But wasn't that how so many romances began? A chance encounter, a mutual interest, the sharing of a moment or two... Maximilian was torn between head and heart, and only time would tell where fate would lead him.

Chapter Eighteen

Maximilian arrived back at the inn just as the bells of Saint Paul's were striking six O'clock. It was far earlier than he had intended, but he had been glad to leave the company of his friends and walk from Mayfair in solitude. He had made up his mind to share the bottle of wine with Delphine that evening. He would ask her about her father and of her life as a child at the inn. It would interest him to know more about her, and whilst he knew he was playing with his feelings – even risking a broken heart once again – it felt as though an inevitability lay ahead.

You've come this far. Why stop now? he thought to himself, as he opened the door to the inn and stepped into the parlor.

He had half expected to find Delphine there, but instead, it was the maid, Bessie, who greeted him.

"Good evening, my Lord. I trust you had a pleasant day," she said, and Maximilian nodded.

"Pleasant...enough," he replied, not wishing to enter into the full details of what had transpired at the home of Sir William.

"Shall I serve your supper in the dining room now, sir? Or will you wait?" Bessie asked.

Maximilian looked around in vague hope. There was no sign of Delphine, and his heart sank, for he had so wanted to be greeted by her smiling face and kind words.

"Is… Delphine…your mistress, forgive me, my hostess…is she here?" he asked, unsure of how to refer to Delphine given their previous intimacies.

The maid smiled and shook her head.

"She's had to go out, sir. But I'm to give you your supper if you'd like it. We've a delicious broth, followed by stuffed lamb's heart, and a steamed pudding with marmalade," she said, beckoning Maximilian to the dining room.

"I'll freshen up and then come down. Will you bring me a jug of hot water?" he asked, and Bessie nodded.

"Yes, sir, and your things – your trunks, sir. They've arrived from Berkshire," the maid said.

The words brought Maximilian great relief. He had been existing in the same shirt and breeches for several days, and whilst he was always meticulous at his toilet, he was beginning to long for a clean set of clothes.

"Ah, excellent. Are they upstairs?" he asked, and Bessie nodded.

"It took all three of us to haul them up, my Lord," she said, and Maximilian felt suddenly embarrassed.

"Forgive me," he said, but the maid only smiled and shook her head.

"We're used to it, sir," she said, and Maximilian smiled – he could well imagine the arrival of the earl and the marquess bringing with them any number of trunks and bags.

Maximilian made his way upstairs. He was disappointed not to see Delphine, but he had noticed the bottle of wine standing on the table by the cellar door and felt certain she would honor his invitation to drink it with him. Bessie brought up a jug of hot water and Maximilian washed his face and hands. He opened the larger of the two trunks and took out a fresh shirt and breeches. Dalton had been meticulous in his packing, and Maximilian was pleased to see his various possessions – his clothes, books, and keepsakes all neatly arranged inside.

And my poetry books, what a blessing, he said to himself, taking out a volume by Coleridge which he intended to read during dinner, if it was to be taken solitarily.

He stripped off and washed himself, changing into the clean shirt and breeches. He combed his hair and doused himself in rose-water from a bottle tucked into one of the side pockets in the trunk. Everything he needed was there, and Maximilian now realized he had a choice before him – to stay or go. He had instructed Dalton to have his things sent on with the intention of making for the continent. The Seven Bells was only ever meant as a place of refuge along the way.

But now… I don't know what to do, Maximilian thought to himself, as he glanced at himself in the mirror.

Dalton had packed his razor blade and Maximilian was now clean shaven, neat, and respectable. He looked every bit a gentleman. He smiled at his reflection in the mirror, imagining how he would look to Delphine. It was a vain, but pleasant thought. He took a deep breath and readied himself to go down for supper, hoping it would not be long before Delphine appeared in the dining room.

* * *

"Your usual table, my Lord? I trust everything was as you wished it to be?" Bessie said, as she met Maximilian at the door to the dining room.

"It was, thank you. I feel much better for a change of clothes and a good wash," Maximilian replied.

Bessie led him to the table in the corner, which was laid for one. He sat down, taking out his volume of Coleridge and flicking idly through the pages. Maximilian was devoted to poetry; it lifted his soul. How he longed to be able to write in such a way as to bring the ethereal alive on the page.

'Tis the middle of night by the castle clock, and the owls have awakened the crowing cock; tu—whit! tu—whoo! And hark, again! the crowing cock, how drowsily it crew... he began to read.

The poem was called *Christabel,* and was one of his favorites. So absorbed was he in the text, he did not hear the sound of footsteps approach, until a voice above him caused him to startle.

"Still here, I see. We thought you'd be gone – now your trunks have arrived," – it was the earl, though unusually, he was not accompanied by the marquess.

Maximilian sighed and closed his book. He knew he would have no peace now, especially as the earl now pulled out the opposite chair and sat down.

"I've not made my plans yet," Maximilian replied.

"Well, don't dally," the earl replied.

Bessie now came to the table carrying a bowl of broth, and she glanced apologetically at Maximilian as she set it down in front of him.

"Some bread, my Lord?" she asked.

"I'll have the broth, too. I'm waiting for Jacob. Serve it here," the earl said, as Maximilian sighed and took up his spoon.

He knew he was not going to get any peace that evening.

"I trust you had a pleasant day?" he asked, and the earl nodded.

"Very pleasant. We were guests of the Lord Mayor himself at the Mansion House. A lavish luncheon, drinking all afternoon...it was splendid. We declined to stay for dinner, though I'm sure the invitation would've been forthcoming," the earl said.

Maximilian gave a wry smile. He could imagine the earl and the marquess awaiting the invitation, even as its issuer would be reluctant to entertain them longer than was necessary.

"And now a quiet evening beckons," he said, and the earl nodded.

"There's a lot to think about. When are you leaving?" he asked.

The question was asked in such a pointed manner as to take Maximilian by surprise. It seemed the earl and the marquess had exhausted their attempts to oust him, and now they could only hope his departure would come soon.

"I'm not sure I intend to leave," Maximilian replied, knowing the reaction his words would gain.

"Not leave? But you have to. You only came here on your way to the continent, didn't you?" the earl demanded.

"I came here uncertain as to the future, and that uncertainty remains," Maximilian replied.

Bessie now brought the earl's bowl of broth and offered him the breadbasket, which he batted away with an impatient hand.

"But...why would you want to stay here? There's nothing for you here. She doesn't want you," he declared, the pitch of his voice now growing higher.

It was the same story, but without the company of the marquess, the earl appeared to wear his emotions more readily on his sleeve. He had been drinking, too, and the effect of the liquor now brought forth a truer reckoning of his feelings.

"Doesn't want me for what?" Maximilian asked, setting down his spoon and fixing the earl with a hard stare.

"To love, you fool. She's not in love with you. She can't be. She's in love with me," he declared, and Maximilian could not help but laugh.

There was a tragedy in this declaration, but one which Maximilian was not about to dissuade. There was no doubt in his mind – Delphine was *not* in love with the earl.

"And what could possibly make you believe that?" Maximilian asked.

The earl faltered for a moment, as though he had never considered why Delphine might be in love with him, but had rather assumed it, even as its truth was far from discernible.

"How could she not be?" the earl replied. Maximilian rolled his eyes.

"Has she told you as much? Has she made those feelings clear by word or deed?" he asked.

The earl looked uncomfortable.

"Well...not in so many words. But I can tell by the way she looks at me. She always comes and talks to me," he said.

"She talks to everyone. It's her job. She's the landlady. You're deluded," Maximilian replied, shaking his head as he pushed away his half-eaten bowl of broth.

The earl appeared distressed by this uncomfortable truth, even as Maximilian could offer little by way of comfort to him. He thought the earl a foolish creature, devoid of reason, and deluded in his thoughts. If he truly believed Delphine was in love with him, then he was very much mistaken. Maximilian did not know whom Delphine was in love with – *if* anyone at all – but he was not about to retort with a similar claim, even as his own wishes tallied with those of the earl. He, too, hoped Delphine was in love with him, and it was certainly a strange thing to admit.

"Deluded? An insult! I'm planning a grand gesture. You'll see. I'm going to show her the depths of my feelings. No mere gift, no… it will be something far grander. She'll not be able to resist me," the earl replied, and rising to his feet, he stormed out of the dining room, just as Bessie appeared from the kitchen to collect the plates.

"I'm sorry about that, my Lord," she whispered, but Maximilian only smiled and shook his head.

"Oh, it's quite all right. I've grown used to it. The inn would be a dull place without their presence," he replied.

Bessie smiled and nodded.

"They certainly add…character, my Lord," she replied diplomatically, taking up the half-finished bowls of broth and returning to the kitchen.

Maximilian had just opened his book of Coleridge's poems again when approaching footsteps caused him to look up.

"Have you seen Robert?" Jacob asked, and Maximilian nodded.

"He just...stormed off," he said, not particularly caring where the earl had gone, but merely thankful it was away from him.

"Good, I've endured his company all day," the marquess replied, and without invitation, he sat down in the chair recently vacated by the earl.

It was strange to encounter the two men separately. They came as a pair, or so it seemed. Maximilian had never seen one without the other. They were inseparable, even as it had been an interesting exercise to observe the earl alone, his true colors revealing themselves more readily.

"You tire of his company?" Maximilian asked, and the marquess scowled.

"He thinks she'll agree. But she won't, you know," he said, and Maximilian gave him a quizzical look.

"She?" he asked, though he suspected he knew precisely to whom the marquess was referring.

"Delphine, of course. He thinks he'll marry her and that'll be that. He gives no thought to me, of course. But she won't marry him. She'll marry me," he said, and he banged his fist down hard on the table.

Maximilian was surprised that this conflict had not already emerged. From the outset of his acquaintance with the two aristocrats, it had seemed clear that both could not have what they desired – the hand of Delphine in marriage. One was going to be disappointed, and despite their coming as a pair, this conflict had seemed inevitable.

"Is that so?" Maximilian replied.

It would, he reasoned, be interesting to hear the marquess' impression, even as he felt certain the earl would not agree.

"It stands to reason. She's always favored me. Robert always leaps in first with his favors and his compliments. But her eyes are drawn to me. She'll marry me, not him. You'll see," the marquess replied.

Maximilian nodded, but he knew the marquess' chances were the same as those of the earl. Whoever Delphine might favor; it was neither of them. They were both of them tragic figures, for whom Maximilian felt sorry – as exasperating as they may be.

"And when might this occur?" Maximilian asked.

"When I present my grand gesture to her. You'll see it soon enough. I was a fool to present her with a mere gift. No…she wants to see one's true feelings. I see that, now," he said, and Maximilian nodded.

"Yes… I'm sure she does," he replied, and the marquess smiled.

"Robert and his foolish words. But words mean nothing without action," he said, rising to his feet.

"Nothing at all," Maximilian replied, humoring the marquess, who it seemed had convinced himself of his own chances in securing Delphine's hand.

"Wait and see. But say nothing to Robert. He'll only grow jealous of me. When Delphine sees my gesture…she'll know I'm the one for her," he said confidently.

Bessie now returned from the kitchen with the dish of stuffed lamb's hearts on a silver platter. Maximilian feared the marquess would insist on dining with him, but with a nod of his head, he hurried off towards the stairs with a spring in his step.

"It's not often they're apart," she said, a note of suspicion in her voice.

"They're no better apart than together. I feel…sorry for them," Maximilian said, and the maid looked at him curiously.

"Forgive me, my Lord, but… I don't quite follow you," she said, setting down the platter on the table and serving the lamb's hearts onto a plate.

"They're both in love with your mistress, but it's clear from my conversations with her as to her feelings for them, in return," he replied.

Bessie blushed.

"You're right, my Lord. She favors another," she said, and Maximilian looked up at her curiously.

He had not believed his words would elicit such a response. If Delphine favored another, who was it? He was not about to ask the question directly. To do so would be far too forthright, but his mind was now racing with possibility.

"She favors another. So, the earl and the marquess are to be disappointed?" he said, and Bessie nodded.

"It's not my place to say it, though, sir. But she wouldn't marry either of them – not for all the tea in China," she replied, and curtseying to Maximilian, she hurried back towards the kitchen.

Maximilian's mind was now alive with possibility. Did he dare believe that the one whom Delphine favored could be himself? She had gone above and beyond in her hospitality, so much so that he could not imagine the favored one being any other but him.

Though she may have a suitor I know nothing of. Where is she now? In the arms of an artisan, perhaps? he asked himself.

But such thoughts seemed ridiculous in the face of Delphine's recent behavior. The bottle of wine stood on the table by the cellar. They were to share it that very evening, and if Delphine really did have another interest beside Maximilian, then she would surely be playing a very dangerous game.

But so did Frances, Maximilian told himself, and his previous anxieties now returned, and he cursed the name of his once betrothed for poisoning his mind against the fairer sex.

He could not trust them – any of them – even the slightest of doubts was enough to make him think twice about the evening ahead. But there was no doubt in Maximilian's mind as to his desire, even as he felt uncertain of where it might lead. He toyed with the stuffed lamb's hearts until Bessie returned to clear the plates, apologizing for his lack of appetite.

"Is something on your mind, my Lord?" she asked, stacking the empty dishes on the silver platter.

"Has your mistress returned from her errands?" Maximilian asked, and Bessie nodded.

"She's going to bring your pudding out to you, sir – marmalade sponge with custard," she said, smiling at Maximilian as she returned to the kitchen.

Maximilian's heart skipped a beat, and he watched the kitchen door, waiting for Delphine to emerge. When she did so, there was a radiant happiness in her look. Maximilian could not help but think how beautiful she was, and how much he desired her.

"Good evening, my Lord," she said, setting the marmalade sponge down in front of him.

"Good evening. I...missed you earlier," he said, blushing a little under her gaze.

"Forgive me, I was running errands. The work of an inn never ceases," she said, and Maximilian nodded.

"It's of no consequence. I hope we might still share the bottle of wine later on?" he asked, and Delphine nodded.

"I've been looking forward to it," she said, smiling at him in such a way that Maximilian wished the smile would last for eternity.

Chapter Nineteen

Delphine had been annoyed at being called away from the inn that afternoon. She had hoped to see Maximilian on his arrival back from wherever it was he had been, but a problem with one of the ovens had necessitated a visit to the blacksmith, and she had been embroiled for some hours in the intricacies of the part required. It had been almost eight O'clock by the time she had arrived back, and the dinner service was almost over.

"They're not speaking to one another. The earl came barging in here telling us he'd take his dinner in his room, and the marquess is in the snug, dining alone. I've never seen them apart," Alice had said in bewilderment, after the story of the strange behavior of the earl and the marquess had been relayed.

"Do you think they've fallen out with one another?" Bessie had asked, but Delphine told them both not to get involved.

Whatever game the earl and the marquess were playing, it was not for them to get involved. But despite these words, Delphine *had* found it odd to learn the earl and the marquess were dining separately. The atmosphere in the dining room as she had taken out Maximilian's pudding was quiet and reserved. It felt strange not to be confronted by the earl and the marquess with their various demands and running commentary on whatever matter they had chosen to devote their attentions to. Still, Delphine was glad to have some peace and quiet, particularly with the bottle of wine and Maximilian's invitation beckoning.

"Do let me know when you're ready to share the bottle of wine. I'm quite happy reading this book of poems until you are," Maximilian said, as Delphine now returned to collect his empty dishes.

He held up a copy of a work by Coleridge, a poet whom Delphine was unfamiliar with, but whom she would be only too glad to learn more about.

"It won't take me long. Perhaps you'd like to join me in the parlor in a few moments? I'll bring some glasses and the bottle of wine," she replied, feeling excited at the prospect of sharing the evening with Maximilian.

She had been looking forward to this all day, and her earlier disappointment at not having seen Maximilian during the day was now forgotten. She returned the dishes to the kitchen, took down two glasses and a bottle opener, before preparing to return to the dining room to pick up the bottle of wine from the table by the cellar door.

"Are we to finish up here, ma'am?" Bessie asked. Delphine turned to her and nodded.

"Yes, why don't you both go to bed early for once? I can manage here," she said, and the maid and the cook looked at one another and smiled.

"If you're sure, ma'am?" Bessie said, and Delphine nodded again.

"Very sure, thank you," she hurried out of the kitchen, snatched up the bottle and stepped into the parlor.

To her utmost relief, the earl and the marquess were nowhere to be seen. The parlor was empty, except for Maximilian, who was sitting in the window reading his book by the light of a candle.

"Ah, you're here. Splendid," he said, as Delphine came to sit opposite him.

"I trust you had a pleasant day?" she said, as she uncorked the bottle.

Her father had taught her how when she was young. It was all in the twisting, or so he had explained. The cork popped, and the bouquet of the wine filled the air. It reminded Delphine of her father, and she was surprised at the force of the emotion which overwhelmed her. This was his favorite wine, and now she was sharing it with Maximilian. It felt poignant and meaningful, even as she had been unprepared for just how it would feel.

"I was at a reunion of sorts. Some friends from Oxford, dining at the home of Sir William Blake. They were all there with their wives and their successes. I must say... I felt rather out of place," he replied, as Delphine poured the wine into their glasses.

"Out of place? But why should you? You have your own successes. You don't need to be like them," she said, but Maximilian shook his head as he took the glass she passed to him.

"It wasn't that I envied them. Quite the opposite, in fact. I'd have been just like them. Cut from the same mold. If I'd married Frances, then I'd be sitting amongst them with the same lack of concern, the same self-satisfaction, the same opinion of myself as they have of themselves. I'd have known no different. But looking at it from the outside, if you will...well, I didn't like it all," he said, raising the glass to his nose and breathing in the aroma.

Delphine pondered this for a moment. She knew little of the intimacies of aristocratic circles – though she had observed much of their ways in service at the inn. But human nature was no different, whether prince or pauper. It was easy to become complacent with one's own lot, to think one's own position the only one that mattered, and one's own way of doing things the right way alone. Maximilian had been forced to take a different way, and in doing so, he had come to see the faults in that which he had left behind.

"And what does that mean for you?" she asked, raising her own glass to her lips, and taking a sip.

The taste was just as she remembered, and she could picture the smile on her father's face at the pleasure which the vintage brought him.

"My possessions arrived today from Berkshire. I've no attachment there anymore, save my father's title. I can go where I please, do as I please, be whoever I please. I've a sense of freedom now, one I'd not known in many years," he replied.

Delphine was unsure of what to make of these words. Was he saying he intended to leave The Seven Bells? Leave London? Leave her...?

"Then you've left the past behind. Those people, your friends, you don't have anything in common with them anymore?" she asked, and Maximilian nodded.

"They're pleasant people, on the whole. But they have what they wanted – what they were always destined to have. But I...well, I've got possibility in my heart, the possibility of what might be," he said, and Delphine smiled.

She hoped that possibility might include her, even as she could not be certain it would. His feelings for her were a mystery, one which she was uncertain how to solve. The thought of causing him to fall in love with her to teach him a lesson about women was long gone. It had all been a foolish fancy, but this...this was very real. Her feelings were real, her sorrow at the possibility of him leaving her was real, and what she wanted now was real...

"A lot's changed for you and all very quickly, too. I can only imagine how that must feel," Delphine said, taking a sip of wine.

But she reminded herself that she, too, knew the suddenness of change. Her father's death had brought with it great upheaval and the possibility of change. A new way lay open to her – she could choose her destiny, and that was both exciting and terrifying, too. She wanted her father's legacy to continue. She wanted to be the landlady of The Seven Bells, but she wanted something else, too –

for herself and not the benefit of others. Her heart had been stirred by her feelings for Maximilian, and unexpectedly so. She took another sip of wine, knowing the possibility of its effects, and smiled at him.

"It feels liberating, I suppose. I have every choice ahead of me, but those choices are...open possibilities," he said, swirling the wine around in his glass.

"But what do *you* want? Isn't that all that matters?" she asked, and he sighed.

"I've spent my whole life preparing for something. That's the lot of the hereditary line. I've spent my life preparing for the moment when my father dies. It sounds barbaric, but it's the truth. I'm to be the Baron of Fermony. That's my destiny. Ever since I've been old enough to understand, that's what I've been told. I've never considered anything else. I was to inherit my father's title, and along the way, I was to marry and produce an heir, who would live with precisely the same expectation as I. It's a never-ending cycle, and one I can't necessarily recommend," he replied.

Delphine could not pretend to understand entirely what he was saying, though she had always grown up knowing she was to inherit the inn from her father. She had no brothers, no male cousins, no distant relatives who might make a claim. Since her youngest days, Delphine had known she would continue her father's legacy, even as it was up to her to decide how she might inhabit that legacy for herself. The drinking of the wine seemed a final act, as though her father's memory could at last be laid to rest – happily and at peace. The inn was hers, but her life was there to do with as she pleased, and she realized it now.

"But you'll still inherit the title, won't you?" she said, and Maximilian nodded.

"I will, that's right. But I won't be married to Frances Stott. I won't be the same as all of them – all my friends, the ones I told you about," he said, and Delphine nodded, fixing him with a searching gaze.

"What *do* you want to be like?" she asked.

It was a searching question, one without an easy answer. She wondered for a moment if she had overstepped the mark and asked a question beyond that expected in whatever form of intimacy now existed between them. Maximilian, too, looked surprised, but not perturbed. He smiled at her and shook his head.

"That's the problem. I don't really know. I know I don't want to be like that, but then I wonder...what do I want to be like? I've thought about that a lot, recently. When I came here from Berkshire, I was so full of anger towards...well, women, I suppose," he said.

Delphine smiled. She was glad to hear that word – "*was*." She had hoped to change his mind about women, and perhaps she had, indeed, played a small part in doing so.

"But no longer?" she asked.

"What's the point of being angry about the past? What's done is done. I can't change Frances' mind, nor would I want to. I'm glad not to be marrying her. Not now I know what she's truly like. No, these things happen for a reason. I realize that now," Maximilian replied.

He had finished his glass of wine, so Delphine poured him a second, topping her own glass up with just a drop.

"I dare not drink too much," she said, knowing the effect it would have on her.

"But what about you? What about your story? I know a little, but I don't know it all. Where are you going?"

It was a strange question, and for a moment, Delphine felt confused. She was going nowhere, happy, instead, to be in his company and have no other expectations placed on her.

"I...well, I'm happy here," she said, but he shook his head and smiled.

"No, I mean in your life, in what's to come. Will you always be the landlady of The Seven Bells?" he asked.

Delphine thought for a moment. Two weeks ago, she would

have said "yes" without hesitation. The inn was all she knew, and it had been all she had ever wanted to know. She was wedded, not to the idea of marriage, but to the idea of legacy – her father's legacy. But Maximilian's arrival – or rather, the feelings she now had for him – had changed that. She wondered if she could have both, as impossible as that seemed.

"I don't really know. I suppose...it's an open possibility. There's so much I might do, though my course seems clear for now," she replied.

He nodded and smiled, keeping his gaze fixed on her, even as Delphine felt the effects of the wine going to her head. Had she said too much? Had she embarrassed herself in front of him? She was not used to talking to a man in such a way, nor to being listened to by a man in such a way. The earl and the marquess were never interested in what she had to say, but only in themselves. This was different, Maximilian was different. He was like no man she had ever known before, and the effect he had on her was one no man had ever had on her, either.

"To be the landlady of The Seven Bells? What was it like to grow up here?" he asked, and Delphine blushed.

"Oh, you don't want to know about all that, surely?" she asked, but he shook his head and smiled.

"I want to know all about you. Please...won't you tell me?" he said.

Delphine smiled. She was only too happy to talk about her father and the life they had lived together. She had so many memories, and whilst she and Bessie and Alice often talked about the past, it felt special to share those memories with Maximilian.

"I was born here, but my mother died when I was very young. I don't remember her, though my father always told me I was just like her and growing more so every day. He used to tell me he loved me twice – first as his daughter and second as the image of my mother. He missed her terribly, but the two of us were happy together – we truly were," Delphine replied, thinking back fondly to all she and her father had shared together.

"But it must've been a strange place to grow up – surrounded by men like the earl and the marquess. Was The Seven Bells always a refuge for the aristocracy?" he asked.

"My father wanted it to be a place of welcome. It once had a dubious reputation – when my great-grandfather first had it – and was the haunt of smugglers who used it to smuggle rum up the Thames. The cellar was full of barrels, or so my father told me. But gradually, over the years, things changed. I remember the first time the earl and the marquess came to stay. I thought them very funny," Delphine said, smiling at her memory of the two men arriving on a wet day in November, wet, cold and hungry. They had demanded a bottle of brandy and a dish of jugged hare within moments of stepping inside the inn.

"What stories there must be. My own youth was spent in misguided pursuits – hunting, fishing, chasing across my father's estate on horses. I knew nothing of the outside world, nor did I wish to. I suppose it was not a bad thing," Maximilian said, taking another sip of wine.

Delphine found herself feeling quite lightheaded, even as she poured more wine into their glasses. She could happily have remained in his company forever and never tired of his conversation.

"Won't you read a poem to me?" she asked, glancing at the volume of Coleridge lying on the table in front of Maximilian.

He smiled at her and picked it up, flicking through the pages with a nod.

"*No cloud, no relique of the sunken day distinguishes the West, no long thin slip of sullen light, no obscure trembling hues. Come, we will rest on this old mossy bridge! You see the glimmer of the stream beneath, but hear no murmuring: it flows silently...*" he began, as Delphine closed her eyes and allowed the words to wash over her like a gentle wave lapping at the shore...

Chapter Twenty

Delphine awoke with a start. She had not meant to fall asleep, but as she sat up and blinked, she realized it was morning. The early morning sun was streaming through the parlor windows, and dust was dancing in the shafts of light. The fire in the hearth had burned to ashes, and the two wineglasses and the bottle stood empty on the table in front of her.

Goodness me, did I really sleep all night long down here? she asked herself, though the answer seemed clear enough.

At that moment, footsteps on the stairs caused her to look up and, to her surprise, and embarrassment, Bessie appeared in the parlor.

"Oh, ma'am... I didn't think you'd be down yet. I've not laid the fires yet," Bessie said, but Delphine shook her head and rose to her feet.

Her head was hurting, and she steadied herself on the table, glancing again at the empty bottle and recalling that delicious sense of calm and peace which had come over her. Maximilian had been reading her a poem, and then...

"It's all right, Bessie. You're not late down. I'm...early in my rising," Delphine replied, hoping the maid would not suspect she had been down here all night long.

"Shall I light the fires, ma'am? Alice won't be long," Bessie said, and Delphine nodded.

"Yes, we'd better get ready for breakfast. They'll all be down soon," she said, stifling a yawn.

Bessie glanced at the empty bottle of wine and the two glasses. She smiled at Delphine, who knew it was foolish to try to hide the truth from her.

"Did the baron's son enjoy the wine, ma'am?" Bessie asked, and Delphine nodded.

"I believe so. But I was…oh, I've been foolish. I fell asleep, Bessie. I don't know when he went to bed. Goodness knows what he must think of me. He was reading me a poem by Coleridge. It was about a nightingale, and then… I can't remember," she said, blushing as Bessie smiled at her.

"I'm sure he doesn't think badly of you, ma'am. You've always said a glass of wine does you no good," Bessie replied.

She began raking out the fire in the hearth, and Delphine made her way into the kitchen, busying herself with preparations for breakfast. Despite the maid's words, she felt embarrassed at the thought of encountering Maximilian that morning – what would he think of her for falling asleep whilst he was reading?

"Good morning, ma'am. I trust you had a pleasant night?" Alice said, as she bustled into the kitchen a few moments later.

The clatter of pots and pans which now erupted made Delphine's head ache even more, and she closed her eyes and sighed. This was going to be a long morning, and as they prepared the breakfast, she wondered if she had made a complete fool of herself the previous evening. She remembered the conversation – the sharing of childhood stories, and Maximilian's lament over his friends, but there had been more to it than mere pleasantries. Delphine had felt a sense of intimacy with the baron's son, and there could be no doubting her feelings for him. But were they feelings he shared?

"I've laid the tables, swept out the hearth and set a fire to warm the dining room, ma'am. They'll be down soon – the earl and the marquess, though after yesterday, perhaps they'll come down separately," Bessie said, smiling and shaking her head.

Delphine had entirely forgotten the dispute between the two aristocrats. It seemed petty in comparison to her own questions about Maximilian.

"Well, I'm sure they"ll sort out their differences," Delphine replied, sitting down at the kitchen table with a sigh.

Bessie and Alice glanced at one another.

"Is everything all right, ma'am?" Alice asked, and Delphine looked up and gave a weak smile.

"Oh…yes, I'm sorry. It's just…well, I shared the bottle of wine with the baron's son last night. It was one of the ones my father favored – his favorite, in fact. It reminded me of him, and then there was the conversation, and…oh, I don't know," she exclaimed, putting her head in her hands.

Bessie came to sit down next to her and put her arm around Delphine's shoulders.

"It's not a game anymore, is it, ma'am?" she said, and Delphine looked up and shook her head.

Whilst Bessie and Alice were in her employ, they were her closest friends, too. She had confided so much in them, even as there were things she still held back from them. She loved them as sisters, but at times she knew she kept them at arm's length, worried at the thought of sharing her feelings with them too readily.

"I… I thought we'd teach him a lesson, that's all. I wanted him to see that not all women are like the one who spurned him," Delphine replied, shaking her head.

"But you've fallen in love with him, haven't you, ma'am?" Alice said, and she, too, came and sat next to Delphine and put her arm around her.

Delphine nodded. She had admitted as much to herself, and now she admitted it to them, too. She *was* in love with Maximilian, and whilst it was a most delightful feeling, it was a feeling which felt incomplete. To be in love was not necessarily to be loved. It took two hearts to be so entwined, and Maximilian's feelings for her remained a mystery still.

"And you've surely shown him that," Bessie said, with a reassuring tone.

"But does he feel the same? Is he in love with me?" Delphine asked, her voice now choked with emotion.

She realized now she had barely given Maximilian a chance to redeem himself, and now she regretted her plan bitterly. If only she had allowed those feelings to grow by themselves, and without the forced gesture of false intention. She had never known such feelings before, nor imagined the hurt and uncertainty they could cause. Once again, Bessie and Alice glanced at one another, now with anxious expressions on their faces.

"You can't know that either way, ma'am. Not until he tells you. But...well, you've spent time together. He clearly enjoys your company, and you've done so much to make him feel welcome and comfortable. I don't see how he couldn't fall in love with you – he'd be a fool not to," Bessie said, and Alice agreed.

"You're both so kind. But I don't know...with his possessions arrived from Berkshire, what does that mean? Is he going to leave? Is he going to go to the continent as he said he would?" she asked, her distress now rising.

If Maximilian left, Delphine knew it would break her heart. It felt foolish to admit it, but it was the truth. Her feelings for him were overwhelming, and now she could not imagine her life without him. Perhaps he had already gone, and with a sudden start, she rose to her feet.

"What's wrong, ma'am?" Bessie asked, as Delphine's eyes grew wide with fear.

"It's...is he still here?" she asked, glancing towards the kitchen door, as though beyond it lay her entire destiny.

It was remarkable how her heart had been so taken up with her feelings for a man she barely knew.

"He wouldn't have left without saying goodbye, ma'am. Why don't you sit down, and I'll make us a pot of tea," Bessie said, patting Delphine's arm as she spoke.

Delphine was still looking fearfully towards the door into the dining room, but she sat back down, putting her head in her hands and reminding herself of how readily the effects of the wine had come over her.

"I just wish...it was as simple as the game I'd thought it would be," she said, shaking her head.

"But that's the problem, ma'am. Real life isn't like a game, and when you play with your emotions like that...well, it doesn't always end well," Alice said, smiling at Delphine, just as the kitchen door shot open with a bang.

"Are we going to be served any breakfast this morning, or am I to send out to Fortnum and Mason for a hamper?" the earl exclaimed.

"You can wait a few moments. I'm still heating the pans," Alice replied, wagging her finger at him.

The earl drew himself up and advanced towards the cook, who did precisely the same.

"Heating it to a burning point, are you? Just ready to char the breakfast like you always do?" he asked, as Alice rolled up her sleeves as though she were about to enter the pugilistic ring.

"Burned? I've never burned your breakfast, though I'd like to often enough. Coming in here, accusing me of such a thing. I'll show you," she said, and picking up a rolling pin, she shook it at the earl, who seemed momentarily perturbed, and dodged backwards around the table, as Alice gave chase.

"You burn everything, and you put too much mustard in the

sauces, and your cakes always fall – I've never tasted such awful food as you send out of this so-called kitchen," the earl cried, dodging Alice's rolling pin, which now crashed down on the table, sending pots and pans flying.

"You ungrateful swine. You've never got a good word to say about anyone. Nothing's ever right, is it? Not for you, nor for your friend. I'll chase you out of this inn, you wicked man," Alice replied, as the earl dodged from side to side, avoiding the strikes of the rolling pin.

It was a bizarre dance, with each of them stepping this way and that, exchanging insults in what was surely a boiling over of the tensions which had been brewing ever since the earl and the marquess had arrived.

"That's enough," Delphine exclaimed, rising to her feet, and snatching the rolling pin from Alice's hand.

"She started it," the earl said, folding his arms and scowling.

"And I'll be the one to finish it – burned breakfast, indeed," Alice retorted, jabbing her finger at the earl, who stuck his tongue out at her.

"I'll make the breakfast," Delphine said, and the earl smiled.

"Excellent. In that case, I'll have two eggs, fried in dripping, with bacon, sausages, tomatoes, mushrooms, and fried bread. Make sure you fry it extra crispy – you know how I like it. And coffee, I must have a pot of coffee at once," he said, and turning on his heels, he marched out of the kitchen.

Delphine sighed, as Alice breathed murderous threats under her breath.

"I'll make the coffee, shall I, ma'am?" Bessie asked, and Delphine nodded.

"Thank you, Bessie. I'll start cooking the breakfast," she said, even as Alice began to protest.

"I'm sorry, ma'am. I didn't mean to get upset. But he just...he knows just what to say to make me angry," she said, and Delphine smiled.

"It's all right, Alice. But you can't chase our guests around the kitchen with a rolling pin – as much as I think the earl rather likes the sport. I'll cook the breakfast today. It'll give me something to distract myself with. I don't want to see the baron's son," she said, and Alice nodded.

"You'll have to see him eventually, ma'am. But I understand. I'll help Bessie with the serving – and I promise I'll keep a civil tongue when it comes to the earl and the marquess," she replied.

Delphine was glad of an excuse to remain in the kitchen. She knew it was churlish to avoid Maximilian, but she felt embarrassed at having fallen asleep in his company and wondered what would happen when next she encountered him. She had been foolish to get so upset and reminded herself she had a job to do – the inn would not run itself.

"The marquess wants the same as the earl. It appears they're on speaking terms again," Bessie declared, when she entered the kitchen a few moments later.

Delphine was frying sausages in a large pan over the grate, holding it at arm's length as the fat spat at her in the heat.

"Is the baron's son here?" she asked, turning to Bessie, who looked suddenly uncomfortable.

"No, ma'am, he hurried out. He didn't want breakfast. I don't know where he went." she replied, and Delphine's heart fell.

Did this mean he did not want to see her? Tear welled up in her eyes, even as she knew it was she who had fallen asleep, and she who had hidden herself in the kitchen…

"Well…perhaps he'll be back later on," she said, forcing a smile to her face. Bessie nodded.

"I'm sure he will, ma'am. He didn't have anything with him – just his coat and hat," she replied.

Delphine was about to reply, but a shout from the earl drew Bessie's attention, and Delphine returned to the pan of sausages.

I hope he'll be back, she thought to herself, even as she was unsure what she would say or do when he did…

Chapter Twenty-One

Maximilian was sitting on the steps of Saint Paul's. He had left the inn early that morning and followed a course in no particular direction, arriving at the cathedral just as the bells were chiming for matins. He had not wished to endure the attentions of the earl and the marquess at breakfast and had been only too glad to inform Bessie he was going out.

I hope Delphine doesn't think badly of me, he said to himself, for he had left in such a hurry there had been no time to wait for her.

She had been cooking breakfast in the kitchen – he had spied her through the door as Alice had bustled out with a plate of eggs for the earl and the marquess. There had been a strange atmosphere in the dining room that morning, as though Maximilian had chanced upon the end of an argument, and he wondered what had transpired as the earl and the cook glowered at one another.

But Maximilian's thoughts had been focused on Delphine. He had slipped away the evening before, not wishing to wake her after she had fallen asleep during his reading of Coleridge's poem about a nightingale. She had looked so very peaceful with her head resting back in the snug by the window, her long red hair trailing down her shoulders, her cheeks with just a hint of blush to them, her lips full and firm…she really was very pretty. He had thought about her a great deal that night, tossing and turning, and finally getting up to ready himself for the day ahead. He had no definite plans, only feeling a walk would surely help to clear his head.

But I've not got very far, have I? he thought to himself, as he gazed up at the towering dome of Saint Paul's above.

A group of ladies were making their way up the steps to matins, and Maximilian watched their progress, imagining their piety at prayer. One of them turned to him, and to his surprise, he recognized her as none other than Lucy – Rupert's wife – who now hurried over to greet him.

"An early riser," she said, as he stood hastily to his feet and took off his hat.

"Forgive me. I didn't realize you'd be here," he said, and his friend's wife smiled.

"I like to come to matins here when we're in London. I'm with my cousins," she said, glancing back towards the group of young ladies who were waiting for her at the top of the steps.

"You mustn't let me delay you," he said, but she shook her head and smiled.

"Don't worry. We're awfully early. They were worried about you yesterday – the men, I mean. They thought you'd made a mistake in coming to London without a plan," she said, and Maximilian smiled.

"They don't need to worry about me. I'm quite content in my decision, though…well, I've a lot to think about," he said, and Lucy smiled.

"I could tell you were distracted by something. You left so suddenly, and I wondered… well, perhaps there was something you wanted to leave for, or someone," she said.

Maximilian was somewhat taken aback by her perception, but

what she said was entirely true. He *had* left for a reason, and the reason had been Delphine.

"I...well, when you put it like that," he said, and Lucy smiled.

"There's no harm in it. I heard Annabella's side of the story, but she rather tries to defend the indefensible. You're the wronged party in all of this. It was you whom Frances behaved appallingly towards. I know we always talk of spurned women and wicked rakes – but it's not always the case. Sometimes, women are just as much to blame. My sex can be...vicious," she said, and Maximilian nodded.

He liked Lucy a great deal. She had a sensible head on her shoulders – not like the chattering, gossiping women he had so often encountered at balls and soirees. The sort he had fled Berkshire to avoid. Here was a woman who understood.

"I don't wish to hold a grudge against Frances. The circumstances are as they are. But...well...you're right. It might sound pitiful, but I was in love with her, and I believed she was in love with me. But the opposite was true. She was laughing behind me back," he said, shaking his head with a sigh.

The memory of his humiliation was still fresh in his mind, and it brought him pain to dwell on it. Lucy slipped her hand into his and squeezed it.

"Then all the more reason to seize happiness once again. You don't deserve to live in misery, Maximilian. Whoever this woman is, why not give her a chance?" she said, and Maximilian blushed.

Well, I..." he began, just as a call came from the top of the cathedral steps.

"Come along, Lucy. The organ's started playing," one of Lucy's cousins called.

"Remember what I said. You deserve to be happy. Take a chance – you've nothing to lose," Lucy said, as she hurried off up the steps towards the cathedral.

Maximilian watched her go. He pondered her words, smiling to himself at how obvious his distractions had been during his visit to the home of Sir William Blake. But what was he to make of her exhortation. In Maximilian's mind, there was everything to lose. He had known the pain of a broken heart, and he wondered if he could risk enduring that again. He barely knew Delphine, even as he knew his feelings for her were certain. Maximilian was in love with her, and the more he thought about her, and the more time he spent with her, the more that love grew.

Then I can't hold back any longer, he said to himself, as he walked aimlessly through the London streets.

Something was drawing him on – his feelings for Delphine, and a hope she had proved her sex to be more than Maximilian's own prejudices made them out to be. He wanted to tell her as much, even as he was unsure of how to do so.

But it's how she feels about me that matters, he thought to himself, and it was that uncertainty which held him back, even as his heart was sure of how he felt.

* * *

"Well, if I can be trusted not to burn them, I'll boil some chickens and make a stew," Alice said.

Delphine, Bessie, and the cook were discussing the menu for the evening. Breakfast had been cleared away, and the earl and the marquess had gone out for the day, leaving only a few guests to be served at luncheon. There was still no sign of Maximilian. Delphine hoped it would not be long before he returned. She was torn between her embarrassment and her desire to speak with him. What would she say?

"I'm sure it'll be delicious, Alice. I'll help you," Delphine said.

"But what about serving at the tables, ma'am? Am I to do it all myself?" Bessie asked.

"Well... I couldn't ask you to do everything. It's just..." Delphine began, and Alice patted her on the arm.

"It's all right, ma'am. We'll see to the serving. You can mind the stew. I'll tell the earl and the marquess it's being made by your fair hands. You could serve them a lump of coal and they'd be happy," Alice said, shaking her head and smiling.

Delphine was grateful to them both, and she spent the afternoon helping Alice prepare the stew. They boiled two chickens to make a stock, adding vegetables and pearl barley. The smell was delicious, and when dinner was served, the stew received compliments from all the diners.

"Is the baron's son there?" Delphine asked, for she had not left the kitchen all afternoon, fearful of encountering Maximilian by chance rather than design.

She had rehearsed her words and intended to apologize to him for falling asleep the evening before.

"He's sitting in his usual place, ma'am. Do you want to take his dinner to him, or shall I?" Bessie asked.

Delphine pondered this for a moment. It might be better to allow Maximilian to enjoy his dinner before speaking to him. It would get cold otherwise, and she ladled out a bowlful of the stew and placed a large hunk of bread on the side, passing it to Bessie with a smile.

"You take it now, Bessie. I'll come out later and speak with him," she said.

Bessie nodded and took the bowl just as Alice entered the kitchen, shaking her head.

"The earl says your stew is "beyond comparison," and I'm to tell you how much he's enjoyed it. The marquess said the same," she said, rolling her eyes.

Delphine smiled. It was only a simple stew. But she knew the earl and the marquess were only playing their usual games. She thought about Maximilian, wondering what he was thinking.

"I'm sure they did," Delphine replied, turning her attentions to the pudding.

It was an apple pie, which had now been baking in the oven for an hour. She took it out, watching as steam rose in a plume from the neatly cut hole in the top of the pastry, which had turned a golden, buttery brown.

"It smells delicious, ma'am," Alice said, as Delphine set the pie down on the kitchen table.

She would take the pudding out to Maximilian herself. She cut a large piece, pouring cream over it and sprinkling it with grated nutmeg.

"I'll take this," she said, as Bessie stepped forward to pick up the dish.

"If you're sure, ma'am," the maid said, and Delphine nodded and took a deep breath.

"I'm sure, yes," she replied, before stepping through the kitchen door into the dining room.

It should have been an easy few steps to Maximilian's table in the corner. Delphine intended to place the dish in front of him, smile at him, and apologize. He would then tell her not to worry, that there was nothing to apologize for, and invite her to sit down. It had all played out in her mind a dozen times that afternoon. Peace would be restored, and the storm in the teacup would be abated. Delphine would realize she had worried needlessly, and she and Maximilian would return to that happy intimacy they had previously shared. Perhaps Maximilian had not even discerned a problem between them...these were Delphine's thoughts as she left the kitchen, but an interruption from across the dining room caused her to pause.

"Miss Delphine, I offer you this ballad in token and appreciation of my heartfelt love for you," the earl called out, springing from his chair and crossing to the middle of the dining room. He sank into a low bow, as Delphine turned to him in astonishment.

Maximilian, along with all the other guests, looked up as well. Delphine stared in horror at the earl, who had pulled out a small volume from his pocket and was flicking through it to find his place, clearing his throat, and making odd humming noises as he did so.

"It's really not necessary," Delphine exclaimed, but the earl was not listening to her and to her horror he began to sing.

"When young and thoughtless, Delphine said,
No one shall win my heart;
But little dreamt the simple maid,
Of love's delusive art.
At ball or play,
She flirt away,
And ever giddy be;
But always said,
I ne'er will wed,
No one shall govern me.
No, no, no, no, no, no,
No one shall govern me..."

This song – the protagonist of which was in fact named Laura, and whom the earl had reimagined as Delphine – went on for several more verses and was sung in such a way as to drown out any protests on the part of its audience. Delphine could not believe the earl's ridiculous behavior. He was like a man possessed, and the song culminated in a climax of warbling, as though the earl were imitating a performer on the Covent Garden stage.

"Enough!" Delphine cried out, flinging the plate of apple pie and cream straight at the earl, who looked shocked at this assault during what was clearly meant to be a gesture of romance.

"But I thought you'd like it," he said, as the marquess stepped forward.

"You didn't sing it properly. I've got a song. She'll like that better," he exclaimed, and was about to begin singing himself, when Delphine snatched up a jug of water from a nearby table and threw it over them, shouting at the top of her voice as she did so.

"I don't want your songs, I don't want your foolish tributes, I don't want any of it. Do you hear me? I'm not in love with either of you. I want to be left alone. That's all I want," she cried, and the two men looked at one another aghast.

"Miss Delphine, we didn't mean..." the earl began, but Delphine now threw the water jug at them.

Both men ducked, and the jug smashed against the far wall of the dining room, before Delphine fled, sobbing up the stairs. She ran to her bedroom, shutting the door behind her and turning the key in the lock. Tears rolled down her cheeks and her whole body trembled with upset and anger.

Oh, why? Why must they do this? I don't love them. I don't want anything to do with them. I just want to be left alone, she sobbed to herself, sitting back against the door with her head in her hands.

Her emotions were fraught, and her frustrations, her fears, her sorrows – all of it – had burst forth in that moment. She was breathing heavily, her senses slowly returning, even as she could hardly believe what she had done. She could only imagine what her father would have said – she had thrown a dish of apple pie and cream over the earl, then doused him and the marquess in water, before throwing the jug at them. These were the actions of a madwoman, and Delphine felt astonished at herself for acting in such a manner.

I should apologize to them...but...oh, why won't they listen to me? They won't listen to me, she exclaimed to herself, her fists clenched as tears rolled down her cheeks.

At that moment, Delphine heard footsteps in the passageway outside her bedroom, and then came a gentle tapping at the door. She presumed it was either Bessie or Alice, come to reason with her and inform her of the displeasure she had caused the earl and the marquess. They certainly would not remain at The Seven Bells now, and Delphine could only imagine the slander which they would spread – her name, and that of her father, would be ruined.

"Go away, Bessie. I don't want to know about it," Delphine called out.

There was a pause outside the door, and the awkward shifting of feet.

"It's... Maximilian," a voice called out gently. Delphine's eyes grew wide with horror.

In her anger at the earl and the marquess, Delphine had quite forgotten that Maximilian had been privy to the whole sorry scene. He had seen the madness take hold of her, and now she could only imagine what he must think of her.

"I... I'm sorry," she replied, trying her best to keep her voice steady, even as she feared facing him.

The door was shut, and she had turned the key in the lock. Delphine rose to her feet, leaning against the door and imagining Maximilian on the other side. What was he thinking? Was he angry with her? Astonished? Sympathetic?

"You've nothing to be sorry for. As usual, they've both behaved like utter fools," Maximilian replied.

Delphine sighed. It was true, but her reaction to their behavior had been nothing short of extraordinary.

"I... I don't want to talk about it. I've made a fool of myself, too," she said, not wishing to face him, not wishing to face anyone after the spectacle she had made.

"Not in front of me, you haven't. You might finally have made them realize the error of their ways. I'd have done precisely the same. Anyone would've. You've nothing to be ashamed of, Delphine," Maximilian said.

Delphine wiped her sleeve across her eyes. She had stopped crying now and was prepared to believe what Maximilian was saying. He was right. The earl and the marquess *did* need to be shown the error of their ways. They had failed to listen to reason, and she had done the only thing she could think of – she had confronted their own ridiculous behavior with something equally so.

"But... I shouldn't have lost my temper like that. It wasn't right. They're my guests and...oh, I wanted so much to follow in my father's legacy, but...perhaps I'm just not meant to be landlady.

Perhaps it was all just nonsense," Delphine replied, feeling the tears well up in her eyes.

"Won't you open the door, Delphine? We can talk about it," Maximilian said, but Delphine did not want to see anyone in that moment, not even him.

"I'm sorry," she said, and running to her bed, Delphine threw herself down and sobbed into the pillow.

She missed her father, and she was so confused as to her feelings for Maximilian. She could not believe he would want to speak to her — not after the madness of what she had done that evening. She felt overwhelmed by her own failures, and now she wanted only to shut out the world and all its consequences.

"I'll be downstairs if you need me, Delphine. Don't worry. It'll be all right, I promise," Maximilian called out, but Delphine did not know how it possibly could.

She continued to sob as his footsteps disappeared along the corridor. Then he was gone.

I've been such a fool, she told herself, burying her head in the pillows and wanting only to forget everything that had happened.

Chapter Twenty-Two

Maximilian sighed. He had stood listening at Delphine's door for a few moments, the sounds of her sobs broken only by the occasional sniff. He had tried his best to comfort her, but her refusal to open the door had meant there was only so much he could do. He wanted to make her understand she was not at fault, and that anyone would have been pushed to breaking point by the ridiculous behavior of the earl and the marquess.

It's their fault, he thought to himself in frustration, as he retreated along the corridor towards the stairs.

Maximilian had watched — first in bemusement and then in horror — at the scene which had unfolded in the dining room earlier that evening. He had felt terribly sorry for Delphine — made a spectacle of and serenaded by the drunken earl. But the sight of her throwing the dish of apple pie and cream — the dish meant for his pudding — followed by the water jug, had been a panacea for his own frustrations with the earl and the marquess. They had got their just desserts — quite literally.

When Delphine had fled, Bessie had rushed from the kitchen

with a damp cloth, dabbing at the earl's waistcoat, as he stood in complete shock at what had transpired. The marquess regained his composure somewhat sooner, but both men had appeared astonished at Delphine's response, as though they had never expected her to behave in such a way. Maximilian had slipped away at that moment, believing his presence more needed at Delphine's side than offering sympathy to the earl and the marquess – a sympathy he did not possess.

But Delphine's reaction had surprised him. She had not wanted to talk, nor had she even opened the door to him. Had he done something wrong? Her actions had reminded him of Frances, and the day he had discovered her infidelity. She had locked herself in her bedroom, too, and flown into a rage at the merest suggestion of their talking to one another. Perhaps this was the same, and Maximilian was reminded of just how little he understood of women.

And I suppose it'll always be the same, he said to himself.

Maximilian did not particularly want to return to the parlor or the dining room. He could only imagine the scene there – the earl and the marquess trading insults with one another or lamenting their sorry failure at a romantic gesture. But neither was it yet time to go to bed. The night was still young, and Maximilian fancied he would take a walk as far as Saint Paul's, or along the river. He took the back stairs towards the kitchen, intending to slip out by the side door, but as he came down the stairs, he had heard voices through the kitchen door – the maid and the cook, and what he heard astonished him, and his eyes grew wide with horror.

"I knew she shouldn't have done it. She put far too much pressure on herself – all this business about making the baron's son fall in love with her. She's worked her fingers to the bone, bless her – and for what?" Bessie was saying.

"For nothing but upset. She can't make him fall in love with her. All those empty gestures...what did she hope to gain from it? And now she's simply upset herself. I've no love for the earl or the marquess, you know that, Bessie, but they're not the only ones to blame. She's got herself all worked up over this. I knew it was a bad idea," the cook replied.

Maximilian stood by the door, listening intently. He could hardly believe what he was hearing. Had Delphine merely been nice to him so as to force his hand? To make him fall in love with her? Surely it wasn't the case...

"I played my part in it, too. I know that. I encouraged her. But I didn't think it would end like this. She'll have locked herself away in her bedroom for the whole night. We'll never coax her out," Bessie said, and there was a clattering of pots and pans.

"But she didn't believe it would end like this, either. Forget the plan, forget all that silliness. She's got true feelings. She can't hide them, can she?"

," Alice said, and Maximilian could hear her tutting as she banged a saucepan on the stove.

But he had heard enough, and he shook his head, his mind racing with what he had heard. It was too incredible for words, too awful to comprehend, and tears welled up in his eyes. He had been deceived again. Maximilian had to steady himself on the doorframe, catching his breath as he realized the awful game he had been played. The kind words, the attentions lavished on him, the special meals, the bottle of wine...all of it had been designed with one thing in mind – to make him fall in love with her as part of some wicked game she was playing. Maximilian could hardly believe what he was hearing.

She's betrayed me. She's the same as all the rest. That's all, isn't it? They're no different. Women are all the same, he exclaimed to himself, feeling suddenly sick to his stomach.

Maximilian had allowed his feelings to get the better of him. He had allowed himself to trust a woman, after vowing never to do so again. But he had thought Delphine was different, that she was not like the rest, not like Frances. But the maid's words had proved otherwise. It had all been a game – nothing less – and Maximilian had been played for a fool. He shook his head, sighing as tears rolled down his cheeks.

I'll show her. I'll make her sorry, he told himself, and pulling open the side door, he stalked off into the night.

* * *

Maximilian stayed out all night. He wandered aimlessly through the streets, arriving eventually at the pleasure gardens in Vauxhall where he availed himself of various distractions, dancing with any number of women in the ballroom, and finding a taste for brandy and tobacco.

"You must come to the Aldershott ball tomorrow evening. We'll all be there," one of the women – a coquettish slip of a girl in a yellow dress with an oversized headpiece made of wax fruit and flowers – said to him, fluttering her eyelids.

"I'll be there," Maximilian told her, and she had run off to join her friends, giggling and pointing to him,

Maximilian cared nothing for the woman or so he told himself. But he could not be so callous as to simply cast his feelings aside. His heart was breaking, and he was torn between anger and sorrow. She was a foolish creature like all the others. But his intentions were no longer chivalrous. He had nothing but contempt for women, and he would gladly go to the Aldershott ball if only to treat the women there with the same scorn their sex had treated him.

If women can use me for their own twisted pleasures, then I can do the same, he had told himself, before staggering back in the direction of the inn.

It was to be his pleasure that morning to confront Delphine with the news of his discovery of her ploy. The façade was gone, her true nature revealed, and Maximilian was looking forward to seeing her squirm under the uncomfortable revelation he was now privy to.

She'll deny it, of course. Women are wily creatures. Like Eve and the serpent. It was so at the dawn of time, and so it is now, he said to himself, as he banged at the door of the inn and called for admittance.

It was Bessie who opened to him, staring at him in surprise as he stepped over the threshold and pushed past her.

"Where's your mistress? Still locked in her room, is she?" he demanded, and the maid nodded.

"Yes, my Lord…but…she had that terrible upset last night," Bessie began.

Maximilian laughed.

"Ah, yes, she was terribly hard done by, wasn't she? The earl and the marquess, those two wicked men," he said. The maid stared at him in confusion.

Far from feeling aggrieved at the behavior of the two aristocrats, Maximilian now thought them both to be on his side – they had succeeded in upsetting Delphine, and after what she had done to him, it was thoroughly deserved.

"She won't be long, my Lord. I'm sure," Bessie said, but Maximilian snatched at the set of keys hung at the maid's waist.

"One of these ought to do it – don't you think?" he exclaimed.

Bessie tried to prevent him from taking the keys from her and a struggle would have ensued had not footsteps on the stairs caused them both to look up.

"What's happened? What's going on?" Delphine asked, staring at the scene in disbelief.

"It's his Lordship, ma'am. He's gone quite mad," Bessie cried, wrenching the keys from Maximilian's grip, and shrinking back against the door in fear.

"Mad? Is that what you believe me to be? Oh, I don't think so. And no madder than a woman who pretends to be a man's friend, his confidant, his intimate – and all for her own nefarious games. To make me fall in love with you. That was your ploy, wasn't it?" Maximilian exclaimed, pointing at Delphine, who gasped.

She came forward, shaking her head and holding out her arms to him.

"Please, it's not like that. You don't understand," she said, but Maximilian only laughed.

"I heard it all last night – the maid and the cook discussing your little plan together. You had it all worked out, didn't you? What was I to do? Fall in love with you and then be humiliated for your own entertainment? I don't understand why, but I do understand how. The meals, the intimacies, the wine – I trusted you, I actually trusted you, after all I've been through at the hands of your kind. I thought you were different. I wanted to think you were different. But you're not. You're just the same as her – the same as all of them," Maximilian exclaimed, and he banged his hand down on the nearest table with such force as to shake the whole parlor.

Delphine shook her head, tears rolling down her cheeks. But Maximilian felt no sympathy for her. She had brought it on herself, entirely on herself.

"I...you don't understand. I wanted to..." she began, but Maximilian had heard enough of explanations.

He no longer cared for the explanations of women. Frances had tried it, too. She had used those same words – she had told him he did not understand. But Maximilian understood all too well. He knew what Delphine had done, and it made him feel sick.

"I don't understand. Is that so? Well... I think I understand it very well. You're all in on it, aren't you," he said, turning to Bessie and pointing his finger at her.

"Please, sir. It's not like that. The mistress didn't mean anything by it, she didn't," Bessie whimpered.

"Then toying with the feelings of a man already heartbroken means nothing, does it?" he demanded, growing angrier with every passing moment.

"Please, let me explain," Delphine said, but Maximilian had heard enough.

He did not want explanations, he did not want excuses, he did not want to be coerced and manipulated. For once, Maximilian was going to have his say.

"You're not going to explain. You'll have my things made ready. I'm leaving this inn immediately, and you'll never see me again. Your little ploy didn't work, Delphine. You've not got what you wanted. Do you hear me?" he cried, and turning on his heels, he wrenched open the door and hurried out onto the street, slamming it behind him with such force that the windows rattled.

And good riddance, he told himself, not caring if he never saw Delphine again.

One thing was certain – Maximilian would never trust a woman ever again, and now he intended to use his anger and hatred to good affect at the Aldershott ball that evening, where any woman would be fair game to his wrath...

Chapter Twenty-Three

Delphine collapsed, sobbing on the parlor floor. Bessie came to put her arms around her, holding her close.

"There, there, ma'am. Don't you cry. Oh, I'm so sorry," she exclaimed, as Delphine clung to her.

"It wasn't supposed to be like this, Bessie. It wasn't supposed to be like this," she wailed.

"I don't know how he knew. He must've overheard Alice and I talking last night...but we said nothing to make him think...oh, I don't know what to do," Bessie exclaimed, as Delphine sobbed.

At that moment, Alice came bustling in from the kitchen and she stared in horror at Delphine and Bessie, both of whom were sitting on the parlor floor, wrapped in one another's arms.

"Goodness me, whatever's the matter?" she exclaimed, and Bessie gave a brief precis of what had just occurred.

The cook shook her head and tutted.

"I knew no good would come of it. You shouldn't have led him a merry dance, ma'am. But your heart was in the right place, I know that much. Now...don't you cry. Come along, let's get you into the kitchen and sit you down. We don't need another scene like last night, do we?" she said, and between them, she and Bessie helped Delphine to stand.

"He didn't let me explain. I know it was a game at first, but it didn't continue as one. I didn't want it to be one. I wanted him…" Delphine exclaimed, cursing herself for her stupidity.

"I know, ma'am, but…if he's got the wrong idea into his head, and don't forget…he's been hurt himself," Alice replied, as they led Delphine into the kitchen and sat her down.

Bessie hurried to make a pot of strong tea, and Delphine buried her head in her hands and wept. She was not about to blame her friends for speaking out of turn. They had been overheard, but it was Delphine who had begun the deception. But that deception, that attempt to make Maximilian fall in love with her, had ceased to be a game. It was real, and far from making him fall in love with her for the sake of teaching him a lesson, Delphine now wanted him to fall in love with her as she had fallen in love with him. She wanted each of them to love the other in deepening of the intimacies they had already shared.

"But what can I do now?" Delphine said, looking up through teary eyes as Bessie poured the tea.

The maid and the cook looked at one another and shook their heads.

"It's always better for the truth to be known, ma'am. There's nothing to hide now. Perhaps you can tell him how you feel. He might've calmed down later on when he returns. Let him have his anger for now – he deserves it after all he's been through. He couldn't trust women – and now he has fresh reason not to. It won't be easy to convince him of the opposite," Alice said, as she sat down next to Delphine and pushed the cup of tea on its saucer towards her.

Delphine nodded and sniffed. She pulled out her handkerchief and dabbed at her eyes. Alice was right, Maximilian had every reason to be angry. He had already been betrayed by a woman, and now he would surely feel a fresh sense of betrayal in her actions, too. This was not what she had intended, and her troubles with the earl and the marquess seemed to pale into insignificance next to that which she had caused for herself.

"I suppose it's up to him now, isn't it?" she said, and Bessie nodded.

"You'll see soon enough what he means to do, ma'am. But don't hold your hopes up. He might want to leave. He might want to go to the continent or back to Berkshire, or anywhere away from here. I'm sorry, ma'am," she said, and she put her arm around Delphine and held her close.

Delphine felt defeated. She had never known the vagaries of the heart, and her first foray into love had proved a disaster. It seemed foolish to think she might truly have caused Maximilian to fall in love with her, even as she knew she had fallen in love with him.

"This is what a broken heart feels like, isn't it?" she said, shaking her head with a sigh, and realizing how much pain there could be in love.

* * *

Maximilian had never felt so angry. To be betrayed once was bad enough, but twice, and by another woman - one he had come to trust...

I'll show them. I'll treat them with nothing but contempt, he told himself, as he stalked the streets.

He spent the day on Regent's Street and Piccadilly, shopping in the fashionable arcades and shops. He bought books at Hatchards, and clothes for travelling abroad. That was now his intention – to leave London as soon as possible and make for the continent. He would never allow himself to become a fool to a woman ever again, and as the evening came, he took a carriage to the Aldershott ball, which was being held in the upper rooms of a house in Mayfair.

"You're very welcome, my Lord," Sir Arthur Aldershott told him, after Maximilian introduced himself and explained his reasons for attending.

"I hope you don't mind my arriving like this. But I met some of your guests at the pleasure gardens in Vauxhall last night. They were most insistent I join you," Maximilian said.

His host nodded. Sir Arthur was a man known in social circles as something of a womanizer. He was an elderly gentleman who had never married but was never short of female company. He smiled at Maximilian and gave him a knowing look.

"And I'm glad they did. Please, this way," Sir Arthur said, pointing Maximilian through a pair of double doors and into the ballroom.

It was a large room, with long windows on one side, and a raised platform at one end where a quartet of musicians were tuning their instruments. Double doors led out onto a terrace on the opposite side to the windows, and tables were set with refreshments and bowls of punch on either side. A throng of well-dressed ladies and gentlemen – more ladies than gentlemen – thronged the room, and amongst them Maximilian could see the object of his intentions, the woman who had invited him at the pleasure gardens, and the woman he intended to enact his revenge on.

"Oh, how wonderful of you to come! I didn't know if you would," she exclaimed, hurrying over to him.

She smelled of rose water and her cheeks were blushed with rouge. Her yellow dress and bizarre headwear had been replaced by a purple ball gown and a fascinator of peacock feathers. She fluttered her eyelids at him and smiled.

"Won't you dance?" he asked, as the music now began.

"Oh, yes. I'd love to dance. What's your name?" she asked, for despite their intimacies of the previous night, such details had not yet been shared.

"Ma... Andrew," he said, smiling at her, as she blushed.

"And I'm Lavinia. Lavinia Dawson, my father's the Member of Parliament for Billingsgate," she said, as he put his arm around her, and the music began.

"And mine's...a knight of the realm," Maximilian replied.

He had no intention of telling her the truth about himself, not even his real name. He wanted her to fall in love with an illusion and to suddenly break that illusion, shattering it in a sudden departure so as to reclaim something of the power he felt he had lost. To treat Lavinia in such a way would be a small – yet triumphal – retort to the terrible treatment he had been subjected to at the hands of the fairer sex. Maximilian knew it was wrong to treat an innocent woman in this way – Lavinia was perfectly pleasant – but Maximilian felt he could not rid himself of his burning anger without this small display of power, however insignificant it might seem.

"Oh, really, how wonderful. And you dance so well," Lavinia said, as they whirled and twirled across the dance floor to the sounds of a waltz.

Other couples did the same, and dancing amidst the throng, Lavinia told him all about herself. This was her second season, she was nineteen years old, but would be twenty the following month. She had an elder sister, Violet, who was courting an officer of the king's militia, and she split her time between London and the family's small estate in Suffolk.

"It sounds as though you have a charmed life, Lavinia," Maximilian said, as the dance continued.

"Oh, but it's missing one thing. I'm yet to fall in love. I want to, you know. I've dreamed about it for so long – a man to meet and fall in love with. You know...quite by chance, just as they do in stories," she said, giggling as Maximilian spun her around.

"Do you fall in love easily?" he asked, enjoying the illusion he was creating.

"I don't know, really. I suppose I do, perhaps. But that's not a bad thing, is it? You're not married, are you?" she asked, looking at him with slight hesitation.

"No, Lady Lavinia, I'm not married. You needn't worry about that," he replied, and Lavinia giggled.

"At the pleasure gardens, you never know. Some of the men forget to take their wedding rings off. It's awfully embarrassing when they realize," she said.

The music now came to an end and the two of them stepped out of the dance. Maximilian suggested they take the air on the terrace and Lavinia thought this was a very good idea, still giggling as Maximilian led her outside. It was a starry night, the moon was high in the sky, and casting its silvery light over a formal garden laid out below.

"Shall we walk amidst the box hedge?" Maximilian asked, pointing to the steps leading down from the terrace.

"Oh, yes, I think that's a very good idea," she said, giggling again.

She was beginning to get on Maximilian's nerves, but he was willing to humor her in preparation for the final insult. They crossed the terrace and made their way down the steps to the formal garden below. It was laid out in a square with a sundial and a fountain at its center, the paths lined with clipped box hedge, the scent of which filled the still warm air of the late evening.

"The moonlight's very beautiful, isn't it?" Maximilian said, as they came to the center of the garden, where the fountain danced in the silvery light from above.

He knew just what to say to charm her, and now she gazed up at him in such adoration as to make him feel suddenly guilty at what he was about to do.

"Oh, yes. I love the moonlight. It makes everything look so beautiful, doesn't it?" she said, smiling up at him.

"I think so, and what a wonderful evening we've had together," he said, as she moved closer to him and slipped her hand around his waist.

"Oh, Andrew…" she said, raising her lips as though she expected him to kiss her.

But he stepped back, realizing the foolishness of what he was intending. This silly creature had done him no wrong. She did not represent the entirety of her sex, nor could she be held accountable for their crimes towards Maximilian. The anger he had known earlier was abated, replaced by a sense of abject sorrow. This was not him – to stoop to the level of those women who had wronged him…his feelings were confused, his heart trembling, as he bowed his head and sighed.

"I'm not called Andrew," he said, and Lavinia looked at him in astonishment.

"What do you mean?" she asked, and Maximilian shook his head.

"I'm sorry, Lady Lavinia. I've played you a dirty trick. I came here for the wrong reasons. I'm not who I said I am. I'm…just a foolish man who trusted too much," he replied, and before Lavinia could question him further, Maximilian rushed across the garden.

He raced up the steps, pushing past the couples on the terrace and back into the ballroom where the musicians were playing another waltz.

"Leaving so soon?" Sir Arthur called out, but Maximilian ignored him.

He wanted only to flee, away from the dreadful possibility he had come so close to realizing. He had wanted to hurt that poor creature, and he realized now what Frances and Delphine had caused him to become – bitter and vengeful. Frances' betrayal had wounded him deeply, but Delphine's had felt a more bitter blow. He realized now he had never truly loved Frances – it was his pride which had been dented by her actions, but this…this was different. His heart was truly broken. But bitter and vengeful was not who he was, even as he had desired to be so for a short while. There was nothing left but to flee and to make his way to the continent and begin anew. Maximilian would never trust another woman, not as long as he lived – that was his vow, and it would be one to live by, come what may.

"The Seven Bells," he called out, climbing into a waiting carriage outside the house in Mayfair, and sitting back, he sighed, brushing away a tear at the thought of how close he had come to turning into the very thing he so detested.

Chapter Twenty-Four

It was not late when Maximilian returned to the inn. His stomach was rumbling, and whilst he did not relish the thought of encountering Delphine, he was at least prepared to be civil to her. The dining room was empty, and so was the parlor, though he could hear voices coming from the kitchen.

"She's terribly upset…" Bessie was saying, as Maximilian listened.

He knew they were talking about Delphine – who else could they be talking about? But his feelings towards her did not allow for sympathy. She had made a rod for her own back, and that was that. He rudely banged on the door and called out to the servants for something to eat.

"Is this an inn or not? Bring some supper," he shouted, no longer caring whom he insulted as he nursed his own wounds.

Bessie appeared tentatively at the kitchen door.

"Oh, my Lord, I'll bring you some supper – we've mutton chops and anchovy sauce with potatoes," she said, looking at him nervously.

Maximilian did not care what he ate, so long as he could eat it quickly and go to bed. He intended to leave first thing in the morning and never see Delphine – or any of the cast of characters which inhabited this accursed inn – again.

"Just bring me it. I don't care what it is. And something to drink, too," he said.

The maid nodded.

"Wine?" she asked, but Maximilian shook his head.

Wine no longer seemed palatable in the face of what had occurred. It was wine which had been used to seduce him, and wine which had proved to be the poisoned cup.

"Ale," he snapped. Bessie nodded and hurried back into the kitchen.

Maximilian slipped into his usual seat and rested his arms on the table. He sighed, glancing around him and noticing a small portrait on the wall. It was amongst a dozen others, and he had not noticed it before. But the subject was obvious – it was Delphine, but in the first flush of youth. She was smiling, though with a shy look on her face, and there was no mistaking the beauty into which she was to grow. He gazed at the painting for some time, his feelings for Delphine still confused.

But that's just what she wanted. She wanted to confuse me. She wanted me to fall in love with her...and she's got her wish. No doubt she's laughing at me and with... he thought to himself, as a terrible idea occurred to him.

What if this whole endeavor had been dreamed up with the earl and the marquess? It all made sense now – or so it seemed. It had all been an act, an elaborate ruse, one designed to make Maximilian sympathize with Delphine's plight – all the more reason for Maximilian to fall in love with her.

I see it all now, he said to himself, as Bessie brought out a plate of mutton chops with potatoes and a tankard of ale.

"Will there be anything else, sir?" she asked, her hands trembling as she set the plate down in front of him.

"The truth," he replied, looking up at her sternly.

Bessie shook her head and stepped back; her eyes wide with fear.

"I don't understand, my Lord," she said, and he snarled at her.

"You know perfectly well what I mean!. Your mistress – Miss Delphine. I want the truth about what you and the cook were talking about. All this business about her pretending to be in love with me or making me fall in love with her. Let's have it," he exclaimed. At his words, Bessie began to sob.

She was frightened, but Maximilian did not care – he wanted an answer to his question, and the maid was going to give it to him.

"Please, sir…it's not how you think. My mistress never meant any harm by it. It's not true. She's a good person, she only…" she began, but Maximilian interrupted her, filled with rage at a weak attempt to excuse the inexcusable.

"A good person? Who kicks a man whilst he's down? You know why I came here, and you know it's precisely for the reason I now sit and suffer again, because of womankind," he exclaimed. Spitting out these last words, he picked up the plate and flung it against the wall, where gravy left a trail running down the plaster.

Bessie turned and fled, banging the kitchen door behind her as Maximilian sat back and heaved a deep sigh. It was all too much – betrayal, deceit…he was a broken man, and his heart was broken, not once, but twice. He *had* fallen in love with Delphine. Truly and completely, and those feelings remained, despite everything that had now occurred between them. He picked up the tankard of ale and took a long draught, shaking his head and wishing he was far away across the sea, beginning a new life in a far-off place.

And that's what I'll do. I'll go where I please, I'll do as I please, and I'll never allow another woman to grow close to me again. There are no women – only liars who toy with men's hearts like creatures from another world. Devils, that's what they are. Tempters, just as Adam was tempted and fell, he thought to himself.

As he sat pondering, Maximilian heard footsteps on the stairs, and he looked up to find Delphine herself standing there. His outburst against Bessie had assuaged his rage, and now he felt only a sense of sorrow at what had passed between him and the woman he had so readily fallen in love with.

"Oh, I didn't realize you'd be back…" Delphine said, looking alarmed at the sight of Maximilian, who shook his head and waved his hand dismissively.

"It's your inn, isn't it? You can come and go as you please. I'm a guest in your inn, and can do the same," he said, rising to his feet.

He wanted to go to bed. The day – and the night before – had exhausted him. He would sleep until he awoke and then he would leave. Delphine could send his things on after him, care of the shipping company.

"My Lord, I…" she began, but Maximilian snarled at her and shook his head.

"I don't want to hear it. What more is there to say?" he said, and it seemed Delphine was now overcome by emotion.

She stepped forward with tears on her eyes, and as she did so, she fell to the floor in faint. The crash shook the dining room, and Maximilian instinctively rushed to her side, lifting her head and cradling her in his arms.

"Delphine? Are you all right? Can you hear me?" he exclaimed.

The noise had brought Bessie and Alice running from the kitchen. Bessie screamed, and Alice rushed to Delphine's side.

"What happened to her?" she demanded, looking accusingly at Maximilian, who stammered in response.

"Nothing…it wasn't anything I did. We were talking and then she fainted," he replied, feeling suddenly terrified at the thought of having done something to cause this dreadful scene.

Perhaps she had fitted – he had heard of women having the most dreadful fits at moments of over excitement. He looked at Bessie and Alice in desperation.

"We'd better send for the doctor," Bessie said.

"Ah, yes, a doctor – though they're all quacks, aren't they? Can a doctor help? She needs to get to bed. Some brandy – yes, some brandy to revive her," he exclaimed, his mind racing with possibility.

"It's you shouting, that's what's done it," Alice said, shaking her head and grimacing at Maximilian.

He was in no state to disagree – one moment she had been sobbing and the next...

"Oh, I've been a fool. Oh, Delphine... I'm so sorry," Maximilian cried, even as tears rolled down his cheeks.

He could hardly believe what had happened. It was all too terrible for words. His feelings for Delphine were certain – he *was* in love with her, even as that love had been forced through falsity.

"Fetch the brandy, Bessie. We'll try to revive her," Alice said, and she pulled Delphine from Maximilian's arms into her lap, as Bessie rushed to bring the brandy bottle.

Maximilian stood back, shaking his head. She was dead – he was certain she was dead. He had killed her. Panic was rising in him, his heart beating fast in his chest, his palms was sweaty.

"What have I done? Oh... Delphine, I love you. I've been a fool. I'm sorry I was so angry. I know you don't love me – you can't love me. But I love you. Oh, with all my heart, I love you," he exclaimed, holding his head in his hands.

Bessie returned with the bottle of brandy, holding it open under Delphine's nose in an attempt to revive her. In Maximilian's mind, all was lost. He had killed her. He had not struck a physical blow, but the force and cruelty of his words had surely overwhelmed her to the point of expiring. She had tried to tell him she was sorry. She had tried to explain, but in his arrogance and self-pity he had ignored her – worse than that, he had rejected her.

"Hold it closer, Bessie. That's it. Come on now, ma'am, won't you wake up?" Alice implored her.

But Delphine remained motionless, and tears rolled down Maximilian's cheeks as he stared at that tragic scene, seemingly powerless against it.

"Oh, ma'am, please wake up..." Bessie begged, clutching at Delphine's hand as she remained motionless in Alice's arms.

Chapter Twenty-Five

Maximilian was shaking his head, despairing at the possibility of what to do. He knew nothing of medicine, and the thought of summoning a city quack to administer pills and potions filled him with dread – Delphine would sooner be poisoned than wake up. But still her eyes remained resolutely closed, and Bessie drew back the brandy bottle and replaced the lid.

"Cold water, Bessie," Alice said, and the maid hurried back to the kitchen.

"She's not...dead, is she? Oh, please don't say she's dead," Maximilian exclaimed, voicing his worst fears.

The cook looked up at him with a disdainful look and rolled her eyes.

"No, sir, she's not dead. She's fainted. Women are prone to fainting when they've had a shock, and you've obviously given her one," she said, as Bessie returned from the kitchen with a jug of water and a cloth.

They were just wringing out a compress when footsteps on the stairs announced the arrival of unwelcome company. It was the earl and the marquess, who stared in disbelief at the scene taking place before them.

"What's all this? Miss Delphine? What's this fiend done to you?" the earl exclaimed, rushing forward to kneel at Delphine's side.

He clasped at her hand, raising it to his lips, as the marques came to do the same on the other side, scowling at Maximilian, who felt entirely helpless in their sight. He could not bear the thought of having harmed her, even as his heart and mind were torn by what she had done to him.

"I've done nothing to her. You must believe me when I say so. We were talking and..." he began, but the earl now sprang to his feet and turned on him.

"You've killed her. I'll summon the magistrates, I'll have you hung for this, I'll... I challenge you to a duel!" he cried, and he raised his fists in a stance, challenging Maximilian, who stepped back and shook his head.

"I'm not going to duel with you whilst Delphine lies there. I won't do it. I didn't do it. I didn't harm her. Don't you understand that?" he exclaimed, even as the earl continued his challenge.

But now the marquess gave a loud exclamation, and all of them turned to see Delphine opening her eyes. Bessie and Alice were holding the damp compress to her forehead, and she looked up, blinking in the lamplight, for darkness had begun to fall outside and Bessie had brought a lamp from the kitchen.

"What's... I don't understand..." Delphine stammered.

"It's all right, ma'am. You've had a nasty turn, that's all. You're awake now, see," Alice said, helping Delphine to sit up.

Maximilian breathed a sigh of relief. In his shock, he had truly believed he had killed Delphine, and to see her revived brought joy to his heart. Their previous quarrels were forgotten. The earl turned, looking both relieved at the sight of Delphine awake, and somewhat disappointed at not having been able to discharge his intentions to duel.

"Delphine – this blaggard tried to kill you," the earl said, even as Maximilian stepped forward to protest.

"I did nothing of the sort. We were talking and then you fainted. I didn't do anything…" he exclaimed, as Bessie and Alice helped Delphine to her feet.

"You've done enough damage for one day," Alice said, shaking her head.

They helped Delphine into a chair. Maximilian felt powerless. He was angry…but the sight of Delphine lying in a faint in front of him had brought him back from his sense of betrayal. He wondered now if there was more to story than he had allowed it to be told. No longer did he want to shout and rage at her, but instead to hold her and comfort her. She still appeared dazed, gazing around her, as Bessie urged her to drink a cup of water.

"I'll make you some tea, ma'am," she said, bustling off towards the kitchen.

"And we'll remain at your side, Delphine. You can't be left alone – not with *this* man," the earl said pointedly, grimacing at Maximilian, who sighed.

He knew he was not welcome, and Delphine was not of sound enough mind to protest. He nodded to the others and turned to go to bed.

"I'm going to my rest," he said, feeling suddenly overwhelmed with tiredness and unable to think properly about anything.

"Maximilian…" Delphine murmured.

"Let him go, my dear. Let him think about what he's done," the earl said, and Maximilian made his way to bed, his heart heavy with sorrow at all that had transpired between them.

*　*　*

Delphine sipped the cup of water, which Bessie held for her. She was still feeling dazed and could barely remember anything of what had caused her to faint as she had done. She and Maximilian had been arguing and then…

"You had a nasty fall, Delphine. That wicked man…he *will* upset you, won't he?" the earl said.

He was holding Delphine's hand, and the marquess was doing the same with the other. Delphine gave a weak smile. Their concern was clear, even as Delphine knew it was unnecessary. It was not Maximilian who had caused her to fall. They had merely been talking, and she fainted. After that, she could only vaguely remember hearing as though from a distance or underwater…

He told me he loved me – he said it to Bessie and Alice, didn't he? She exclaimed to herself, not wishing to voice her thoughts for fear of what the earl and the marquess would do in response.

"You don't need to worry. I'll be all right," Delphine said, looking from the earl to the marquess and back.

Both men glanced at one another with anxious expressions on their faces.

"She's deluded. It's the fall. She must've bumped her head," the marquess said, and Delphine smiled.

"I didn't…really, it's quite all right. I'm all right," she said, but the earl and the marquess both shook their heads.

"You're not all right, Delphine. We must help you. Summon a doctor, Bessie," the earl said, indicating to the maid, who glanced at Delphine as though for reassurance.

"I don't need a doctor. Really, they're all just quacks. You've all done more than enough for me – some tea, Bessie. That's what I'd like," Delphine replied, and Bessie hurried off into the kitchen to make the tea, leaving her with the earl and the marquess.

Alice who was watching tutted and shook her head.

"The mistress doesn't need the tea of you fussing around her either. Step back and give her some space," she said, but Delphine shook her head.

"It's all right. They're only being kind – they're always being kind," she replied.

The earl and the marquess looked at one another in surprise.

"We're concerned for you, Delphine," the earl replied, and Delphine smiled at him.

"I know you are. You've always been so, even if you've a strange way of showing it," she said.

Perhaps it was the bump to the head, or the realization of the foolish game she had played, but Delphine no longer saw the earl and the marquess as foils to her happiness. They had always been there for her, always concerned, always the first to defend her from whatever perceived threat accosted her. She wondered if she had perhaps overreacted towards them – particularly with regards to their gifts and songs.

"But you know we are, Delphine. We love you," the earl said, and the marquess nodded.

"Truly, we do. You're like...a sister to us," he said, and Delphine smiled.

"Then why not treat me as such? Why all these silly gestures and over the top reactions? I can't marry both of you – one of you would be left unhappy and I couldn't bear that. No, I don't want to marry either of you and leave the other bereft. But I would like the two of you as my friends – my dearest friends, my brothers," she said, and the earl and the marquess nodded.

"We feared we'd lost you, Delphine. Seeing you lying there in Alice's arms...it brought us to tears," the earl said, and the marquess nodded.

"To tears...yes, oh, we're sentimental old fools. But you, Delphine...you mean more to us than you'll ever know," he said, and he raised Delphine's hand to his lips and kissed it.

"Then perhaps we can begin again – no more eccentricity and foolish gestures. Let's just be the closest of friends," she replied, and both men smiled.

"I'd rather that than lose you, Delphine. I love you, but you're right, that love could never be at the expense of Jacob's happiness, nor his at mine, I'm sure," the earl said, and the marquess nodded.

"Then we're at peace," the marquess replied.

"But you do love him, don't you – the baron's son, I mean. For all his faults, you do love him," the earl said.

Delphine thought for a moment. What the earl said was true. She *was* in love with Maximilian. She had not meant to fall in love with him. She had *meant* to teach him a lesson about womankind – that not all women were the same as Frances Stott. But in doing so, Delphine had inadvertently proved the opposite, or so it surely appeared to Maximilian. He would think her nothing more than an imitation of the woman who had betrayed him, proving, beyond doubt, his belief in the wickedness of the fairer sex. How could he trust a woman ever again after what Delphine had done?

"But it's me that's at fault..." Delphine replied, and she explained to the earl and the marquess her plan and everything that had come about because of it.

"So...he wasn't the womanizer we believed him to be? He wasn't trying to seduce you?" the marquess said, once Delphine had finished her explanation.

"He had nothing to do with it. It was all me," Delphine confessed, as the earl and the marquess looked at one another in astonishment.

"We were quite beastly to him, when all this time he only wanted to be left alone," the earl said, shaking his head.

"Well...you weren't to know the truth, were you? I'm sorry, I've behaved so foolishly. But I just wanted to show him not every woman is like her. I've not done a very good job of it," Delphine said, sighing.

Bessie returned with the tea, and they each drank a cup, a ponderous silence reigning. It was all a terrible mess, and Delphine could see no way of reconciling with Maximilian. This was her fault, even as her heart was broken over what she had done. Her game had so quickly turned into a truth, blurring the lines between fantasy and reality. She had so quickly come to love him, and now she ached with longing for what might have been.

"I think it's time you go to bed, Delphine. Perhaps things will seem better in the morning," the earl said.

Delphine wanted somehow to resolve the situation that very night. But she knew it was not possible. Perhaps Maximilian would speak to her in the morning, and she clung to those distant words she believed she had heard in the midst of her faint.

He does love me, he said so, but oh...can he forgive me? she asked herself, as the earl and the marquess helped her to bed, and it seemed there was nothing more she could do that day than close her eyes and try to sleep.

Chapter Twenty-Six

Delphine passed a restless night. Her dreams were filled with images of Maximilian – the shared bottle of wine, the happy conversations, the anger on his face, the look of betrayal, the...

"Oh!" Delphine exclaimed, waking suddenly, and sitting up with a start.

The early morning sun was filtering through a gap in the curtains, and she rubbed her eyes, the moment between dreams and reality blurred as the events of the previous day returned to her. She sighed and yawned, lying back down, and pulling the blankets up around her. She did not want to get up, nor did she want to see anyone that day. She would hide in her bedroom; the inn could go to the dogs for all she cared...

"Ma'am? Are you awake?" Bessie's voice came from beyond the door, and she tapped on it gently, causing Delphine to startle.

"I... I don't want to see anyone, Bessie," she called out, but the handle of the door turned, and it opened, revealing the maid bearing a tray on which was placed a steaming cup of tea.

"You can't hide in here all day, ma'am, and I need to tell you... the baron's son, he's gone," she said.

At these words, Delphine gave an anguished cry and pulled the blankets up over her head. She had expected as much, but to be confronted by the ugly truth…it was too much to bear.

"Did you see him go? Did he say anything?" she asked, peering out at Bessie, who now brought the tea to Delphine's bedside.

"I didn't see him, ma'am – not to talk to, at least. We were in the kitchen – it's past seven O'clock, and we heard footsteps. I thought it was you at first, but then the door banged, and I rushed out to see him hurrying off towards the stables," Bessie replied.

Delphine sighed. She was trying hard not to cry, but tears were welling up in her eyes, and now she rolled onto her side, knowing all was lost. She had been a fool, and she had no one to blame but herself.

"It's too awful, Bessie," she moaned, and the maid sat on the side of the bed and put her hand on Delphine's shoulder.

"Come now, ma'am. This isn't like you. Where's your fighting spirit? You've made your peace with the earl and the marquess. They're downstairs having breakfast now – they're behaving quite differently. It's remarkable. They wanted to know how you are. Won't you come down and see them? You need some company at a time like this," Bessie said.

Delphine rolled over and looked up at the maid, who smiled and patted her arm. She knew she was only wallowing in her own misery. Her father would be ashamed of her. With a determined sigh, she sat up and nodded.

"You're right. I'll come downstairs. Perhaps…oh, I don't know, but you're right, I need company, and not just my own," she said.

Bessie left Delphine to dress. She washed her face, brushed her hair, and put on a fresh dress, before standing in front of the mirror and taking a deep breath.

You can't wallow in self-pity. He's gone, she told herself, even as she felt a desperate need to apologize to him.

She wanted to explain and to make him see reason. Even if he could not forgive her, then surely, he deserved to hear the truth – and wanted to hear the truth.

But if he's gone... she thought to herself, as she left her bedroom with a heavy heart and made her way downstairs.

The dining room was mercifully quiet, and only a few of the guests were having breakfast. The earl and the marquess were eating slices of bread spread thickly with marmalade, and they did not seek to summon Delphine to their table, as was their usual custom. But Delphine approached them herself. She wanted their company, as strange as it seemed to admit it.

"Good morning, Delphine. Did you manage to sleep?" the earl asked, and Delphine nodded.

"A little, but he's gone...that's what Bessie told me. He left first thing this morning," she said, fighting back the tears.

"I saw him saddling his horse, but he took none of his possessions with him. Presumably they remain here," the marquess said, taking a bite of his bread and marmalade.

"I...don't know. But...oh. I don't know what to do. I want to explain the truth to him. I was going to do so this morning, at least to allow him to understand. But it's hopeless now," Delphine said, and she sank down into an empty chair at the table and put her head in her hands.

The earl put his arm around her to comfort her.

"There, there, my dear, don't cry," he said, but Delphine could no longer hold back the flood of tears, and she sobbed openly.

The marquess gallantly took out a large spotted handkerchief for her, and the earl poured a cup of coffee, which he pushed towards her.

"You must drink something, my dear," the marquess said.

"Oh, I've been such a fool. I'm so sorry," Delphine said, feeling a sudden sense of guilt over how she had behaved towards the two aristocrats, who had only ever had her best interests at heart – as eccentric as they had been in expressing them.

"You've nothing to be sorry for, Delphine – nothing at all," the earl said.

Delphine was about to reply when a loud knocking came at the door of the inn, and she looked up to find Bessie hurrying to answer it.

"Visitors at this time?" Bessie said, tutting and shaking her head.

Delphine sat up; her hopes raised that this might be Maximilian returning. But it was not the baron's son who stood on the threshold, but rather a man dressed in the livery of a coachman, with battered epaulettes and a crooked tricorn hat on his head.

"I've come with a message from Lord Blane. He makes for his Bedforshire estate, Fermony Grange. You're to send his possessions on from here," the man said.

Delphine rose to her feet and hurried to the door.

"Are you taking him there? Do you know where he is now?" she asked, imploring the coachman, who looked somewhat taken aback.

"He rides himself, miss. He paid me a shilling to relay the message," the man said.

Delphine's face fell. She would have gone that very moment and followed the coachman to wherever Maximilian was waiting. But such thoughts were merely foolish, and she nodded and turned away.

"We'll send his things," she said, sighing as she returned to her place at the earl and the marquess' table.

The coachman left and Bessie closed the door of the inn as Delphine took a sip of coffee and shook her head.

"That's it, then. It's lost. I've made an utter fool of myself, and for what? A silly game," she exclaimed, cursing her own stupidity, even as the earl and the marquess shook their heads.

"We all do foolish things for love, Delphine. You're no different, though less foolish than Jacob and I," the earl replied.

Delphine looked up at him and gave a weak smile.

"What would I do without you two fools? You're my favorite fools in all the world," she said, as a tear ran down her cheek.

The earl laughed.

"Well, you don't need to do without us, but perhaps...we could help you?" he said, and Delphine looked at him curiously.

"It's very kind of you, but I don't know how you can. ..." she said. The earl shook his head and interrupted her.

"I've got an idea," he replied, as he leaned forward and smiled.

***

Maximilian was riding hard. He had left London behind him, and was now galloping along country lanes and across farmland in the direction of Fermony Grange. He had barely slept the night before, so full of anxiety over what had occurred. The sight of Delphine lying motionless had terrified him. He had truly thought she was dead, and that it was the shock of his words and anger which had killed her. To see her revived had brought relief to his heart, but he could not have remained in her company any longer. His feelings were confused, even though he still loved her and wanted only to be with her.

But she betrayed you, he kept telling himself, knowing in his heart that he had not allowed her even to explain herself.

There was so much he did not know, not least how the game had turned into something more. Maximilian felt certain Delphine had feelings for him, feelings he shared, but could he ever forgive the way those feelings had begun?

I shouldn't. It'll only end in tragedy. Think about Frances. Think about what she did to you, he told himself, as the gates of his father's estate came into view.

It felt as though Maximilian had never left, and he wondered how he would be received. He had no intention of remaining there for long, even as he was uncertain where to go.

But how can I go anywhere when I love her? he asked himself, filled with anger for allowing his heart to be so overtaken.

And that was the problem. Maximilian was in love with Delphine, even though he believed she had betrayed him. He could not rid himself of that love, nor could he rid himself of the feeling that he had left too hastily and without allowing Delphine to explain her actions. He felt guilty, and as he rode up the long drive towards the house, he wondered again if he had made a terrible mistake.

"My Lord?" Dalton, the butler, exclaimed, as he opened the front door to Maximilian a few moments later.

"I won't be staying long, Dalton. Inform my father," Maximilian said, throwing off his traveling cloak.

The butler looked confused.

"But my Lord. I don't understand. We sent your things on. Your father believes you're on the continent. He's staying at the home of Lord Farnbrough. He left yesterday and won't be back for a week," the butler replied.

Maximilian was glad to hear this. He had no desire to explain himself to his father. He did not even know why he had returned home to Berkshire. It was all so confusing. His heart was torn, his mind was confused, and it felt as though there was nothing left to hold onto, nothing stable by which to orientate himself. He felt like a ship lost at sea, desperately searching for a sore.

"Very good. I'll take some refreshments in the drawing room," Maximilian replied.

The butler gave a curt bow. It was not his place to question Maximilian's actions, and now Maximilian made his way to the drawing room, slumping down into an armchair by the fire with a sigh. He had brought with him only a volume of poetry, stuffed hastily into his pocket. He pulled it out and began to read

"*And a good south wind sprung up behind;*
The Albatross did follow,
And every day, for food or play,

Came to the mariner's hollo!
In mist or cloud, on mast or shroud,
It perched for vespers nine;
Whiles all the night, through fog-smoke white,
Glimmered the white Moon-shine.'
God save thee, ancient Mariner!
From the fiends, that plague thee thus!—
Why look'st thou so?'—With my cross-bow
I shot the albatross…"

It felt to Maximilian as though he had done the same, and Coleridge's words rang true in his heart. Delphine was not his enemy. She had done so much for him, but he had cast her aside without even allowing her to explain – he had shot her down, even when she had done nothing but be kind to him. This was Maximilian's darkest hour, and he sat for the rest of the afternoon, brooding in the drawing room. Rain was lashing against the window, and a wind whistled around the house. He had almost fallen asleep, fatigued from his journey, when the door opened, and the butler appeared looking somewhat perturbed.

"Visitors for you, my Lord," he said, and Maximilian sat up in surprise.

"I'm not expecting any visitors," he said, but at that moment, and to Maximilian's great surprise, the earl and the marquess barged past the butler and entered the room.

"We had to come. You've made a terrible mistake," the earl exclaimed, as Maximilian rose to his feet in astonishment.

"You should've stayed. She's devastated," the marquess continued, and Maximilian looked from one to the other in utter disbelief.

"You mean…" he began, but the earl interrupted.

"Let's put all this nonsense behind us. We've been fools; we know that. But we've come here with Delphine's blessing. We want to make amends, we want to bring the two of you back together," the earl exclaimed.

There was a sense of desperation in his voice, as though everything depended on this moment. The change which had come over him was quite remarkable, and Maximilian did not know what to say.

"I don't know if I can…" he started, but the earl sprang forward and seized him by the hand.

"But you must. She's in the most terrible state. She didn't mean any of it. She only did it to stop us from being such fools. We love her, but we don't want to marry her – neither of us. She's like a sister to us. Won't you understand that? It's you she loves – it's not some game anymore. Perhaps at the beginning it seemed so, but not anymore. You've got to believe me," he said.

Maximilian pondered this for a moment, then shook his head.

"I can't… I'm already betrothed to be married," he replied, and the earl and the marquess stared at him in utter disbelief.

Chapter Twenty-Seven

Delphine was restless. She had tried to help Bessie and Alice in the kitchen, and she had made an attempt at packing Maximilian's things into his trunks. But she had been reduced to tears at the sight of his empty bedroom, his clothes strewn across the floor. He had left in such a hurry that everything was in disarray. It was all a terrible mess, and so were her feelings. She felt confused and overwhelmed.

"Sit down, ma'am. You're in no state to do anything," Alice had told her, tutting and shaking her head after Delphine had dropped a large bowl of chopped onions onto the floor.

"I'll clear it up," Bessie said, hurrying to help.

Delphine sank into a chair at the kitchen table and put her head into her hands. She felt pathetic – useless and ridiculous. A man should not have this effect on her, and she could only imagine what her father would have said if he had been there.

"Oh, it's no use. I can't do anything," she said, shaking her head.

Bessie came to put her arm around her.

"I know it's hard, ma'am. But you've got to put him behind you. Sometimes we don't always get the ending we want. I know you want to tell him you're sorry, but…he's gone, and he's not coming back. It'll get easier as the days go by. But for now…let us look after you," she said.

"Bessie's right, ma'am. You're experiencing your first heartbreak. It's never easy, but time heals. He's gone, and you've got to let him go," Alice said, turning from the stove and smiling at Delphine.

Delphine was glad she was not on her own. Bessie and Alice were the most loyal friends, but she had not told her friends about the earl and the marquess' offer. They had set off at once for Berkshire, taking a carriage, and promising to return with news by the evening. But Delphine did not know what they could hope to achieve. They could not hope to bring Maximilian back, and given the history between them, she did not think the baron's son would welcome their arrival.

"I'm so glad to have the two of you. I don't say it often enough, but you're my family, and I love you both dearly," Delphine said, smiling at Bessie and Alice, who came and put their arms around her.

"And we love you, too, ma'am," Bessie replied.

Their tender moment was interrupted by a commotion in the dining room.

"Oh, here comes trouble. They'll be demanding something," Alice said, scowling towards the door.

But Delphine rose to her feet and took a deep breath.

"It's all right, I'll go and talk to them. Things are…much better between us now," she said, as she hurried out of the kitchen door and into the dining room.

There she found the earl and the marquess divesting themselves of their traveling clothes. They were both soaking wet and splattered with mud, as though their journey had been made in the utmost haste and through terrible weather.

"Ah, my dear, you must come and sit down," the earl said, with a grave look on his face.

Delphine looked at him curiously. Surely, he could not be bringing news of a worse nature than she already knew. What could be more terrible than finding love and seeing it destroyed before even its first blooms had risen?

"Did you…see him?" she asked, tentatively.

The earl and the marquess sat down at their usual table and beckoned Delphine to join them.

"We saw him, yes…but I'm afraid I've got some terrible and upsetting news to share with you," the earl replied.

Delphine took a deep breath. She could not imagine what he was about to say. Her heart was already broken, her happiness destroyed, and all by her own stupidity. She had no one to blame for herself, and if the earl was about to tell her of Maximilian's anger, then it was surely all she deserved.

"But what? I don't understand," she said. The earl and the marquess looked at one another and shook their heads.

"He's getting married, Delphine," the earl replied.

* * *

It took a few moments for Delphine to realize what the earl had said. Surely, she had misheard. She shook her head and stared at him in disbelief.

"I…no, that can't be true. What do you mean?" she asked, but the earl nodded.

"It's true. He's getting married, here, in London. He told us himself," he said, as tears welled up in Delphine's eyes.

She fought them back, but it was no use. She began to sob, clinging to the earl, who now put his arms around her.

"There, there, my dear. Don't worry. We'll look after you. I'm sorry to be the bearer of such tragic news. He told us he'd made a spur of the moment decision, it was all rather hurried, but he'd return to London in the coming days. He's going to come here..." he said, and Delphine looked up in astonishment.

This was only a twisting of the knife. She could not believe Maximilian cruelty. Even in the face of her own behaviour. Did he not realize the hurt he would cause her? To stay at the inn on the day of his wedding seemed the most terrible insult. Her anger rose, and she pulled back from the earl's arms, banging her fist on the table as she did so.

"No, I won't allow it. He can't," she exclaimed.

"But he is. I don't understand it either, Delphine. But he's going to make a point of marrying from here. Presumably in Saint Paul's, though I don't know how he can possibly have made the arrangements so soon. It seems quite incredible to me," the earl said, shaking his head.

Delphine could not understand it either. The whole thing seemed too incredible for words. Had Maximilian been courting this woman at the same time as his flirtations with her? If so, he was as much to blame as she, over what had transpired between them. Did the woman even know of their dalliance? She deserved to, and now Delphine felt only anger at herself having been so tricked.

"It must've been those times he went out so mysteriously – the ball, his visit to a friend, it was all a foil, wasn't it?" she exclaimed.

"You mustn't upset yourself, Delphine," the marquess said, but Delphine *was* upset.

She was angrier than she had ever been before, and she rose to her feet with a grim look on her face.

"I'll tell him just what I think of him," she said, as she realized she would have the chance to confront Maximilian on his return.

It was the strangest feeling, a bizarre turn of events which hardly made sense. Was this merely a deliberate attempt on Maximilian's part to spite her? Did he want revenge?

"Oh, Delphine, please, you mustn't upset yourself," the earl implored, repeating the marquess' words.

But Delphine was beyond comfort now. She knew just what she was going to do, and now she was determined not to give in to whatever wicked scheme Maximilian had devised.

"I'll show him," she said, clenching her fists, as she resolved to teach Maximilian the lesson he deserved.

* * *

Delphine did not have Maximilian's trunks sent back to Berkshire. A message was received the following day to the effect that they were to expect the return of the Baron's son the following Monday and that preparations for the wedding were in hand. There was no intimacy in his words, only a stark formality as he issued instructions as to the preparations he desired. In an added insult, he wrote of his intention to bring his bride to the inn and demanded that a lavish dinner was to be served, the expenses for which were included.

Delphine could not refuse his request. She could not afford to do so, and reluctantly, she set about making the preparations. As to the identity of the bride, no one knew. The earl and the marquess offered their speculations, but Maximilian had revealed nothing to identify the mysterious woman, only that she could be found in London and would be revealed on the day of the wedding. Delphine was trying her best to concentrate on the practicalities, even as she brooded on how she would greet the errant bachelor.

"I don't know how you can allow it, ma'am," Alice said, shaking her head as she vigorously mixed the batter for a fruit cake which was to be the centrepiece of the wedding breakfast.

"We've got bills to pay, Alice, and I can't refuse, can I? Imagine what people would say? No, we must…bear the weight of it," she replied grimly, as she counted out bottles of wine from a crate and stacked them in the corner of the kitchen.

It was to be a lavish feast, and Maximilian had written to say that a hundred guests were expected and that footmen would arrive to serve the meal. It was all very strange, but Delphine was determined to have her say. She would not stand idly by and watch this spectacle, so clearly designed to humiliate her. She had come to the conclusion that this was Maximilian's revenge. Not only against her, but against the whole of her sex. She could only feel sorry for the woman he was to marry, assuming she, too, was part of Maximilian's plan for vengeance.

Perhaps he was plotting it all this time. Perhaps I was his pawn, too, she thought to herself, as the day of the wedding approached...

Chapter Twenty-Eight

Delphine rose early on the day of the wedding. Everything was prepared, and she, Bessie, and Alice had stayed up late the night before to ensure all was ready. The dining room had been transformed, and was now set with long tables, covered in white cloths, with silver cutlery and crystal glassware. They were to use the best crockery, and large vases had been filled with pretty bouquets of flowers to decorate the tables.

The kitchen, too, was ready, and on the table stood the cake, iced, and decorated with sugared flowers, waiting to be cut by the bride and groom. Alice was already at work, preparing haunches of beef for roasting, whilst Bessie sat peeling potatoes, which would be roasted alongside the meat. Delphine was counting the additional bottles of wine which had arrived from one of the merchants on the dockside, and it seemed all was ready.

"What time does he arrive?" Alice said, as she stacked logs onto the fire beneath the range.

"Soon, I presume. I really know nothing about the ceremony. He sent instructions for the meal and the decorations. I've changed the sheets in his bedroom. I presume he and the bride will spend the night here," Delphine replied.

Alice shook her head and tutted.

"I'd like to see her. I wonder what she's like? Some aristocratic woman, no doubt. He's behaving like a vicious snake," she said.

Delphine could only agree. It was spiteful of Maximilian to parade his bride in front of her. There was no doubt this was an act of revenge. But Delphine had already prepared her words. She would tell Maximilian she was sorry for the way she had behaved, but that she was not above considering his pettiness an insult. She would be gracious and magnanimous, but she would not be cowed by him, nor by his bride.

"It's not her fault, though. He's persuaded her, somehow, but… well…that's that, isn't it?" Delphine said, shaking her head.

As she was speaking, there came a loud knocking at the door of the inn, and Delphine took a deep breath, imagining this to be the arrival of Maximilian.

"I'll go, ma'am," Bessie said, and before Delphine could protest, she had hurried out to answer the door.

But it was not Maximilian whom she returned with a moment later, but rather, a large box, which she handed to Delphine with a puzzled expression on her face.

"What's this?" Delphine asked.

"I don't know, ma'am. A coachman just arrived with it. It's come from Berkshire, addressed to you," she said.

Delphine put the box on the kitchen table and opened it as Bessie and Alice looked on. Inside, to her amazement – and indignation – was a wedding dress. It was sumptuous – of ivory and lace, with a long trail and veil, all wrapped in delicate paper scented with rose water.

"The swine…" Delphine exclaimed.

Maximilian had sent her the dress for his bride. It was an utter humiliation; one she could hardly dare to believe.

"To send the dress to you, ma'am…that's wicked. You should

cut it up," Alice said, pointing to a large pair of scissors hanging from a hook on the wall.

But Delphine shook her head. She would ignore the insult, even as it grieved her bitterly. This entire charade was designed to humiliate her, and now she wondered what would happen when Maximilian himself arrived. Would he come with his bride? Would she know what Delphine had done? She had no more time to ponder this, before a further knocking at the door brought her back to her senses.

"This must be him," she said, as Bessie and Alice looked at one another fearfully.

"It's all right, ma'am. We're both here. We'll get through this together," Alice said, as Delphine drew herself up and went to answer the door.

* * *

If Delphine had imagined a change in Maximilian, then she had been mistaken, for whilst an insurmountable gulf now existed between them, it had been only a few days since they had last been in one another's company. Maximilian was precisely the same as she remembered him, and to her own dismay, her feelings for him were the same, too. As she opened the door, she found the man she had fallen in love with, and despite her anger towards him, that love remained.

"Good day, Delphine," he said, in a disinterested tone, stepping over the threshold uninvited.

He looked around the dining room, surveying the preparations for the wedding, and nodded in approval.

"You'll see we followed your instructions," she said, feeling suddenly terribly awkward and embarrassed in his presence.

She wondered if she could really let fly her anger against him, even as she knew she would regret not speaking her mind. She was torn between an apology and a sense of betrayal, and she fought back the tears welling up in her eyes and clenched her fists in frustration at her herself and at him.

"Yes, it's all most acceptable. I couldn't think of a better place to celebrate my marriage than here," he replied.

Delphine could hardly believe what she was hearing. By his tone, his words, and his demeanor, it was almost as though he had no awareness of what he had done. It felt as though he had simply cast all thoughts of her aside and was treating her merely as the landlady of The Seven Bells, and not as the woman with whom he had presumably fallen in love, and with whom he had shared such intimacies. Perhaps they had never existed, and again she wondered if it was she who had been played a fool.

"I'm glad you approve. You're to change in the upper room. I've tidied it for you and changed the bed. But your bride isn't here. Her dress arrived," Delphine added, knowing she sounded meek and pitiful in her tone.

He nodded, still gazing around him at the arrangements.

"Yes…she'll be here soon enough. Keep the dress down here until she arrives. I'll go and get ready," he said, and before Delphine could reply, he hurried off towards the stairs and disappeared up onto the landing.

Delphine sighed. A tear rolled down her cheek, and she wondered how she could possibly say the words she wanted to in the face of such bizarre indifference. Bessie emerged from the kitchen with a questioning look on her face.

"Did he…?" she began, but Delphine shook her head.

"He didn't do anything, Bessie. It's as though I never meant anything to him. And perhaps I didn't. I'm beginning to think he played the same game with me as I did with him. I feel so foolish," she exclaimed.

Everything was prepared. The wedding was about to take place, and Delphine knew she would be a witness to her own heartbreak.

"You're not foolish, ma'am. He's just playing a wicked game

with you. He's nothing but a rake. I'm sorry, I shouldn't say so, but…oh, I wish he'd never come here," Bessie said, putting her arms around Delphine to comfort her.

"No, you're right, Bessie. It would've been better if he hadn't," Delphine replied.

She was mourning the death of her father, and Maximilian's arrival had come when she was at her lowest. She had been vulnerable, and allowed herself to be swept up in comforting feelings which had paid no heed to sense or reason.

"My poor mistress, I only want you to be happy," Bessie said, still with her arms around Delphine.

"Perhaps I'm not meant to be," Delphine replied.

They were still awaiting the bride. Indeed, none of the guests had yet arrived, and Delphine was curious as to when this woman would appear. She had thought about telling her the truth and begging her to reconsider the match. But it would only be a fool's errand, and Delphine could only imagine the anger with which Maximilian would greet any attempt at interference. She was beaten, and she knew it.

"But what happens now, ma'am? Do we just wait for him?" Bessie asked, and Delphine nodded.

"There's nothing more we can do, Bessie. We have to wait. We've no other choice," Delphine replied.

They did not have long *to* wait. Maximilian was soon heard on the stairs and appeared in the parlor just after the earl and the marquess, who stood eyeing him silently. Delphine had begged them not to make a scene, and she was grateful that they stood tight-lipped, as Maximilian surveyed the scene once again. He was dressed in a frock coat and tails, with a blue cravat at the neck, a white shirt and breeches, and highly polished black boots. There was no doubting he looked very handsome, even as Delphine tried to push her feelings for him aside.

"I see everything's ready," he said, turning to Delphine, who looked at him curiously.

"But no one's here. There's no bride. I want...I want to talk to you," she said, glancing at the others.

The earl and the marquess looked uncertain, but Bessie and Alice beckoned to them, and the four of them retreated to the kitchen. Delphine and Maximilian were left alone, and she looked at him uncertainly, wondering what to say, even as they had come to the moment she had longed for – a chance to speak the words on her heart, words which remained confused, but which needed to be said.

"I'm not waiting for anyone," Maximilian replied.

Delphine now grew angry – he was playing games with her. Perhaps there was no wedding, no bride, no guests – this may all be an elaborate game, and she fought back the tears as she pointed at him angrily.

"Stop playing games, Maximilian. Why all this charade? Why do you delight in tormenting me?" she demanded.

"But I'm not..." he began, even as she interrupted him.

"You take flight before I can explain myself, you announce a marriage to a woman I've never heard of – not that it's my place to question you, but...oh, you didn't even allow me the time to explain! To say I'm sorry," she sobbed.

"But I'm here now, and I'm waiting for the bride," he said, and to Delphine's astonishment, he smiled at her.

This was perverse. He was going to humiliate her in front of this woman. It made her so angry and yet so sad, too...

"But she's not here. You sent her wedding dress here. You're standing here waiting for her, and you expect me to do so, too," she stammered, as he stepped forward and caught her by the arms.

Her legs felt weak, and it seemed as though she was about to faint again, when his words caused her to gasp out loud.

"I do, Delphine, because I need you to say yes," he replied.

"I...me? To say yes to what?" she asked, staring up into his eyes as he gazed down at her with a smile.

"To marry me, Delphine. You're the bride I'm waiting for. The dress is for you. This is all for you," he exclaimed, even as Delphine shook her head in astonishment.

She hardly dared to believe what she was hearing. Did he really mean it, or was this yet another wicked ploy designed to humiliate her? He himself had been betrothed, and that betrothal had been broken at the moment of happiness. Was he intending to do the same?

"But...how can I be? How can it be? You can't marry me. Not after what I've done. You were so angry..." she stammered.

"But I never allowed you to explain, did I? I never allowed you to tell me the truth. You're just as much in love with me as I am with you. What began as a game was merely a prelude to a truth. Please...tell me I'm right? I thought of nothing but you as I rode back to Berkshire, and when the earl and the marquess came to see me, I realized they'd come as envoys to tell me your true feelings. Forgive my own little game, but won't you do me the honor of being my wife? Marry me, Delphine. It's all prepared. I only need you to say yes..." he said.

And now he kneeled in front of her, taking her hand in his and gazing imploringly up at her with a look of such love as to bring tears to Delphine's eyes. She did not have to think, even as she was overwhelmed by what he had done, by what he had said, and what he was now promising. This was no game. She realized that now. This was real. It was everything she had come to desire.

"I do say yes. And I'm sorry for my own game, my own foolishness. But you've got to understand, it meant nothing, because all too soon I realized it wasn't a game. I didn't want it to be a game. I wanted it to be real. My feelings for you are real, but it took me a while to understand them," she said, as Maximilian rose to his feet and put his arms around her.

In that moment, it felt to Delphine as though all her troubles were gone. She hardly dared believe it was true, but the truth was standing before her. No more games, no more heartache, only the coming together of two hearts as one. There had been so much uncertainty, so much pain, so much separation. But all that was passed, and now she gazed around her at the preparations for the wedding – *her* wedding.

"I was making myself miserable, and for what? My own stubbornness. If only I'd let you explain, Delphine. And why shouldn't you have played a game with me? I came here bitter and angry. I treated you appallingly, and yet you saw beyond that to the person I could be if only my wounds were tended. I'm so grateful to you," he said, and Delphine smiled.

"I could've gone about things very differently. I *should've* gone about things differently. The others warned me… I should've listened. I didn't know what I wanted. I've never been in love, and now I never want to be without it," she said, as she rested her head on his chest, and he held her in a loving embrace.

"And you don't need to be. You won't be. And neither will I. It was hard for me to trust again. I thought I'd made a terrible mistake, but I know now I hadn't. We were just…a little blinded by it all," he said, and Delphine nodded.

At that moment, the kitchen door opened, and Bessie peered out cautiously. When she saw Delphine in Maximilian's arms, her eyes grew wide with astonishment.

"I…ma'am? Is everything all right?" she asked, and Delphine smiled.

"It's all right, yes, Bessie. Tell the others to come out. We've got some wonderful news to share," Delphine said.

Bessie called to the others, and Alice, the earl, and the marquess appeared, looking confused.

"Delphine? What's happened? Where's the bride?" the earl said, looking suspiciously at Maximilian, who smiled.

"She's right here, sir – *Delphine* is the bride, and this is *her* wedding. And I think, given her dear father isn't here to perform his duties, it would only be right if the two of you, her dear friends, and the men who came to remind me of what love really means, have the honor of giving her away," he said.

The earl and the marquess gasped, and Delphine quickly explained what had transpired and how she and Maximilian were to be married that very day.

"Then you'd better get into your dress, ma'am," Alice said, and she hurried back into the kitchen and appeared a moment later with the box containing the wedding dress.

Delphine smiled, and Bessie now beckoned her to follow her upstairs.

"I'll help you, ma'am. Come this way," she said, and with a glance at Maximilian, who smiled and nodded, Delphine hurried off to get ready for the wedding – her wedding, and the moment she had never believed could come.

Epilogue

Delphine stood in front of the mirror, gazing at herself as though in a dream. She was dressed in the ivory wedding gown. It fitted perfectly, and the long trail flowed down her shoulders and back, curling around her waist, as Bessie helped to pin up her hair.

"You look beautiful, ma'am. Truly, you do," she said, smiling at Delphine, who blushed.

"And so do you, Bessie," she replied, for Maximilian had provided new dresses for both the maid and the cook.

She had never allowed her mind to wander to this point, to imagine what it would be like to be a bride adorned for her wedding day.

"I never thought this day would come. I never believed I'd be married," she said, turning to Bessie, who had tears in her eyes.

"Your father would be so proud, ma'am. I wish he was here to see you now," Bessie said.

Delphine nodded. She wished it, too, and she imagined what her father might say if he was here now. He would surely be proud of her, and proud to walk her down the aisle.

"I hope he'd think I've done well," Delphine replied.

"And you have, ma'am. You've continued in his legacy. That means more than anything," Bessie said, and she put her arms around Delphine and embraced her.

A knock came at the door. It was Alice, and she had come to tell them that a carriage was waiting to take them to Saint Paul's.

"In the cathedral? Goodness, it's going to be quite an occasion," Delphine said, her eyes growing wide with astonishment at the thought of such a grand occasion.

They made their way downstairs, where Maximilian and the earl and the marquess were waiting for them.

"You look beautiful, Delphine," Maximilian said, smiling at her, and Delphine blushed.

"It's like a dream," she replied.

"It will be our honor to escort you, Delphine," the earl said, offering Delphine his arm.

The marquess did the same, and Delphine was only too happy to allow them to lead her out of the inn to the waiting carriage. Maximilian went ahead, and with Alice and Bessie, the rest of them climbed into the carriage for the short journey to the cathedral. The bells were peeling, and when they arrived, the steps were lined with well-wishers, all of them cheering and waving.

"But who are all these people?" Delphine exclaimed, for she had never seen any of them before.

"Friends of Maximilian, I presume," the earl said, as the carriage came to a halt.

Maximilian was standing at the top of the steps, and the earl and the marquess now led Delphine through the crowd, all of them waving and cheering.

"Congratulations, I'm so glad you've found happiness together," a beautifully dressed woman on the arm of a handsome gentleman said, as Maximilian now came to greet them.

"This is my friend Rupert, and his dear wife, Lucy," Maximilian said, and Delphine held out her hand to them.

"I'm glad to meet you... I'm sorry, this is all somewhat overwhelming," she said, glancing at Maximilian, who smiled.

"It's all happened rather fast, hasn't it? But why delay happiness? Come now, we've got a wedding to attend," he said, and beckoning to Delphine, he led her up the cathedral steps, followed by the crowd.

As they came to the door, a short man with gray hair wearing a long frock coat stepped out of the shadows. Maximilian stared at him in surprise, and now he gave a curt bow to Delphine who had never seen him before in her life.

"Father, what're you doing here?" Maximilian exclaimed.

"I couldn't stay away from my own son's wedding, could I? I'm not the ogre you think me to be. Dalton told me what you'd planned. I congratulate you, my boy. A beautiful bride, and so much her father's daughter. I often enjoyed your father's hospitality, Delphine. God bless you both," he said, as Delphine and Maximilian smiled at one another as they made their way up the steps.

The doors of the cathedral were open, and the long marble aisle stretched out beneath the dome. A surplice clad clergyman was waiting for them, and now the organ began to thunder a wedding march.

"This way, my Lord. You're fortunate the Archbishop was available to grant you a special license. A happy day for you all," the clergyman said, and he led Maximilian down the aisle, whilst Delphine and the others waited for their signal.

"It's quite incredible, isn't it? But you're sure this is what you want?" the earl said, turning to Delphine, who nodded.

She had never been more certain of anything in her life. Through the turmoil and confusion, her feelings for Maximilian had remained – they had only grown stronger. That morning, she had believed all to be lost, but instead, it was only the beginning of something wonderful to come. The guests filed into the pews, the organ was at its zenith, and the clergyman nodded to her, as Maximilian stood at the far end of the aisle.

"Here we go," the marquess whispered, as the three of them made their way sedately forward.

When they came to where Maximilian stood beneath the dome of that great church, which was flooded with light from the morning sun, he turned to her and smiled.

"Will you marry me, Delphine?" he asked, and Delphine nodded.

"I will," she replied, as the earl and the marquess stepped back and the clergyman cleared his throat.

"Dearly beloved, we are gathered together here in the sight of God, and in the face of this Congregation, to join together this man and this woman in holy Matrimony; which is an honorable estate, instituted of God in the time of man's innocence, signifying unto us the mystical union that is betwixt Christ and his Church..." he began, reading aloud from the prayerbook.

And so, Delphine and Maximilian were married. They made their vows and promised to be faithful to one another in good times and bad. Maximilian gave Delphine a ring, a symbol of their union, and after the final blessing, they shared a kiss.

"I love you with all my heart, Delphine," Maximilian whispered, as their lips parted.

"And I love you, too," she replied, slipping her hand into his, as they turned to face the congregation.

Bessie and Alice were in floods of tears, and it amused Delphine to see the earl and the marquess in a similar state, clutching at one another as they sobbed.

"Oh, it's simply beautiful. A fairytale, a love story, worthy of Shakespeare," the earl exclaimed, as the two men hurried forward to be the first to congratulate the newly married couple.

"Well...we owe the two of you a debt of gratitude," Maximilian said, and the earl and the marquess looked at one another in surprise.

"Us?" the marquess said, and Maximilian nodded.

"For coming to Berkshire as you did. I knew I loved Delphine with all my heart, but I wasn't sure how she felt about me. I thought it had all been a game, but when you came to tell me of her sorrow, I realized the truth. I'm sorry I played a game with you. The thought came to me quite in the moment – the pretense of a marriage arranged for another, but in fact our own," he said, turning to Delphine, who smiled.

"We're only glad to see Delphine made happy," the marquess said, and the earl nodded.

"But you won't get rid of us so easily. We'll still make the inn our regular haunt. Someone's got to keep an eye on you," the earl said, grinning at Delphine.

"And I wouldn't have it any other way. Where would I be without my two favorite aristocrats?" Delphine asked, and both men blushed and shrieked with laughter, so much so that the clergyman who had conducted the service raised his eyebrows.

"Though we could do with less complaining about the food," Alice said, as she and Bessie came to congratulate Delphine and Maximilian.

"Oh, but that was always just a game, my dear – you're the finest cook we know. In all of London, nay, England, nay, all the world, there isn't a finer cook than Alice," the earl said, putting his arm around her and causing her to blush a deep shade of red.

"Oh...well, if you say so... I hope you'll enjoy the brisket I've roasted today," she said, and the earl smiled.

"I'll insist on a second helping. Come now, to The Seven Bells – my stomach is rumbling and I feel in need of a celebration," he exclaimed, and he and the marquess went off arm in arm down the aisle, calling out loud greetings to the assembled guests, as Delphine and Maximilian shook their heads and laughed.

They were greeted now by all manner of well-wishers. The guests were all acquaintances of Maximilian, and Delphine was introduced to his friends from Oxford, including Sir William Blake, who greeted her warmly.

"How glad I am to see Maximilian made happy at last," he said, as he kissed Delphine on both cheeks.

"And he's made me very happy, too," Delphine replied, glancing at Maximilian, and smiling.

The guests and well-wishers were invited to the inn, and Delphine and Maximilian rode together in the carriage, accompanied by Bessie, Alice, the earl, and the marquess.

"I've got footmen coming to serve the meal," Maximilian said, as they arrived back at The Seven Bells.

Delphine glanced at Bessie and Alice, both of whom looked surprised.

"You mean...?" Alice said, and Maximilian nodded.

"You're our guests. You'll be waited on for once," he said, and the maid and the cook clapped their hands together in delight.

A footman now emerged from the inn and opened the carriage door for them. Maximilian helped Delphine down, and Bessie took up the trail of her dress. The other guests were arriving, having hurried after the carriage through the narrow streets around Saint Paul's. A happy and jovial atmosphere hung in the air, and Delphine and Maximilian led the way inside, where they found everything prepared for the celebration.

"Are we really to be waited on? I feel I should be doing something," Alice said, as a footman led them to their places.

"Just enjoy it, Alice. You deserve it," Delphine replied. The cook shook her head, as she sat down at the linen-covered table, where silver cutlery and crystal glassware glinted in the sunshine pouring through the windows.

Delphine and Maximilian sat at the head of the table, and now the earl called the guests to attention by tapping a knife against a glass.

"Today is an unexpected day, but a happy one, nonetheless. *The* happiest of days. Delphine has long been the dearest of friends to us, and we give thanks for the joyful celebration we've witnessed today. And so, before we begin this lavish meal, I want to offer a toast to the bride and groom," the earl said, raising a now charged glass to Delphine and Maximilian.

"Thank you," Delphine said, and the earl toasted them.

"To Delphine and Maximilian. May their lives together be long and happy. God bless them," he said, and the rest of the guests repeated his words.

Delphine turned to Maximilian and slipped her hand into his.

"Thank you," she whispered, as he leaned forward and kissed her.

* * *

The celebrations lasted for much of the day. The meal was served, and Alice continued to protest at being waited on, insisting she did something rather than sit idly sipping the wine which was rapidly making her merry. When the feast was over, the tables were pushed back, and a quartet of musicians played so that the guests could dance and revel. It was the most joyful of days, and as she danced with Maximilian, Delphine knew she had found her happiness.

"What do we do now?" she asked, when the festivities were over.

"I want you to come with me to Berkshire. I want you to see Fermony Grange and my estate," he said.

Delphine was doubtful for a moment. She was uncertain whether she could leave the inn for such a length of time.

"I... I'm not sure. What about The Seven Bells? What about Bessie and Alice?" she asked, and Maximilian smiled.

"I'm sure with the help of the earl and the marquess they can manage. We'll come back soon enough. I want us to run the inn together – that's what your father would've wanted, isn't it?" he said.

At these words, Delphine was filled with relief. She had been worrying about what might become of the inn now she and Maximilian were married. Would she be expected to perform the tasks and duties of an aristocratic woman? The thought of giving up The Seven Bells and abandoning her father's legacy had filled her with a sense of sorrow, and now she threw her arms around Maximilian and kissed him.

"Oh, do you really mean it? How wonderful," she exclaimed, and he smiled at her.

"I want you to be happy, Delphine. That's all. We'll run the inn together – you'll have to teach me everything I need to know. Especially about wine," he said, and Delphine smiled.

"I'll be only too happy to do so," she replied.

After thanking their guests and leaving the inn in the capable hands of Bessie and Alice, Delphine and Maximilian set off in the carriage for Berkshire. The earl and the marquess had assured Delphine they would remain to "assist," and with peace now reigning, the happy couple left London without a care in the world.

"You'll like Berkshire, I'm sure," Maximilian said, as they sat back and watched the city turn into countryside.

Delphine had never left the confines of London. It was all a remarkable new experience for her, and she gazed out of the window in delight as the countryside rushed past. The journey to Berkshire would take them well into the evening, and, as dusk fell, she settled back in Maximilian's arms, grateful to him for all he had done, and all he would do for her.

"I can't wait to see it and share it with you. So much has changed in just a day. It's difficult to imagine," she said, as she rested her head on his shoulder.

"But we've both found the love we deserve," Maximilian said, with a kiss on the top of her head.

"I never thought I'd get married. I didn't know how it would be possible, and I feared you wouldn't want to remain at The Seven Bells," she said, closing her eyes as fatigue came over her.

"I think it's a wonderful place. What better life could there be? But I fear a time will come when responsibility means we must return to Berkshire on a more permanent basis. But those days are far ahead. My father remains strong, and I've no doubt fate will decide the rest," Maximilian replied.

But he was right – those concerns lay far ahead in the future, and for now, Delphine could only feel a happy sense of purpose at what was to come. This was meant to be, their love was meant to be, and Delphine knew that whatever happened, she and Maximilian would remain strong. They had come through so much already. The game was over, and life stretched out before them, filled with possibility for whatever they decided it should be.

Extended Epilogue

I would like to thank you all from the bottom of my heart for reading my book **"Miss Delphine's Dangerous Game"**!

Laurence and Henrietta?

Visit a search engine and enter the link you see below the picture to connect to a more personal level and as a BONUS, I will send you the Extended Epilogue of this Book!

EXTENDED EPILOGUE

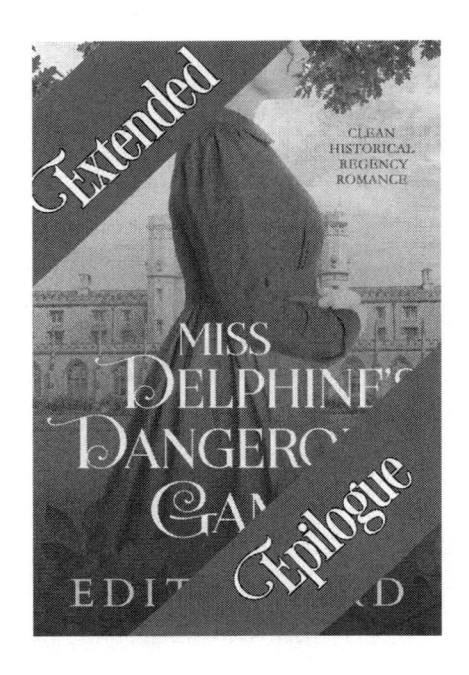

https://edithbyrd.com/eb-022-exep/

I would be honored if you could spare a little time to post your review!

A Message from Edith Byrd

Thank you all very much for reading my book to the end!

I strongly believe that every story needs to be told, but it is truly a great story if it is worth reading. I really hope mine was worth your trouble!

I would like to thank from the bottom of my heart my friend and colleague Fanny Finch. I had been her fan for a long time before she gave me the opportunity to work alongside her as a beta reader, and later she inspired me into taking up writing.

She was gracious enough to help me start my careet as an author with our cowritten novel and my debut and for that I will be forever grateful!

As a parting gift I offer some advice: if writing is your dream, it is never too late! All you need is the will to take a risk and good people around you to nudge you on and never let you quit!

Faithfully yours,

A MESSAGE FROM EDITH BYRD

About Starfall Publications

Starfall Publications has helped me and so many others extend my passion from writing to you.

The prime focus of this company has been – and always will be – *quality* and I am honored to be able to publish my books under their name.

Having said that, I would like to officially thank Starfall Publications for offering me the opportunity to be part of such a wonderful, hard-working team!

Thanks to them, my dreams – and your dreams — have come true!

Be a Part of Edith Byrd's Family

I would like to thank you all for supporting me in my first steps as an author.

If you're not a member of my family yet, it's never too late! Stay up to date on upcoming releases and check out my website for exclusive gifts, romance suggestions, and lots of surprises!

http://edithbyrd.com/free-gift/

Social Media:
- Facebook - http://edithbyrd.com/facebook
- Goodreads - http://edithbyrd.com/goodreads
- Bookbub - http://edithbyrd.com/bookbub
- Amazon - http://edithbyrd.com/amazon-follow

Also by Edith Byrd

Here are all my books!

I try to have the majority of my books priced extremely low as I believe everyone should be able to escape from reality no matter the circumstances..

If you have read some of them click on the Titles below or type the link next to the title and post your review!

- Winning a Lady's Love before Christmas - http://edithbyrd.com/AmB001
- How to Lie your Way into a Lady's Heart - http://edithbyrd.com/AmB002
- What the Duke is Hiding - http://edithbyrd.com/AmB003
- Letters, Lies and Love for Miss Melody - http://edithbyrd.com/AmB004
- How to Cook your Way into an Earl's Heart - http://edithbyrd.com/AmB005
- The Duke who Saved me - http://edithbyrd.com/AmB006
- Destined Hearts in Troubled Times - http://edithbyrd.com/AmBS1
- How to Close the Deal of Love - http://edithbyrd.com/AmB007
- The Double Identity of a Bewitching Lady - http://edithbyrd.com/AmB008
- The Secret of a Lady's Past - http://edithbyrd.com/AmB009
- From Convenience to Love - http://edithbyrd.com/AmB010

- Walking with a Baron - http://edithbyrd.com/AmB011
- Love behind a Ghost Story - http://edithbyrd.com/AmB012
- A Lady for the Widowed Marquess - http://edithbyrd.com/AmB013
- Eternal Hearts - http://edithbyrd.com/AmB014
- How to Survive Love - http://edithbyrd.com/AmBS2
- The Arranged Courtship - http://edithbyrd.com/AmB015
- An Earl's Heart taken by Storm - http://edithbyrd.com/AmB016
- The Duke's Second Chance at Love - http://edithbyrd.com/AmB017
- Regency Wallflowers - http://edithbyrd.com/AmBS3
- From Duchess to Governess - http://edithbyrd.com/AmB018
- For the Love of a Broken Lord - http://edithbyrd.com/AmB019
- Falling for the Duke's Other Face - http://edithbyrd.com/AmB020
- The Lord Behind the Letters - http://edithbyrd.com/AmB021

Printed in Great Britain
by Amazon